JJ Gre

FIRST DOWN

Bella
BOOKS
2013

Bella Books, Inc.
P.O. Box 10543
Tallahassee, FL 32302

Printed in the United States of America on acid-free paper
First Bella Books Edition 2013

Editor: Nene Adams
Cover Designer: Kiaro Creative

ISBN 13: 978-1-59493-362-2

Dedication

This book is for Mel. It may seem like a simple statement, but everything about her was more complex than I can ever give words to. In the few short years that I was blessed to have her in my life, she changed my world. She took my hand and guided me out of the closet. She taught me what it is to be in love. She showed me how to live with passion, energy and enthusiasm. She gave me strength, and when I was lucky, she let me give some back. Although she's moved on to a better place, where her pain has been lifted from her, I know that she remains with me, every day. Thank you, Mel, for everything. This is for you, Buddy.

Acknowledgment

First and foremost, I want to thank my family. I know that's cliché, but I am blessed that it is well warranted. Your insanity and inspiration contribute in equal measure to my accomplishments. Next, my friends and first readers, especially Little Mel, Ryan and Roomie. Thanks for being sounding walls, dramatic inspiration, comedic relief, and even my shoulders to cry on. Third, Cami, for crafting the awesome little cartoon me in my Bio. Fourth, thank you, for actually reading my story. I hope you like it. Last but not least, my unworthy gratitude to Our Lady and the Big Guy Upstairs. Can't really say much more than that. Thank you all.

About the Author

Loyal Friend
Daughter
Sister
Domer
Introvert
Structural Engineer
Ultimate (Frisbee) Player
Searching
Coloradish
Out and Proud
Pet Lover
Writer
Dreamer

CHAPTER ONE

Detective Rynn Callahan walked into the darkened office, flicked on her desk lamp, and glanced around at the other homicide detectives huddled in pairs over their own work. Sighing, she brought her computer to life with a tap on the keyboard. She was getting used to being a loner, but each day of the past three months without her partner had felt interminable.

Today didn't seem like it would be all that much different from yesterday, or the weeks before that either, but in a police station, she'd learned nothing was certain. As if on cue, her phone rang, breaking the monotony.

"Callahan," she answered.

The lieutenant's voice sounded sharp. "You get anywhere on that case, Detective?"

"Not quite, sir." Rynn rattled off a few quick details of one of her open cases, an assault with suspected domestic violence.

"Well, forget the loser boyfriend. We've got a body, and it ain't no accident. I need you to get out there and take a look."

Rynn's senses jumped to life. "I'll be right there." She pulled on her jacket as the lieutenant gave her the address. Before she could hang up and get moving, he added the one thing she had been dreading since her partner, Jack Samson, took a bullet in the leg.

"Oh, and Callahan—" From his tone when he said her name, she knew she wasn't going to like what came next. "Take Pearson from SVU with you. No more solo work."

Her heart sank. She had been hanging on to the hope that she wouldn't have to take another partner. She'd been with Samson so long that she hated to think their partnership might be over. "Yes, sir. For this case only, or long term?"

He grunted. "We'll see how this case goes, won't we? Go get Pearson and get out there."

"Yes, sir." Her answer was barely out of her mouth before she heard a click ending the call.

She grabbed her notepad and headed to the front desk. Steve Pearson? What did she know about him? She'd heard of a new hire in the Special Victims department about a year ago, but she'd not yet met him. *Oh well, anything I've heard up to this point doesn't really mean much.* After all, she'd heard the rumors circulating about her. She wasn't about to put significant stock in hearsay. She had a homicide to focus on.

In the lobby, Rynn waited while the receptionist, Betty, paged Pearson. When he rounded a corner, she realized he was older than she'd expected, maybe late thirties.

He gave her an appraising glance before speaking first. "You must be Callahan. Just got off the line with the higher-ups. Looks like we're a team now, eh? So where're we headed?"

Rynn gestured toward the door. "Come on, I'll fill you in while we drive."

Although impatient to leave, she held out her hand for a quick introductory shake. Pearson had a firm handshake, but not over the top. Good. She'd come to discover that cops, especially detectives, tended to be people of few words. A handshake could still say a lot, though. Too soft, and it meant either the person might be weak in the field, or they thought that because she was a woman, they should be gentle. Too aggressive, and she knew she was working with the macho type, always out to prove himself a big man.

Whether she had gotten used to working alone, or she'd subconsciously decided to take the lead, Rynn ignored the department vehicles and turned toward her Tahoe once she and Pearson entered the parking lot. She registered the pause in Pearson's step, but he quickly walked around to the passenger side and hopped in without complaint.

Rynn chanced another glance at him as she started the car. Tall. Thin, but well-muscled. Black hair flecked with gray, making his age more difficult to accurately determine. She held to her original guess of late thirties, but that was based largely on his skin tone and unlined features.

She pulled the Tahoe away from the station and offered a bit more of an introduction than they'd shared in the lobby. "Sorry if I was abrupt back there. Just want to get moving on this new case. Crime scenes can go cold really fast, as I'm sure you know."

Out of the corner of her eye, she saw him look at her and nod. "Fine with me. Plenty of time for pleasantries as we move forward. What do you know about our victim?"

"The lieutenant didn't share much. Male, late twenties or early thirties, found dead in his home by an elderly neighbor couple. Apparently, the scene's pretty gruesome. CSI should be there by now, and possibly the ME. That's really all I've got."

Pearson stared out the front windshield while she talked. Again, Rynn wondered about his experience. Well, what better way to find out than to ask?

"So, do you like Pearson or Steve?" She glanced his way, not liking that she couldn't watch him during their first conversation. People—all people, she believed—said more with their bodies than their mouths. She caught him shrugging before she trained her gaze back on the road.

"Either way is really fine with me," he said. "Usually it's Pearson at work. Seems like everyone goes with the last name, so I do too. Outside work, I tend to go with Steve. Only thing

I've ever heard anyone call you is Callahan. I take it that's by choice?"

Now it was her turn to shrug. "Doesn't bother me. Same as with you, I suppose. Samson sometimes uses Rynn. But other than that, it's Callahan. I guess because he's gotten to know me best. I've been partnered with Samson since I made detective."

Pearson smiled. "Yeah. Sounds like you two were the dynamic duo around the station."

His statement piqued her curiosity. Hoping she didn't sound aggressive, she asked, "Sorry, but it seems like you know more about me than I do about you. Why is that?"

She felt him turn a studying glance in her direction. "Well, I did my homework. Didn't you?"

She didn't respond, opting instead to focus on the road. Was that a teasing or a condescending tone in his voice? She had trouble telling without being able to read his body language.

He laughed. "You only heard about me this morning, didn't you?"

She nodded. "Yes. Same conversation as the body call. You've known we were getting partnered longer?" She was going to kill the lieutenant for not giving her more notice.

"They told me yesterday. Said to wrap up what I was working on with SVU this week, with the intention of transferring me to homicide beginning Monday. But when this murder got called in, Monday became today. Honestly, that works fine for me. I requested the transfer months ago and wasn't too sad about leaving SVU more quickly."

Rynn knew she would have to ask him more about that later, but they had arrived at the victim's address. She maneuvered the Tahoe carefully through the street, where the responding officer's patrol car, the ME unit and the CSI van had attracted a crowd of gawkers.

She parked her Tahoe against the curb two houses down. Together, she and Pearson walked up to the front door of the house. Crime scene tape had been put up around the door. A uniformed officer stood a few feet away, watching the crowd.

Rynn flashed her badge at him as she ducked under the tape. The officer barely nodded at them when Pearson followed her lead. Inside, one CSI walked a perimeter search while another took pictures. A conversation in the next room directed her toward a scene of brutal violence.

She stepped into the living room. The victim lay flat on his back in the middle of the room. Blood pooled on the hardwood floor beneath his crumpled body. One leg was bent under at an unnatural angle. The victim was shirtless and barefoot, but wore loose fitting trousers. His face and torso were bruised and mutilated with cuts.

The ME squatted next to the body. "Patrick Boden, age thirty-three. Apparently lived alone." She gestured at the cuts Rynn had noted. "As you can see, there is a great deal of blood. Judging from liver temperature, he's been dead at least twelve hours. Preliminary cause of death is exsanguination due to sharp force trauma. No defensive wounds. Lividity around the wrists and ankles suggests he was restrained at some point, but he was not tied when we arrived."

Rynn nodded. "And the leg?"

The ME stood, stepping away from the body. "The compound fracture is obvious, but I'll need to complete the postmortem to determine more."

Rynn's gaze shifted to the rest of the room. She studied the area, noting the simple décor. Classy. Stylish. Not at all cluttered.

A worn chair in the corner faced a huge flat-screen TV. A tall rack of movies stood next to it, but little else showed much evidence of use. Glancing at the TV, she noted the system, easily the most expensive thing in the room. Wireless surround sound speakers were tucked into corners and mounted on the back wall. Next to the movie rack was a small entertainment center housing a hi-def cable receiver, a Blu-ray player and several gaming systems. The room was clean, no dust bunnies in the corners. A couch stood against the far wall, the single framed poster above it showing a panoramic view of Soldier Field.

She left the ME to transport the body and moved out of the living room, finding Pearson in the dining room talking to one of the CSIs. She listened in for a few seconds before moving on to other things. She might not know much about Pearson's work history, but to assume he was less than fully competent would set them off on the wrong foot entirely.

She worked her way through the house to the kitchen, where she found a uniformed officer talking with a nearly hysterical older woman. Glancing through the window, she saw a man, about the same age as the woman and equally distraught, lingering outside in the backyard.

Rynn moved further into the kitchen. The rear door was splintered at the jamb and a pane of glass had been knocked out. Forced entry. She looked around the rest of the room, taking meticulous notes of her observations.

The officer looked at her as she approached. Rynn thought relief lightened his harried expression. He rushed to introduce her to the elderly woman. "Detective! This is Mrs. Evelyn Walker. She lives next door. She and her husband found the body."

Rynn saw the old woman shudder at his phrasing. She sighed, guessing the officer had little experience with this kind of scenario. People didn't often like to hear their family, friends or neighbors referred to as "the body." Names were best, but at the very least "victim" had a sense of humanity. She nodded at the officer, and he hurried from the room. She stepped toward the woman, who had covered her face in her hands, not so much as glancing up.

Unable to meet Mrs. Walker's eyes, Rynn touched her gently on the shoulder, not at all surprised when the woman burst into violent sobs. She gently led Mrs. Walker to a picnic table in the backyard, and interviewed her and her husband, James, for nearly half an hour before thanking them and rising from the table. The kindly neighbors nodded to her as she started to turn away.

Back inside the house, Rynn reentered the living room.

Pearson stepped over to her. "I've been out front checking with the other neighbors. It seems no one really knew our victim. No one remembers hearing or seeing anything unusual the past day or two. I had one guy tell me he didn't even know someone lived in this house. I guess Boden really kept to himself."

Rynn nodded. "That's fairly consistent with what the Walkers—the couple next door who found the victim—had to say. If I had to hazard a guess, I'd say Evelyn Walker probably makes it a point to know what's going on in the neighborhood. She and her husband knew Boden a little, but it seems our victim was very private. Friendly, polite, often away at work, apparently as a financial advisor. Unfortunately, that's really all they could give me."

"Well, Detective." Pearson motioned to the door. "Anything else you want to see here?"

Rynn shook her head. "Nope. Forced entry, no apparent theft. Let's go back to the station and see what we can find out about Boden."

CHAPTER TWO

Information on the case came in slowly over the next few days. No leads came close to pointing to a suspect, though. Now Rynn mentally reviewed what they knew about the victim.

Patrick Boden seemed a model citizen. He worked for Trabini and Sons Financial Group in downtown Chicago, where he was an ideal employee. He had joined the firm straight out of college, and in the past ten years moved steadily up the corporate ladder. He acted as a consultant to dozens of clients, mostly the average, suburban, middle-class person or couple, helping them plan investments and save for their futures. He had a few higher profile clients, some with multimillion-dollar portfolios, but no one had ever logged a complaint against him.

He always used his vacation time, mostly in the spring. The morning he'd been found dead was the first time any of his co-workers could remember him not being at his desk ten minutes before the start of the workday at eight a.m.

Boden's record was clean, not even so much as a parking ticket. He rarely joined his co-workers for drinks after work, didn't open up much about his personal life, but despite his reserve, everyone seemed to like him and found him friendly and polite.

Their investigation at Boden's office took most of Wednesday since she and Pearson had to make the drive into Chicago. When she got into the office Thursday morning, the ME's report and toxicology screen were on her desk. She waited for Pearson. Together, they went to the morgue to talk with the doctor about the autopsy results.

The most unusual details were the shattered knee and broken leg, both a result of blunt force trauma. There was no sign of healing, leading the ME to conclude that the murderer had caused the injuries. The victim's face and body were slashed multiple times, but the smooth cuts were consistent with a typical large kitchen knife. The number of cuts and inconsistency of depth might indicate an inexperienced killer trying to maximize damage without having the physiological knowledge to target key places.

While much of the report might be used to convict a suspect, it gave Rynn and her partner nothing to follow up on.

By Friday, she and Pearson had made little progress on the case. Rynn felt like she was spinning her wheels. At least she'd gotten to know her new partner better in the last few days.

Pearson was a good guy. Sharp, although he had worked few homicides. It turned out she'd thought he was a new detective because he'd only been in their precinct a little over a year. Before then, he'd worked in Cleveland, but he declined to talk about why he'd moved. That had been the only sensitive subject so far. Other than that, they chatted easily.

Rynn was surprised their partnership worked so well. In the break room that morning, Samson, back to work but limited to light desk duty, heckled her about it, asking her how she could stand working with another man after all the time they'd spent together.

"Rynn, baby, after years together, you ditch me for this lowlife?" Samson made a display of fake sobs.

Pearson played it up and wrapped his arm around Rynn. "You bet, buddy. She's all mine now, and there ain't nothin' you can do about it. This sexy lady and me were meant to be together."

His smile put her at ease. She refused to admit it, but she had been afraid of working with another partner, figuring she couldn't get so lucky twice in a row.

She didn't immediately join the banter, but Samson refused to let it go. "What? You've got nothin' to say to me?" he asked her. "I taught you everything you know! I made you the woman you are today!"

She tossed him a wry smile. "Now, now, Jacky. Don't go saying that too loud. You know your wife was already suspicious of all those late nights we had together, staking out the lowlifes of Kane County."

Samson burst into laughter.

She loved being able to catch him off his guard sometimes. She noticed the question in Pearson's expression and explained. "Mrs. Samson loves me. Usually says I'm the son she never had. She keeps telling her husband here that he's too old and ugly to be spending his days with a pretty little thing like me. She knows Jack can't help being a father figure for me."

"Years together, sure, when it was our real daughter who wanted to spend time with you..." His voice trailed off and he winked slyly.

Rynn punched him on the arm. "I can't believe you brought that up again!"

Another inquiring glance from Pearson prompted Samson to go on. "Gina, our oldest girl, had a bit of a thing for Rynn a few years back. They even went out a couple times, didn't you?"

Rynn couldn't stop the blush heating her face. "Oh, God, we are not talking about this again. No offense, Jack, but Gina just wasn't my type. At all."

She tried to escape back to her desk, but Samson caught her and pulled her into a bear hug. "We've been over this a dozen times. No offense taken. You know I love my daughter, but she's a girl, you know? I just don't much understand her."

"So if she's the girl, what are you trying to say about me?" Rynn feigned insult, but their laughter filled the break room, Samson's the loudest of all.

"Well, honey, it's like you said, you're the son I never had!"

Rynn had been nervous about how Pearson might react to the news that she was a lesbian. She didn't hide her sexuality at work, but she knew some of the other guys in the department could be jerks about it. The last thing she needed was to hit it off with a new partner only to have him wig out because she was gay.

He didn't. In fact, he'd even teased her about it during their lunch break. "So, Jack Samson's daughter, eh?" he deadpanned.

Rynn instinctively stiffened for a second, but when she shot him a glance, he grinned like a Cheshire cat, which earned him a punch on the arm too.

He took the teasing a step further. "Man, you've got stones. Going out with your partner's daughter. Only thing better would be if you dated the chief's kid too." He chuckled, but Rynn thought she saw a shadow cross his face.

"Gina was not my type. She's nothing like her father." As soon as the words were out of her mouth, Rynn scrunched her nose. Crap, had she just set herself up for—

"Are you saying Jack Samson *is* your type?" The grin was back in full force.

Rynn responded by punching him again and brushed off his comment with a short, "Oh, you know what I mean."

Later as the afternoon waned, Pearson sat at the desk across from Rynn's. She looked up when he let out a long sigh and ran his fingers through his short salt-and-pepper hair.

Drifting into a moment of speculation, she considered everything she had learned about him. She'd been right when she guessed his age at late thirties during their first meeting. He had worked primarily in SVU during his time in Cleveland, although he'd done stints in Vice and Homicide. After over thirteen years on the force, as far as he let on, he just decided to up and move to Chicago. But she could tell there was a story he just wasn't ready to share.

Apparently, one year here in Kane County's SVU and he'd had enough of his former partner, Hyler. She had heard horror stories about how Hyler was a macho dick, but she'd never actually met him. Despite knowing she shouldn't listen to gossip, she couldn't help avoiding him. Macho dicks tended to be homophobes too. Fortunately, it seemed Pearson was nothing like Hyler in that regard.

Rynn shook herself from her reverie and glanced at the clock. Four thirty p.m. She pushed her chair back from her desk and cleared her throat to get Pearson's attention. "Well, I'd say you've had a pretty big first week away from SVU. Why don't you take off for the weekend and we'll hit this again fresh on Monday morning?"

Pearson considered her for a second, a shadow of suspicion in his eyes. "I'm not leaving if you're not leaving. I carry my own weight, you know."

Rynn raised an eyebrow. She hadn't expected his defensiveness. "I never said you didn't."

He sighed a second time and rose to his feet. "I'm sorry. I didn't mean to be so touchy. Hyler had a way of dismissing me that rubbed me the wrong way, so after a year of his B.S., I suppose I must be a little sensitive."

Rynn nodded. "No dismissal, here. In fact, I plan to head out soon myself."

He stretched and smiled. "In that case, I will take you up on your suggestion to bail a few minutes early. It's been a good first week, Detective. Hopefully, we'll crack this case next week and the new investigative A-Team will be on our way to the top." He shrugged on a jacket.

Rynn returned his smile and threw him a short wave when he turned to leave. Yeah, Pearson was turning out to be an all right partner so far.

She looked at the open file on her desk. She couldn't really think of much else to do with the Boden homicide tonight.

Fresh eyes on Monday were probably their best bet. She closed the folder and grabbed the mouse to shut down her computer.

The screen had just flickered to black when her phone rang. She grabbed the receiver. "Callahan."

"Rynn, sweetheart, did I just see Stevie leave?"

Rynn smiled at Betty's tone. She had a hunch that the sweet, elderly receptionist in the front station would call him Stevie. "Yeah, I told him to take off."

After a pause, Betty said, "Oh. Well, there's a young woman here who would like to discuss the Patrick Boden case with someone. That's the case you and Stevie are working on, isn't it?"

Rynn leaned forward. "Yes. That's ours."

"Should I have her make an appointment for Monday when you are both here?" Betty asked.

Rynn didn't hesitate. Pearson would understand. "No, no, I'll be out in a few minutes to talk to her." She knew when unexpected witnesses stepped forward, she might never see them again if she didn't set up a meeting right away.

"All right, dear. I'll let her know."

Rynn set the phone down. She was certainly intrigued, but she had to be careful because the other thing about unexpected voluntary witnesses was that, unfortunately, she couldn't always trust their motives or their information.

She rose from her chair. Approaching the lobby from a side corridor, she found the visitor standing with her arms folded loosely across her chest. The posture was an uneasy one, but the beautiful woman didn't fidget or show any other signs of nerves.

Rynn paused just out of sight. Why anxious? Was the woman worried about possessing information pertaining to a murder investigation? Perhaps. Most likely, in fact. She surreptitiously studied the woman and didn't detect fear. Certainly no guilt. She watched a second longer, and couldn't help letting her gaze trace up and down the woman's figure.

The woman appeared determined and looked businesslike in a charcoal-gray power suit. Her sleek, dark brown hair was clipped into an impeccably neat twist at the back of her head.

Rynn shook herself out of her trance and stepped forward. The woman turned sharply at the sound of footsteps, a calm confidence filling her eyes as her gaze swept over Rynn's body.

Rynn offered a welcoming smile, which was met by a stunning look of certainty, any hint of nerves suddenly gone. The woman might have been anxious, but after that barely noticeable appraisal, an almost knowing expression transformed her face. The slightest grin tugged at a corner of her mouth.

The woman spoke first. "You must be Detective Kathrynn Callahan." At Rynn's acknowledgment, she continued. "I'm Toni Davis."

Rynn extended her hand. "Welcome, Ms. Davis. What can I do for you today?" She was impressed by the warm strength conveyed through their brief handshake.

Toni motioned at the front desk. "As I'm sure your receptionist informed you, I'm here about Patrick Boden. I have some information, some very sensitive information, that may or may not pertain to the case, but my client and I have decided to let your office, or perhaps you personally, be the judge of that."

Rynn frowned. "Your client? Are you an attorney, Ms. Davis?"

Toni smiled and shook her head. "Not quite. And you'll have to forgive me for not explaining exactly who I am just yet. You see, I'm a little wary of being overheard."

"Of course. I apologize. Why don't you come back to one of our private conference rooms with me and we'll talk there?" Rynn turned slightly to lead the way, but was stopped short by the slightest touch on her arm.

"Actually, Detective, I'm a bit wary of the whole station. I would be more comfortable if you'd join me for a coffee away from here."

Rynn turned back to study Toni. Meeting her steady gaze, she was struck by the dark chocolate depths, so intense with so many different emotions. Confidence, honesty, yet also caution and perhaps suspicion shone there, so easy for her to read, and so easy to believe.

After a moment's silence, she responded. "That would be highly unusual, ma'am, seeing as you're already in the station."

Toni nodded without offering further explanation.

Rynn pressed. "Is there a particular reason why you prefer to talk elsewhere?"

Again, that slight tug at the corner of Toni's mouth. "As I said, Detective, I'm a little wary of being overheard."

Rynn frowned. "And as I said, our conference rooms are completely private. I wasn't about to take you to an interrogation room with one-way glass, cameras and microphones."

Toni chuckled. "Perhaps not, but I still don't trust these facilities. At least not given the nature of my information."

"What is the nature of that information, exactly?" Rynn challenged.

"Nice try, but I'm not talking here. Though as I mentioned, I suspect you might be interested to hear what I have to say."

"You really think a coffee shop can offer you more privacy than a secure police station?"

"Yes, actually, I do. At least, the coffee shop I have in mind." Toni seemed determined to have the conversation elsewhere or not at all.

Rynn decided to acquiesce. "Well, let me at least get my notepad. If you'll wait here just a moment, I'll be right back, then we'll discuss where we're going."

Toni smiled.

Rynn was beginning to like that smile, even if Toni had proven a bit stubborn. Difficult witnesses could be a pain in the ass, but instinct told her this one was worth humoring. She walked back to her office quickly, questions running through her mind. Who was Toni Davis? What was her relationship to the victim? Why the insistence that they talk elsewhere? Where did she intend to take her? And what, exactly, did she know about Patrick Boden?

After retrieving her notepad, she returned to the reception area to find that Toni had taken a seat in one of the chairs by the door. She stopped briefly in front of Betty's desk, letting her know that she was leaving with Ms. Davis to discuss the case in a location of her choice.

Betty found the situation highly unusual. "Rynn, dear, I didn't think you were supposed to do that, especially not with Stevie being gone already."

Rynn smiled at her motherly tone. "Yes, Betty, I'm well aware, but she simply refuses to talk here. I'm not about to let a potential witness get away for the sake of following protocol. Did you have her sign the visitor's log when she arrived?"

Betty puffed out her chest in feigned indignation. "Of course. Although you may be willing to buck protocol, I pride myself on sticking to it. If you haven't figured it out yet, dear, I am an excellent receptionist. Ms. Antoinette Davis signed in at precisely four forty-eight p.m. this afternoon."

"Of course, Betty. I never should have doubted you."

"Indeed not." Betty smiled.

Rynn turned to leave the station with Toni Davis.

CHAPTER THREE

Toni couldn't completely suppress the smile threatening to erupt when she first saw Kathrynn Callahan. Many of her misgivings about coming down to the police station evaporated. Why? she wondered. Because she felt more comfortable in the presence of a female detective?

No, she knew there was more to it than that. This had been a terrible, terrible week, the pain of loss compounded by her inability to admit to her friendship with Patrick Boden. On top of that, she knew the situation was a thousand times worse for Daniel, and she was one of the very few people to whom he could turn for comfort.

In being strong for him, she had been sapped of her energy. That, coupled with fear and indecision over whether or not she and Daniel should go to the police, had left her nearly exhausted. Over a lunch meeting earlier in the day, they had come to a decision. She would seek out the detectives investigating Patrick's murder. She'd demand privacy and stress the delicacy of their position. If she felt she could trust them, she would share what she knew.

One look at Detective Callahan greatly improved her mood. She recognized the same thing in her that lay at the center of their fears. And she sensed something more, something safe, about the blonde woman who greeted her. She believed immediately that Detective Callahan would understand, and she was no longer so afraid to talk.

Maybe she shouldn't put quite so much stock in a single glance, but Detective Callahan made her insides stir. She prided herself on being able to read people, to almost sense people's character. Yes, she could trust this woman, she decided, but she still did not trust the greater establishment. She and Detective Callahan would have to talk elsewhere.

Detective Callahan resisted the idea, as Toni knew she would.

In the end, Toni won.

When they stepped outside together into the early evening sunlight, Toni turned to the woman beside her. Detective Callahan spoke first. "All right, Ms. Davis. I suppose I'm letting you run this operation. For now, at least. So what are we doing?"

Toni offered her a smile. "Well, first of all, please, call me Toni." She hoped to win the detective's trust sooner rather than later.

Detective Callahan nodded. "Okay. Toni, then. Where are we going?"

Toni noticed the return offer of a first-name basis had not been extended. Fine, she would simply move forward without it. "I thought we might go to a small coffee shop not too far from here. Madeleine's. Ever heard of it?"

Detective Callahan nodded. "This time of day, traffic might be a bit heavy, but I'm comfortable there. I think we'll be able to talk without any difficulties." She shrugged. "I'm still a little surprised that you prefer a coffee shop to a police station, but I'm certainly interested in what you have to say. Or perhaps you just wanted a ride in a police cruiser?"

Toni was pleased at the slightly teasing tone. "Oh, no, I think I'd rather drive myself, if you don't mind."

"Good, because I didn't bring the keys to a cruiser. I hate driving those things. I prefer to take my own car. Shall I follow you?"

"I thought you said you knew how to get there."

Detective Callahan shrugged and smiled. "I do. But I don't much feel like letting you out of my sight until I know what's going on."

Toni chuckled. "Very well, Detective. If you insist. The black car is mine." She gestured at her Lexus.

Detective Callahan gave the car a simple appraising glance and turned toward the back of the parking lot.

Surprising herself, Toni called after her. "Detective?" When the detective looked back, she gave her a devilish grin. "Try to keep up." She winked and turned to her car.

* * *

Rynn stood rooted in the parking lot a moment while Toni strode to her Lexus. She had to shake herself to start moving again. She headed quickly to her Tahoe, although she couldn't help one more glance over her shoulder to take in those perfect legs. Had the new witness been flirting with her? No. *Come on, Rynn, get it together.* She never lost her focus with witnesses and that wasn't about to change. She'd just been caught off guard.

As she pulled her vehicle out of the parking lot behind the sleek black Lexus, Rynn wondered once again about Toni Davis. Exactly who was she? She was impeccably dressed, confident, sharp. The car screamed money, power and speed. She was funny. *Hold on, how is sense of humor relevant to the investigation?*

Rynn shook her head, startled by her reaction.

The drive to Madeleine's was twice as long as it should have been because of the time of day. Rynn generally tried to avoid driving anywhere between five and six o'clock on Friday which, if she were being honest, was half the reason she'd suggested she and Pearson bail early.

The Lexus pulled into a small parking lot behind the coffee shop, and Rynn followed suit. The place wasn't busy, apparently not appealing to evening commuters. Those who needed a caffeine fix to get home could go to one of the hundred Starbucks' drive-through windows littered around the area. Madeleine's catered to a different crowd. She suspected the shop would be much busier later in the evening.

When she killed her Tahoe's engine, she noted a sign in the coffee shop's window advertising an acoustic guitar player performing that evening at eight o'clock. She climbed out of her car and looked over at the Lexus two spaces down. Toni waited by the rear of the car, smiling as she approached. She considered Toni again, realizing that she might have to make a more conscious effort to focus if that smile stuck around.

She motioned to the door. "Shall we?"

Toni nodded and stepped forward. "You've been here before, you said?"

"Maybe once or twice." Rynn shrugged. "Not a lot. It's a little out of the way for me."

Toni reached the door first and held it open for her to step inside. "Yes, it's not the closest for me either, but I've found its benefits certainly outweigh that particular disadvantage." She turned to the counter, greeting the girl behind it with a smile. "Hey kid! How have you been?"

Rynn's glance dropped from the menu board when she heard the girl's friendly reply. "Oh, you know, same old. Maddie's a slave driver, as always. You want your usual?"

Toni and the girl continued to chat. Rynn made a mental note that Toni was obviously a regular. Her eyes flicked to the girl's nametag—Emma—before returning to the drinks selection.

Finally, Toni turned back to Rynn and nudged her arm. "My order's probably getting cold by now. Are you just going to stand there pondering all night?"

Rynn smiled and stepped up to the counter. "Medium hazelnut coffee."

From behind her, Toni corrected. "Make it a large. And throw some foam on top. From me."

Rynn caught a subtle exchange between Toni and Emma. When she reached for her wallet, Toni actually swatted her hand lightly. "No, no, Detective. It's on me."

Thanking her, Rynn started to turn away from the counter but paused when she noticed an inquiring glance from Emma. Toni shook her head, pursing her lips in the negative. She mouthed, "Business," and Emma simply nodded.

Drinks in hand a moment later, Toni led Rynn to a couple of comfortable armchairs at the back of the shop. As daylight rapidly faded outside, the shop's atmosphere became more intimate. Once again, she studied Toni, who took a seat in the chair opposite.

Toni relaxed, tucking one leg under her body. She maintained the position comfortably despite her power skirt, impressing Rynn. Deliberately forbidding her attention from lingering on Toni's legs, she focused instead on her intense eyes.

Rynn's thoughtful consideration met an equally searching gaze. She knew the questions in her own mind, but what was Toni looking for?

* * *

Toni felt comfortable at Madeleine's. She also knew beyond a doubt that her conversation was safe here. Even if someone overheard the gist of what she had to tell the detective, the typical crowd wasn't likely to care.

At this time in the evening, she hadn't expected many people to be in the shop and she'd been right. In fact, she and Detective Callahan were the only patrons. In two hours, it would be a completely different story. Nevertheless, she wasn't willing to rush the conversation. If need be, she thought she could force a move to another location.

Despite her confidence, Toni hesitated to dive right into the reason for their meeting. Instead, she opened with small talk. "Hazelnut, Detective? I would have pegged you for a regular, black, no-frills type." She grinned warmly and sipped her chai tea, never shifting her gaze from the stunning green eyes looking back at her. She saw Detective Callahan's expression flicker with a range of emotions: interest, amusement, curiosity, a touch of impatience. She suspected that the detective didn't like to be kept waiting, but had the patience to sit here all night if necessary.

After a few seconds of silence, Detective Callahan finally responded. "Looks can be deceiving, Ms. Davis."

Doing her best to read the detective's character, Toni's doubts were alleviated by the humor behind the words. She decided to continue. "I hope you're not trying to tell me you're not as trustworthy as you appear?" she asked playfully, though she wanted an honest answer.

The detective shook her head. "Not at all, Ms. Davis. I was just referring to personal preferences." She smiled and added, "On coffee, of course."

What other personal preferences might she have in mind? Toni wondered. Had the detective's gaydar gone off as strongly as her own during their initial meeting? She took another sip of tea. "Coffee." She nodded. "Of course. And didn't I ask you to call me Toni?"

Detective Callahan studied her. "Toni, yes. I apologize. I must admit, I'm not quite used to this."

"This? You mean a coffee shop?"

"No, coffee shops are fine. I was referring more to being lured out of my office by a mysterious woman with the promise of information on a murder I'm investigating."

Toni grinned. "So you're saying I'm mysterious? Do you like mysterious?" *God, am I flirting with a police detective?* Yes. Yes, she was. She couldn't seem to help herself.

If Detective Callahan noticed, her expression didn't let on. "Perhaps. I suppose it depends on the mystery. I like to solve my cases. If you contribute to that goal, I suspect I'll come to like you quite a bit."

Come to? "You don't like me now?" Toni broke their eye contact and looked briefly down into her cup. The pause was long enough to remind her why she was here.

"I didn't mean it like that," the detective said. "I just don't know you at all. Yet."

Toni glanced up. Detective Callahan shifted uncomfortably in her seat. Could it really be so easy to disarm her? She sensed a vulnerability she hadn't expected. Again, she was hit with a strong impulse to trust this stranger. She looked away again, this time gazing thoughtfully out the nearby window. After a moment, she met the detective's gaze once more. *God, her eyes are so green.* Focus. *It's time to start talking.*

She began, "I suppose I should tell you a bit more about myself and why I've *lured* you here."

Detective Callahan smiled briefly at the phrasing.

Toni opened her mouth to continue but paused. It was silly, but… "You're going to think I'm crazy, but can I call you Kathrynn? Or Kate? Whatever you go by with friends." She thought it couldn't hurt to try.

Detective Callahan appeared surprised. "I prefer to maintain a level of professional distance with witnesses. Why would you ask me to change that?"

Toni sighed. "What I'm about to tell you is very personal. Very important. Not something I feel at all comfortable sharing with a stranger. But as I mentioned in the station, I think it might mean something. I…I'm not sure, but it might, and so we've decided to tell you."

"We?" Detective Callahan tilted her head, curiosity painting her strong features.

"Yes, we. My client and I."

"Why are you reluctant to talk to me as a homicide detective?"

Toni stared into her now empty mug. "What I know, what I have to share, hasn't always been treated with respect by the law. I believe you may be different, though. Not as a detective, but as a person. I have to believe that, or else I don't think I can trust you with what I came to discuss."

Her statement was met with silence. The detective finally nodded. "Call me Rynn."

Toni looked up. *Rynn.* It fit her well. "Thank you." Toni paused to gather her thoughts. "Okay, Rynn, I'm sure you must be dying of curiosity. I have only one more request, and I doubt you'll be so agreeable this time."

Rynn narrowed her eyes. Toni hesitated and glanced over her, taking in her striking appearance. Rynn projected calm and strength. She wasn't rough or forceful, which had been her mental picture of a homicide detective.

Rynn Callahan was...Toni didn't know how quite to describe her. The word "solid" came to mind, but with a far more positive connotation than she might have expected. Had someone previously described another woman that way, she might expect a hefty build or an abrasive personality, neither of which Rynn possessed.

Rynn was toned, muscular, but not in a scary, female bodybuilder way. Perhaps a bit androgynous, her dirty-blonde hair was cut fairly short, hanging stick-straight and just below her jawline. Lastly, she had the most stunning emerald eyes Toni had ever seen—eyes which now regarded her coolly, waiting for her to speak.

Uh-oh. Am I pushing this too far? But she had to at least try, though she would be shocked if Rynn agreed. "I need to ask that you not include this information in the file. Act on it as you see fit, but no official record. No one else can know what I'm going to share," Toni said. Then she sat back and waited for Rynn's response.

CHAPTER FOUR

Rynn could hardly believe her ears. She kept her face expressionless, but she was rapidly losing patience. What in the hell kind of game was this woman playing? Toni may or may not be about to tell her something that may or may not pertain to the investigation of a violent murder, and now she wanted her to keep it off the official record?

What could possibly be so sensitive that Toni dragged her from the station to meet in a coffee shop, only to confess to a deep distrust of the law? Rynn was intrigued, to be sure, but the situation was getting more ridiculous. She shook her head. "No, I can't agree to that. If for no other reason than if whatever you have to say helps me in the investigation, I'll need to include it in the case file for the district attorney."

Toni's face fell. She averted her gaze, but nodded. "I thought as much. Will you at least withhold any reporting unless it proves necessary? A man's livelihood is at stake. Should the information become public, his career will suffer, if not end entirely. Your discretion is most welcome."

What in the world was Toni about to tell her? Rynn considered the revised request. Could it hurt? She was surprised when Toni's sadness tugged at her heart. If the need arose, nothing was secret, but she didn't see the harm in agreeing to delay her decision. She took a deep breath. "Very well. I'll wait. But if I need to include it in my report, I will."

Toni turned to her, a slight smile lifting the corner of her mouth. "Thank you, Rynn." She paused. The silence stretched between them. At last, she asked, "What do you know about Patrick Boden's personal life?"

Rynn arched her brow. Now Toni wanted her to disclose information? "Sorry, but I'm here to discuss what you know, not the other way around."

Toni shook her head. "No, I suppose not. If I had to guess, I'd wager not much. Patrick was very careful."

Rynn knew her expression betrayed nothing, but her curiosity was piqued. "Why was that?"

Toni sighed. "He had to be." She paused, her gaze falling to her lap. She quietly continued, "He loved Daniel very much, and he would never do anything to risk Daniel's happiness. Even if that meant returning to the closet to keep Daniel's secret."

Daniel? The closet? So Patrick Boden was gay, Rynn thought.

Toni continued. "We thought about telling you as much as we could without naming Daniel, without risking outing him. But no, we decided...I should say, Daniel decided that wouldn't work. Any detective worth their salt would dig deeper and find out once they knew Patrick had a lover. And I suspect that you, Detective Callahan, would indeed keep digging."

Rynn noted that Toni had used her title and wondered why she'd shifted back to formality. She kept silent and let Toni go on.

"I'm here to tell you Daniel's secret with the hope that you will respect him and show as much discretion as possible in moving forward. You see, Daniel's career depends on being in the social spotlight. Were he to come out now, he could lose everything." Toni turned away, clearly fighting back tears. "At least, everything else. Maybe he's already lost everything worth having. He loved Patrick so much. You never plan on something like this. They thought they would have a lifetime to share. They…oh, they couldn't wait for life after the game so that they could be together. Truly be together."

The game? The game of being closeted? Rynn studied Toni. She wouldn't question or prompt now, sensing it best to give her as much time as she needed.

After a minute, Toni cleared her throat and went on. "Maybe this will make more sense if I explain who I am, and why I have come to talk instead of Daniel himself. I am Daniel's agent. And his friend, but today, I'm acting as his representative." She brushed a tear from her cheek before forcing a small laugh. "At least, I'm trying to, if I can keep it together." She drew in a deep breath. "I'm a sports agent, and I represent dozens of clients across the country, although mostly in the Midwest. Through my business relationships, I have also formed several good friendships. That happens to be the case with Daniel and Patrick. As such, I find myself in the position of knowing what the police likely do not—that Patrick was gay, had a committed lover of over five years, and this lover is a very high profile, very famous individual."

Rynn considered the information while Toni stared out the window, lost in her thoughts. She wondered if Toni even remembered she was there.

"It's tragic enough that Patrick was killed," Toni said, barely above a whisper. "It's all the more horrible because Daniel can't mourn him. He's forced to go on with his life as if nothing has happened, as if he hasn't just lost his soul mate. They were so careful throughout their relationship and Daniel throughout his career.

"I've often wondered if it wouldn't be better for him to come out and damn the consequences. I've wondered if he'd be happier that way, even if the game forced him out, even if his fans turned on him. If he could openly express who he is and share with the world his love for Patrick, would he have been better off? It was never my decision to make, though. Nor will I be that hypocritical. There are people in my life I'm still afraid to tell about my own sexuality."

Rynn tilted her head in surprise at this admission. Her gaydar hadn't pinged in the least when she'd first set eyes on Toni a short while ago. On the other hand, her friends often teased her about having worse gaydar than most straight people.

"If I can't confide in lifelong family friends, how could I expect Daniel to come out to the whole country?" Toni asked. "It doesn't surprise me in the least that we have absolutely zero out gay male athletes actively competing in this country. It shames and disappoints me, certainly. But it does not surprise me." Her voice faded.

Rynn sat quietly, processing what she had been told. This was certainly information she needed for her investigation, but the investigation seemed secondary to the pain flooding Toni's expression. She was shaken from her thoughts by the tinkling of the bell above the door. A group of about eight twenty-somethings walked into the shop, chatting happily. She glanced at her watch. Seven thirty already? Had she and Toni been here that long?

Toni sighed.

Now that Rynn understood the reasons behind her secrecy, she made a quiet offer. "Is there somewhere else you'd like to take this conversation?"

Toni nodded gratefully. "Yes. But honestly, I'm not sure how much more I have to say. You know the gist of it."

Rynn agreed. "The gist, yes. I still don't actually know who Daniel is. You've given me only a first name without a team or even a sport, and you've not indicated if you have any reason to suspect that someone might have targeted Patrick because of his relationship with Daniel." *Or if there's a chance that Daniel is involved*, she added silently.

Dark shadows clouded Toni's eyes.

Rynn nudged her a little. "Is there? Are you aware of anyone bearing a grudge against Daniel who may have been aware of his relationship with the victim?"

Toni shrugged. "Daniel had enemies, yes, but he never actually took any of them seriously. They're so petty. He actually gets death threats from fans of opposing teams. How silly is that?"

"Unfortunately, in my line of work, I've come to find that no reason is too petty for some people to commit murder," Rynn admitted softly. The bell at the door rang a second time. Another group of people walked in. Apparently, tonight's musician was a decent draw.

"Rynn, are you a Bears fan?" Toni questioned.

Rynn shook her head. "Honestly, not really. I take it that Daniel is a Bear?"

Toni nodded. "Yes. And a rather well known one at that. Would you care to go to the game on Sunday? They're playing the Jaguars. Might actually be able to win this one."

Rynn considered the suggestion. Would Toni make her wait two more days for further information? Then again, she doubted Toni would be much use while she checked out Daniel as a suspect. She could get Daniel's name from the team roster and arrange an interview immediately without having to push Toni too much and lose her cooperation. She replied, "I've never actually been down to Soldier Field. I hear tickets are hard to come by."

Toni grinned through the lingering sadness. "Not if you're a sports agent. I represent a couple of guys on the team, and one for Jacksonville as well, actually. Pick you up at the station at ten o'clock? It takes a little while to get downtown and find parking and everything. Also, we can talk in the car that way."

Rynn hated to see Toni's melancholy. She hadn't felt such a tug in a long time. Toni opened her mouth hesitantly, as if she had something more to say, but she remained quiet.

"And don't worry," Rynn went on. "You were right. I completely understand and sympathize with the need for discretion. I promise I will keep this information need-to-know only." Of course, need-to-know meant she would tell her lieutenant and probably Pearson, but it wasn't necessary to tell Toni that. Still, the omission made her feel oddly guilty.

Toni smiled. "Thank you, Rynn. That means a lot to Daniel." She paused. "And to me." She rose from her chair as a group of people settled at the table next to them.

Rynn followed Toni outside. The night air was cool and crisp. The stars shone brightly and a full moon lit the sky. She handed over a business card. "My cell number's on there, if you think of anything else or want to talk to me again before then."

Toni turned to face her when they reached the sleek black Lexus. "Sunday, then?"

Rynn smiled, "It's a date." She said the words without really thinking and was rewarded with a return smile from Toni. *A date? Did I really just say that?* She felt oddly self-conscious, realizing that spending the day with Toni held a strong appeal. She shifted her stance, suddenly wanting to make a quick exit before she embarrassed herself.

Whether or not Toni noticed her sudden awkwardness, she wasn't sure. But her eyes held Toni's a second longer before Toni turned to pull open her car door.

"Sunday," Toni confirmed, slipping gracefully into the vehicle.

Rynn suppressed an unexpected desire to wish her a good night, fearing that might cross the bounds of professional courtesy. As she walked to her Tahoe, she found herself turning to watch Toni's Lexus pull away from the dimly lit parking lot.

CHAPTER FIVE

The crack of lightning and rolling thunder woke Rynn early Sunday morning. The rumble outside matched the lingering foul mood from her futile day before. What should have been a simple exercise in pulling a name from a public website rapidly spiraled downward when she found there wasn't a single Daniel on the Bears' roster, nor had there been in four years. She met briefly with her lieutenant to discuss the new developments and her options. Records requests on the entire roster—and Toni as well—would take longer than waiting to talk to her the next day.

Rynn felt the only progress she'd made was in checking the Bears' schedule. They had played the Monday night game in Arizona five days prior, which meant if Daniel was on the team, he would have an airtight alibi. Millions would have seen him on TV and the team flight had not arrived back in Chicago until after the window during which the murder occurred.

Half awake, she rolled on her side and squinted at the glowing clock. Seven o'clock? It was still so dark outside, she didn't want to believe the time.

Damn, this wasn't just a midnight storm that might dry out by morning, she thought. She rolled back over, her plans for the day drifting into her mind. She looked forward to the football game with Toni, perhaps more than she should have, professionally speaking.

With the storm outside literally rattling her bedroom windows, Rynn began to think that spending the day in bed, or at the very least indoors, was a much better idea. At least the weather would keep her too miserable to enjoy Toni's company much.

She faded into a fitful dream, paced by the rumbling torrent outside. An hour later, her alarm screamed at her, and as usual, she flopped across the bed, blindly slamming the snooze button. She lifted her arms over her head and stretched, still reluctant to climb from the comfy depths of sleep. The rain had slowed, and she heard no more thunder, but the temptation to turn off the alarm and drift back to her dreams was strong, even though eight o'clock was already sleeping in compared to her normal hours. She might typically have to be at work by this time, but that didn't mean she had to like it.

After another minute enjoying the warmth of her bed, Rynn forced herself up, crawled out of bed, and dragged her feet to the shower. As the hot, strong spray flowed over her body, she allowed herself a minute to bask in the massaging water. Afterward, she threw on clean jeans, a casual button-down shirt and a thick, waterproof jacket. Finally, she tied up her low-cut boots, and braved the rain, shocked by the drop in temperature since the day before.

Driving over to the rendezvous, she realized she hadn't eaten breakfast. She wondered if Toni would be hungry as well, and decided it wouldn't hurt to grab some coffee and pastries. Sitting at Starbucks' drive-through window, she realized she didn't even know if Toni liked coffee, given that she'd had tea the other night.

Rynn shrugged to herself and ordered two pumpkin spice lattes, a blueberry muffin, a cran-raspberry scone, and some sort of fruit Danish. She wasn't entirely sure what kind of fruit it was, but she figured all the pastries were pretty tasty.

She left Starbucks and drove her Tahoe to the back of the station's parking lot, where she scanned the other cars for the black Lexus Toni drove the other night. While gazing out the passenger side window, she was startled by the double beeping of a car horn next to her vehicle. Trying to pretend she hadn't just jumped in her seat, she turned to see Toni grinning at her from the Lexus.

Rynn grabbed the coffees and the bag of pastries, then ducked quickly from her car into Toni's. Even in the few seconds it took her to transfer between vehicles, she managed to be soaked by the fine, misty rain steadily falling.

Toni reached across the car and helped her with the two steaming cups, placing them securely in the cup holders while Rynn slipped into the low leather seat. The sweet aroma of pumpkin spice and pastries filled the car.

"Should have known the cop would have doughnuts," Toni teased, inhaling deeply. "Wow, this smells amazing. How did you know I hadn't eaten breakfast?"

Rynn smiled. "I had no idea. I just knew I hadn't. I hope you like the coffee. I wasn't sure if chai tea went well with breakfast pastries." She caught the sparkle in Toni's eye and the soft grin. Was Toni surprised "the cop" remembered what she'd had to drink the other night? She was a detective, after all.

Toni grabbed the bag. "Mmm, they all look good. Which one is for me?"

Rynn shrugged. "Whichever one you want. Or two, if you're hungry. I'll eat whatever's left." She watched as Toni considered for a second before selecting the mystery fruit Danish. When Toni threw her an inquiring look, she shrugged again. "I don't know. I told them to surprise me."

Toni smiled, seeming to enjoy the unknown. She took a tentative bite. Rynn caught herself following the outline of Toni's lips on the pastry. *What the hell are you doing?* She forced herself to look away, surprised by her wandering mind.

Toni was thoughtful for a minute, making Rynn fear she didn't like it. Then she murmured, "I think it's some kind of mixed berry. It's hard to say. Tasty, though. Here, you tell me."

Before Rynn had a chance to protest, Toni held out the Danish to her. She instinctively took a bite. The intimacy of the gesture made it even more difficult to shake her heated thoughts. She chewed the flaky pastry, trying to discern the flavors washing over her tongue. Toni was right, she decided. The Danish was good, but she had no idea what fruit was in the filling. Mixed berry seemed as good a guess as any.

She shook her head. "Still no idea. But I like it." *And I liked you feeding it to me.* She had to glance away to clear her head. Where were these thoughts coming from? She felt nothing like her normally calm, cool, collected self. She hoped Toni couldn't tell she was so far off her game.

Toni took another bite of the mystery pastry before wrapping the rest in its paper and returning it to the bag. She took a careful sip of the coffee nearest her before turning the key in the ignition and shifting the car into gear. On the way out of the parking lot, she swerved slightly to splash through a pothole, throwing a wave of water into the air.

Rynn chuckled at the playful driving, but the realization that she was about to spend the afternoon outside in the chilly rain sent a shiver down her spine as if she had just been doused. "I can't believe I'm letting you drag me to a game in this weather. I'm still dripping just from jumping cars. Do you think the weather will let up at all by game time?"

Toni focused squarely on the road. Her coy expression made Rynn think that she was hiding a smile, but that didn't make sense.

After a moment, Toni responded, "Well, Detective, when I invited you, I had no idea it would rain. The meteorologists seem to have had it backward for the weekend, seeing as they forecast rain yesterday and sun today." She snuck a quick glance at Rynn before turning her gaze back to the road. "If you're worried about catching cold, we could perhaps reschedule," she offered with a grin.

Rynn suspected that Toni had guessed she was far too stubborn to appear like a wimp. "No, no. I'll be fine."

She and Toni chatted idly for another twenty or thirty minutes while the Lexus made its way into the city. The small talk warmed the air in the car as much as the heater.

Rynn realized with some surprise she was extremely comfortable around Toni, and on more than one occasion she made her laugh. It was easy to forget that she and Toni had an ulterior purpose for going together to the football game today. After a few minutes lull in the conversation, she forced her mind back to work and shifted the talk to more serious matters.

"About Patrick and Daniel..." She spoke quietly, knowing the topic change might be upsetting. Sure enough, Toni stiffened slightly before letting out a deflated sigh. When Toni didn't speak, she went on. "How well did you know Patrick Boden?" she asked, alert for Toni's reaction.

After another shaky sigh, Toni spoke softly. "Fairly well. I'm much closer to Daniel, but I came to know Patrick through him. I've been Daniel's agent practically since he entered the league eight years ago. I was still finishing up law school, but I was already working for my dad's firm. He's based in California, and he's been representing athletes for forty years, one of the longest tenures in the profession. Basically, I'd been interning for him since high school. He showed me all the nuances, showed me how to handle the prima donnas without necessarily putting up with their crap."

Toni paused to navigate the thickening traffic before continuing. She filled in the details of Daniel's and her relationship, noting they had bonded over their sexual minority status. She spoke thoughtfully about her dear friend and his lost love.

By now, they were driving through the heart of downtown Chicago, approaching Soldier Field on Lake Shore Drive. Rynn sat in silence while Toni drove the Lexus toward a security cop directing traffic away from the hectic stadium. Reaching the officer, Toni simply lowered her window and flashed a parking pass. The guard moved aside a bright orange traffic cone and waved her through.

The car coasted slowly along the road next to the field while Rynn took in the view of the stadium. Despite the overcast sky and rain-soaked surroundings, she found something impressive about the old stadium with its strange silver addition. She'd grown up watching the Bears, but had never actually attended a game before. The NFL seemed so passionless when she watched it on TV, but she couldn't deny the excitement of the fans milling around the wet grounds, eagerly awaiting the game.

Toni eventually navigated the car through crowds of people and road cones into a parking garage that looked like it had been built right under the stadium.

Rynn turned to her, incredulous. "I thought you said finding parking took a while. Why do I feel like you were pulling my leg?"

Toni grinned playfully at her. "I believe I also mentioned some perks to being a sports agent. Well, good parking is one of them. What takes time is getting here with all the traffic. We did pretty well." She motioned to the clock on the car's console. "It's only eleven thirty. The game is scheduled to start a little after one o'clock, so I guess we have some time to kill."

Rynn tried to convince herself that the glint in Toni's eyes wasn't intended to be mischievous, but she found herself responding with a smile. "Any suggestions? This is my first time at an NFL game. What do you usually do before it starts?"

Toni pulled the key from the ignition, letting the engine fall silent. Rynn stirred, oddly uncomfortable in the dim parking garage. Toni gave her a pensive look and spoke, "I often like to walk by the water, but the view won't be much to brag about today. It looks like the rain has let up, though, if you'd care to take a stroll."

Rynn considered the offer. She was going to sit in the damp cold all afternoon. Did she really want to walk along the waterfront on such an overcast morning? Meeting Toni's gaze, she decided she was game for just about anything, so she nodded in agreement.

She and Toni left the parking garage together, walking away from the busy street they had traveled down a few minutes ago. As they stepped away from the building, she shivered and pulled her jacket around her torso more tightly.

Toni noticed and laughed. "What's wrong, Detective? Too chilly for you here?"

Rynn feigned a glare, thawed a bit by the use of her title in such a playful tone. "No, I'm fine for now. But I take no responsibility for any whining that results from you keeping me out in this cold all afternoon." Her pride didn't allow her to banter with just anyone, but she was comfortable with Toni and enjoyed the warm laugh that her joking complaint caused. "And if I catch a cold, I'm blaming you," she added, sniffling for effect.

"We'll see about that, Rynn. If you're too weak to handle what I've got in mind, I'll just have to nurse you back to health." Toni chuckled again and moved away, fortunately not seeing the flush that heated Rynn's cold face.

She and Toni headed over to the railing standing along the edge of the boardwalk. Because of the unpleasant weather, the water was choppy, rougher than Rynn had expected from Lake Michigan. One benefit of the chill damp was that not too many people had wandered to the water, most still tailgating near their vehicles in the open lots or taking cover under the overhangs of surrounding buildings.

Toni stopped and gazed out over the angry, gray water. "It fits, doesn't it?" she murmured.

Rynn stepped closer and rested her arms on the railing. When Toni didn't continue, she asked, "What do you mean?"

Toni sighed. "The weather. This dark, gray gloom that seems to cover the whole city. It's as if today, the sky feels Daniel's pain and is reflecting it back to us, perhaps because Daniel himself can't show it." She turned to face Rynn. "He didn't want to play today. Didn't want to practice this week. In all the years I've known him, I can't remember another time when he didn't want to play. Even when a teammate died a few years back, shot in a drive-by, he sought solace in the game. He blames himself for Patrick's death. He can't shake the gut feeling that the murder has something to do with him, with his secrecy. I don't know. Maybe it does, maybe not. That's why he decided I should talk to you." She shifted to face the water once more.

Rynn felt a need to comfort Toni. She resisted any physical contact, reminding herself that she had to maintain professional distance. She didn't really know what to say, except what she always said to families in this situation. She spoke quietly, "I'll do my best. If it's possible, I'll figure out what happened and bring Daniel what peace can be had from that knowledge."

Toni nodded without taking her gaze from the water.

They stood together in comfortable silence a little longer. With no other people near them, there seemed little sound beyond the crashing of small waves against the breakwater below. Eventually, Rynn broke the quiet with a question. "You said Daniel is playing today?"

"Yes. He doesn't know how not to play. But I'm worried. His heart is broken. In this game, if you play without heart, you risk getting injured. I wish he would have found some way to take this one off."

Rynn thought for a minute. She had to dig deeper, but was careful to respect Toni's emotions. "Is he a starter?"

Toni turned to her again with a knowing look. "You checked the roster, didn't you?"

Rynn nodded, not explaining herself further.

Toni continued. "He's easily the biggest name on the team, but you wouldn't have found him looking for Daniel. It's his middle name. That's what he prefers with close family and friends. It allows him some distance from the media darling image."

Rynn thought again about the games she'd watched recently and the listing of team members. She glanced over her shoulder at the stadium. The Bears didn't have a lot of big names. They hadn't been very good in recent years. The quarterback, often the most recognizable name on the team, was mediocre at best and leading an anemic offense. No, it was the defense that had kept the team in games recently. Even their Super Bowl run a few years back was due to defense. And the best player on that side of the ball was…

Rynn's eyes widened. Toni smiled slightly, apparently seeing the realization on her face.

"You're telling me that Tommy Rocker, the best safety in the NFL, is gay?" Rynn's voiced her astonishment in a low whisper.

Toni laughed at her surprise. "Yes, that's exactly what I'm telling you. Thomas Daniel Rocker. You see now that he's not just some scrub backup. I don't know about the best safety in the league, but he's had six Pro Bowl appearances in eight years with Chicago, so yes, he's a big player. Can you imagine the backlash if he were to come out?"

Rynn shook her head in disbelief. "He's such a large presence in Chicago sports. How could he possibly have kept his relationship with Patrick a secret?"

Toni turned to look at the stadium and the city beyond. "Very carefully. And often at great cost. Part of my job has been to help him keep that secret. And what time he spent with Patrick was painstakingly planned. He had a private cell phone account under an alias, as did Patrick. They talked frequently, but didn't often see each other. Especially not during the season. Off season was better. They traveled together. All over the world, in fact. They had to get far enough away that Daniel wouldn't be recognized. Both of them were very patient men. I think what kept them going to this point was the belief that Daniel wouldn't play football forever, and once his career was over, they would have the rest of their lives together."

The detective part of Rynn's mind made note of the cell phones, and the fact that Patrick and Daniel had traveled. She'd already suspected as much, having pieced together his co-workers' accounts of Patrick's vacations and the fact that he had a secret NFL boyfriend. Looking back to the stadium, she noted a steady stream of people moving through the gates. She motioned toward them, wondering if she and Toni should head inside.

Toni answered her unspoken question. "I suppose we might as well. Are you excited about your first Soldier Field experience?"

"Looking forward to the game, yes. Not so much sitting in this cold, wet weather, though." Her statement was met by another playful glint in Toni's eyes.

Rynn thought, *Why do I get the feeling I'm missing something here?* But she said nothing more as Toni led the way toward the stadium.

CHAPTER SIX

Toni smiled to herself while she worked her way to the stadium entrance. As the crowd thickened, she subconsciously reached back and took Rynn's hand, guiding her through the security gates and ticket turnstiles. After a few seconds, she realized what she had done and felt a tug of embarrassment, but shrugged it off. *At this point, it would be worse to call attention to it.*

Her hand still grasping Rynn's, Toni headed through the familiar concourses of Soldier Field. The game day smells of popcorn, bratwurst and beer filled the air. She couldn't help being warmed by the familiarity of the sporting festivities.

Despite everything that had happened this week and all the flaws of professional sports highlighted by Daniel's forced life in the closet, she loved this atmosphere. She loved her career, loved the games. No longer able to compete in sports at a high level herself, she was grateful that she had the skill and background to excel in a field so close to athletics.

She also enjoyed being able to treat people to some of the perks she experienced because of her position as agent. She stole a look at Rynn as they slowly progressed along the busy walkway. For now, they were dry and Rynn seemed to be enjoying herself, though she'd made no secret of the fact she wasn't thrilled about spending the day sitting in the rain.

The thought made Toni grin. Rynn had no idea what she'd planned.

Seeing their turn up ahead, Toni glanced down. A quick check of her watch told her the game should be starting in the next half hour. *Okay, show time.* She tugged playfully on Rynn's hand, suddenly aware that somehow, their fingers had become entwined. *It's just because it was crowded,* she told herself. *I didn't want to get separated.* Especially since Rynn had never visited the stadium before.

Toni had surprised her friends with game day plans in the past, but for some reason, she was more excited than usual to surprise Rynn. She led her farther down the ground level concourse, finally pausing in front of an elevator. After pulling an access card from her pocket, she swiped it through the security pad.

Rynn turned to her, an eyebrow raised in curiosity. "An elevator? Aren't these just for handicapped and rich people at a stadium like this?"

Toni laughed. "You know, some might make the argument that being rich is a handicap, but no, the elevator isn't reserved for them. You just have to know the right people."

Rynn nodded, a hint of playful suspicion glinting in her eyes. "Know the right people, eh? So I get to ride in style to my cold, wet seat? No escalators or long, crowded ramps for us?"

Toni couldn't keep the grin from her face. "Something like that."

The doors opened with a ding. Toni waved Rynn inside and followed her. She swiped the access card through another computerized reader, this time punching in a code on the keypad. "Do I have your attention yet, Detective?" she asked.

Rynn gave her a return smile. "You've had my attention since you entered into my station two days ago, Ms. Davis."

Toni nodded. "Good."

With another ding, the elevator doors opened. Toni had the pleasure of watching the astonishment, then comprehension, register across Rynn's face. She and Rynn stepped out onto the plush carpet of the hallway joining the private viewing suites.

Rynn looked at her incredulously. "We're watching the game from here?"

"You didn't really think I was going to make you sit in the cold rain all afternoon, did you?" Toni teased.

Rynn blinked once. "Well, yeah, actually I did."

Toni loved the surprise in Rynn's expression. She wasn't ashamed to admit to herself that she had wanted to impress the detective, and it appeared she'd done just that. Moving closer, she whispered in Rynn's ear, "I know how to treat a woman right, especially on a first date."

Rynn looked shocked.

Toni turned and led Rynn down the hall. She knew she was crossing the line, but couldn't help herself. *Mmm, Rynn's cute when she blushes.*

* * *

Rynn was speechless. First from the surprise of being taken to the private suites, and secondly from the feeling of Toni's warm breath against her ear. She wasn't sure when Toni had taken her hand downstairs in the crowd, but now she couldn't deny the woman was coming on to her. And there was also no denying she liked it.

She tried to shake any suggestive thoughts from her mind as she followed Toni down the hall. After all, Toni was a witness in a murder investigation she was conducting. Surely, she had more self-control than that.

They passed some larger suites with plate glass separating the rooms from the noise in the corridor. Most, Rynn concluded, were occupied by fans milling around, socializing and waiting for kickoff. Occasionally, she and Toni passed a room that had curtains printed with the Bears logo pulled over the glass, offering a heightened degree of privacy.

Finally, Toni stopped in front of a small room, motioning Rynn to enter first.

She stepped inside and was instantly drawn to the massive window in front of her. She looked out on the field below. The room was situated at the thirty-yard line on the north end. Taking in the rest of the room, she saw a massive, flat screen, hi-def TV in the front corner above her head. She turned at the sound of Toni's voice coming from a few feet behind her.

"Replays and commentary," Toni explained. "Don't want to miss any of the action."

Rynn just nodded, not quite having found her voice yet.

Toni smiled at her. "Shall we take a seat?" She moved forward and settled into a plush couch just a few feet away from the window wall overlooking the field. She patted the cushion next to her, shamelessly flirting.

Rynn finally recovered from her shock and rolled her eyes. She couldn't help laughing at Toni's expression of feigned innocence. *Damn, she's sexy.* She gave herself a mental shake, trying to suppress the completely inappropriate thoughts crashing down on her. She wondered how often Toni pulled this stunt on other women, bringing them to a private suite and teasing them with that look. Despite her constant mental reminders that this was a professional meeting, it felt more like a date.

Opting not to sit down yet, Rynn continued to look around the suite. It wasn't a large room, maybe twelve feet square. A folding table stood against the back wall close to where they had entered. She noted the curtains were drawn. Interesting. *I guess Toni likes her privacy.* She briefly wondered why before resuming her assessment.

The TV above her head flashed broadcast coverage of the pregame, the sound turned so low Rynn could barely hear it. That was okay—she didn't really want to listen to the announcers.

Two end tables and the couch were the only furniture in the room, with the TV and a mini fridge rounding out the accommodations. Assorted framed Bears paraphernalia decorated the walls. It was simple, almost cozy, but the location alone demonstrated the money behind it.

Rynn stepped over to the glass window and gazed at the field. She became aware that Toni had moved next to her. They stood in silence for a minute, just a few inches separating them.

Toni was the one to break the quiet. "See number twenty-three? On the sideline down there? That's Daniel. He normally spends warm-ups helping out the other guys, getting the defense ready. He's been the defensive captain for three years." She paused before adding quietly, "The other guys respond to him. He's charismatic. A good leader. I don't know how well he'll be able to lead today, though. Look at him, just milling around the sideline. I've never seen him do that. Never."

Rynn turned to face Toni, responding to the sadness in her voice.

Her attention drawn back to the window, Rynn saw the other players hopping around, getting psyched for the game ahead. Daniel stood with his back to them, barely moving. A coach approached Daniel and leaned close, saying something in his ear. He nodded and reached down to grab a helmet off the bench. Before he pulled it over his sandy blond hair, he turned. She could have sworn his piercing gaze sought out their box.

Toni gasped quietly beside her. Rynn turned sharply at the sound and was taken aback. Toni had drawn a hand over her mouth in surprise, fingertips resting on her lips. Before she could ask what had happened, Toni answered the unspoken question.

"He never wears eye black, especially not with something written on it. I can't believe it." Lost in her own thoughts, Toni stared down at the field, her hand moving to rest on the glass in front of her as if she were reaching out to her friend.

He looked up at their window. Rynn watched him nod once before he turned back to the field.

No longer locked in a silent communication with Daniel, Toni quickly turned and grabbed a remote off the end table. She turned up the TV's volume enough to hear the talking heads.

Rynn studied her companion, who now appreared quite shaken.

Finally, Toni seemed to remember her presence. She sank onto the couch. "He had something written on the eye black," she repeated. "I need to know what. He didn't tell me he was going to do that. I need to find out if he did anything else he didn't tell me about either." She suddenly seemed exhausted, as if a new weight had been laid on her shoulders.

Rynn sat down next to her. "What do you think it says?"

Toni shrugged. "I have no idea. Something about Patrick, I'm sure. But is it something that will mean anything to anyone else? This is a surprise to me. I didn't know he was going to do that," she repeated.

Rynn asked, "Are you afraid he'll come out, that he'll tell the world about his lost love?"

Toni gazed out the window as Daniel walked to the center of the field with the other captains for the coin flip. "I don't know. I don't think he will. At least, not directly. But he may finally give enough clues for someone to figure it out."

"And that's a bad thing?" Rynn frowned, trying to understand the thoughts running through Toni's head.

"Yes. No. I don't know." Toni sighed. "I just want him to be happy, and I know that's gone now without Patrick. I'm afraid he'll do something he regrets out of grief. If he wants to come out, I will support him all the way, but I think there's a right way and a wrong way to do it. If he's ready to face the scrutiny head-on, ready to meet the ones who'll try to crush him, I'll be right there. But I need to make sure he knows what he's doing, and that he intends to do it."

"Are you worried about his career?" Rynn asked.

Toni shook her head. "As his agent, yes. As his friend, no. If he's lost his love for the game, then he should walk away before he gets hurt. I'm not one of those agents who pushes a player to keep going just so I can continue raking in my commission. Daniel is more than a client to me. He's a friend. Now he's hurting and there's not much I can do to comfort him."

Rynn reached over and touched Toni's arm, allowing herself the small gesture. "He knows you're here for him. He looked up here for a reason. He knows."

She heard the TV announcers talking about the start of the game. The Jags had won the toss and elected to defer, which meant Chicago would get the ball to start. Daniel would not have to take the field immediately. Both she and Toni looked up at the screen at the sound of his name.

"…and Tommy Rocker is sporting a little something extra today, as you pointed out earlier, Jimmy," said one announcer. "We're not sure what the numbers on his eye black mean, but I can't recall ever seeing him show off that accessory before. Can you, Bill?"

"No, Bob, still no indication from our studio about what Rocker's eye black message means, but folks, we'll be sure to let you know once we find out. Just after this break, we'll get things started with the Jacksonville Jaguars and your Chicago Bears!"

The scene focused on a close-up of Daniel standing on the sideline with a fiery intensity in his eyes. Rynn didn't see any sadness there. She wondered if a lifetime of athletics had trained him to channel any and all emotion into aggression on the field. Perhaps they were about to find out.

The broadcast cut to a cable logo montage. She turned to look at Toni, who stared blankly at the television screen, and asked softly, "Those numbers on his left side were Monday's date. Do you know the others?"

Toni shook her head slightly. "I can't believe him. I guess that works, as the chances of anyone figuring out what that means must be pretty slim."

Rynn studied her. "You know what the other numbers mean? Zero eight two zero?"

Toni nodded this time. "Yes. It's another date. August twentieth. Patrick's birthday."

Date of birth and date of death. Daniel was indeed memorializing his lost lover for the world to see, but Toni was right. Rynn didn't see how anyone would figure out the message.

CHAPTER SEVEN

It took less than three minutes after the broadcast highlighted Daniel's eye black for Toni's cell phone to ring. She'd known a media scramble was coming and didn't look forward to it. She really wished Daniel had given her a heads-up. She did not want to spend the entire game telling every sports journalist out there that she had no comment on the matter, nor did Tommy Rocker have any statement to release.

After what felt like the twentieth call, Toni finally gave up pacing and threw her phone at the couch in frustration. She knew Rynn had been watching her instead of the game the whole time, and she felt bad to realize they'd only watched a small part of the first quarter.

Daniel had only taken the field once so far, but Jacksonville hadn't really tossed the ball his way at all. The Bears initially managed a couple of first downs rushing before punting it away. After the Bears' second possession also ended in a punt, the Jags muffed it, giving the ball right back the Bears. For better or for worse, the persistence in trying to force the run, with little success, had resulted in the clock running quickly through the quarter.

As the Bears prepared to punt yet again, Toni ran her fingers through her hair and sank onto the couch next to Rynn. Having hoped the day would be more relaxing than work, she had opted to let her hair hang loose this morning. Unfortunately, it now seemed that today would actually be more stressful than a typical day at the office, which, for a sports agent, was saying something.

Letting an exasperated sigh escape her lips, Toni turned to Rynn, who had been sitting and munching quietly on fries and a burger. Toni had almost forgotten that they'd ordered the food from the suite concierge service. She closed her eyes, suddenly feeling overwhelmed.

After a few moments of silence, Rynn spoke. "Sounds like you're pretty popular today."

Toni opened her eyes to Rynn's supportive smile. She shook her head. "I suppose that's one way to put it. Reporters obviously can't reach Daniel in the middle of the game, so they hound me. I'd turn off my phone, but that's what my job is—representing my client."

Rynn nodded sympathetically. "You've had a few minutes quiet at least." She motioned to a second burger sitting on the end table. "You should try to eat something."

Toni glanced at the cold food. "I really don't feel like eating anymore. I'm too tired, and the media vultures have killed my appetite." When her cell phone rang again, she almost ignored it. She certainly wanted to. Looking down at the caller ID, she was relieved to see that it was not another reporter. Tapping the touchpad, she answered wearily, "Hi, Dad."

Her father's joking voice poked at her over the line. "Your boy's causing a bit of a ruckus over there, isn't he?"

Toni said nothing. While he, like the rest of the world, was unaware that Daniel was gay, he did know that their relationship extended beyond the typical player-agent business.

"Even the California sports guys are trying to solve the mystery of Tommy Rocker's eye black message," he said. "So you gonna help an old man out and let me in on the secret?"

With a sigh, Toni mumbled, "Now Dad, you know better than anyone how important client confidentiality is in our business. I learned it from you. Daniel's not talking about it. If he wants to say something later, I'm sure ESPN will tell you all about it."

"Honey, you sound beat up. Is something wrong?" he asked.

She shook her head, despite knowing he couldn't see her. "No, Dad. It's just that I've been fielding questions about the eye black since the game started. It's a little tiring since we have no comment. I'd like to actually watch some of the game, you know?"

He chuckled. Being an agent himself, Toni knew he was familiar with what she was going through. "All right, then, I won't join in the harassment. Are you up in the box?"

"Yes. It's been rainy and overcast all day here."

"Okay. Well, I'll let you get back to it. Don't worry about the media, honey. The devils are insatiable. If Rocker wants to say or do something, he will. Athletes like making waves, and I doubt Rocker's much of an exception. It's our job to dictate the size of the splash, that's all you can do. And I'm sure you'll handle it just fine."

Toni felt a slight smile tug at the corner of her mouth. "Thanks, Dad. I'll talk to you later."

"Goodbye, honey."

Toni tossed the phone back on the couch and leaned her head against the soft cushion behind her. She let her eyes drift closed again, relaxing before a roar from outside the box returned her to the present. Focusing on the game, she watched the tail end of the run as Daniel trotted into the end zone. Interception returned for a touchdown. She smiled, knowing her friend needed a bright spot right now.

* * *

Rynn had been more interested in watching Toni than watching the game. The woman was having a hell of an afternoon. Her phone had rung off the hook for most of the first half, a never-ending string of calls from what she gathered were reporters questioning Daniel's eye black.

Just when it seemed Toni might get some sort of a break, the game really got going, and the phone started ringing again. From listening to Toni's responses, it seemed like more of the same, amplified by the unbelievable game Daniel played. It appeared everyone wanted to know what the eye black meant and if it somehow had any bearing on the game.

Daniel played like a man possessed. Rynn had never seen anything like it. He single-handedly beat the Jaguars. He returned not one, but two interceptions for touchdowns, and snagged a third which led to a Bears' field goal. He'd also been the player to blow up the opposing runners who managed to break into the secondary.

It seemed that Jacksonville flat out gave up going anywhere near him. In the second half, they managed a touchdown by chipping away with the running game, five yards at a time. Using the same tactic, they later put themselves in field goal range for a successful kicking attempt. But nothing got past Tommy Rocker.

With a final score of 17-10, Daniel was the unquestionable difference for his team. As the stadium slowly emptied, Bears fans loudly celebrated their victory. Rynn found herself watching Toni pace the room, talking on her phone and saying, "No comment," to what seemed like every sports journalist in the nation.

Sighing audibly, Toni chucked her phone at the couch. She didn't collapse onto the soft furniture this time. Instead, she went to the window, used her arm as a headrest, and leaned face-first against the glass.

Rynn stood and moved over near her. Though she had intended to offer comfort, she was surprised when Toni turned and flung her arms around her. The hug felt heavy with the stress Toni had been under all day, possibly all week. She didn't know what to do other than return the embrace and offer some support. She wasn't usually an affectionate person. The awkward stiffness she anticipated never materialized. The sweet scent of Toni's hair lingered in her senses. Toni's sculpted body molded into her arms. Despite knowing she shouldn't—Toni was a witness!—she wanted to hang on to the embrace.

After a few short seconds, Toni pulled away, clearly embarrassed. "God, I am so sorry. I don't know what just came over me." She ran a nervous hand through her hair. "I can't believe I just did that."

Rynn remained stuck in place, the soft warmth of Toni's touch burned into her skin and her memory. She quickly came to her senses and tried to relieve Toni's embarrassment. "It's no big deal. I know what a crappy day you've been having. Sometimes you just need a hug, right?" She was warmed by Toni's appreciative smile.

Relaxed, though still noticeably self-conscious, Toni gestured toward the door. "I guess I've kept you captive in my drama long enough. Shall we?"

Rynn nodded and followed her out of the box. They made their way silently back to the parking garage, most of the crowd having dispersed while she and Toni lingered in the suite for nearly an hour. She thought that on a clear and sunny afternoon, celebrating fans might have hung around longer, enjoying a beautiful view of a calm Lake Michigan. But the gray skies and the choppy water behind them did not oblige such a picturesque vision.

While the throngs of pedestrians had thinned, the traffic was fairly heavy when the Lexus pulled away from the stadium. Rynn wasn't sure if Toni was still embarrassed by their impromptu embrace, or simply exhausted by the day's events, but either way, she hadn't spoken a word since leaving the box. The ride home was quiet. Small talk bubbled up every now and then, but overall, she was surprised by how comfortable she felt simply sharing the silence with Toni.

Toni's phone battery eventually died. Rynn suspected that Toni had a charger somewhere in the car, but couldn't blame her for using the excuse to ignore the persistent callers.

Rynn was reluctant to leave Toni behind when they arrived at the station sometime later. After a moment's hesitation, she asked, "You going to be okay?"

Toni faced her a moment before turning away. "Of course. Maybe I'll be able to talk to Daniel later and we can come up with some vague statement to pacify the media. I'm sure once I put out that fire, things will be much less stressful."

Rynn wasn't so sure this was true, given her client's possible connection to a murder, but she didn't want to draw the fact to Toni's attention. Stressful, indeed. Perhaps the hounding media were a good distraction from the pain of loss that seemed to have been shoved to the back of her attention. She nodded and reached for the door handle. "Thank you for taking me today. I enjoyed the game."

In truth, she had barely watched the game, but she wanted to give Toni at least one thing to be happy about today. One look and she knew Toni hadn't been fooled, but still seemed to appreciate the attempt. She closed the Lexus's door, pleased by the faint trace of a smile lightening Toni's weariness.

CHAPTER EIGHT

After years of beating Samson to work, Rynn was surprised when she arrived Monday morning to find Pearson already sitting at his desk. With a start, she realized that she hadn't thought at all about what to tell him regarding her weekend. Hopefully her meeting with the lieutenant at eight thirty would help her address that question.

"Good morning," he greeted her.

"Hey, Pearson." She felt sociable this morning and liked the idea of having another friend as a partner. Taking a seat at her desk, she asked, "How was your weekend?"

He shrugged. "Relatively uneventful. Browns lost again, but that's hardly surprising."

Why was it that the first Monday morning comment from most of the people she knew, especially the men, concerned football? She teased him in response. "You might not want to say that too loud around here. You do know you're in Bears' country now, right?"

He smiled. "That's what I keep hearing. It's not like our teams are even in the same conference, so I don't think people mind humoring my mild, lingering sympathies. It's not like I'm a die-hard fan—at least, not since moving—but I did grow up in northern Ohio." He shrugged. "Speaking of your Bears, I hear they put on a show yesterday. Or at least, ESPN won't shut up about that safety. What's his name again?"

Rynn masked the sudden tension she felt and gave Rocker's name, but said nothing else.

"That's right." Pearson flipped through the file in front of him, apparently unaware of any shift in her demeanor. Perhaps she simply hid it well. "If you listen to the media, he's become the best thing in football since Knute Rockne invented the forward pass."

He went on with the sports talk a little while, just idle, friendly chitchat. Rynn considered whether to fill him in, but decided to wait until after she spoke with the lieutenant.

A few minutes before her meeting, she ran through the facts again with Pearson. As she rose from her desk, he added, "The morgue called just before you got here, said they were finished with the autopsy. With no conclusive findings, they're releasing the body to the family tomorrow. As I understand it, he'll be buried down in Florida after a viewing near where his parents currently live."

Rynn kept her eyes locked on her computer screen. Did Daniel know?

* * *

Toni stood in her fifth-floor corner office, staring out the window at the city skyline in the distance. She couldn't concentrate. No, that wasn't quite true. She just couldn't seem to focus on work.

She couldn't stop thinking about Daniel. She'd never seen that much focus from him before, such intensity, such *passion* that had electrified his whole body during yesterday's game. She knew it was because he couldn't express the love and mourning he felt for Patrick.

She gazed out the window, lost in thoughts of her friend. The phone rang on the desk behind her. Since she'd told her secretary to hold all calls that must mean it was already after six o'clock and Kari had left for the day. After a moment's hesitation, she turned and picked up the receiver.

"Hello?"

"You know, I was beginning to wonder if your secretary had hung up on me again."

Toni covered her eyes with her hand. "Again, Rynn?"

"Yes, again." Rynn's voice sounded teasing. "I've called about a dozen times, trying to get her to let me talk to you. She's a good firewall."

Toni sighed. "I'm terribly sorry about that, Detective."

"Oh, don't be. Actually, I think I might be jealous. Sometimes, I wish I had someone to buffer my calls so effectively."

"I wouldn't have thought you were the type to suffer difficult personal assistants," Toni said. She wondered about Rynn's thoughtful silence, hoping she hadn't offended her.

Finally, Rynn replied. "No, I don't suppose I normally do."

"It's my fault, really. I should have put you on the list of calls to forward through to me. It was my mistake."

Rynn replied lightly, "You mean I'm not on your list of very important people?"

Toni felt a tug somewhere deep in her chest, but hurriedly brushed off the feeling. She returned Rynn's banter. "The list is very exclusive, you know. Not just anyone gets on it. How do I know you're trustworthy?"

A brief pause. "I'm sure in time I'll prove myself to you. If you let me."

Rynn sounded serious. Toni found herself short of breath, the tug in her chest a touch more insistent. She didn't know how to respond, so she changed the topic. "Perhaps. For now, though, to what do I owe the pleasure of your call?"

Rynn didn't immediately respond. Toni mentally kicked herself for messing up the moment. *What moment? There is no moment. She's a detective working a case that you might have information on. That's it.* She shook herself to regain her focus.

"I'm calling about Patrick," Rynn said gently.

Toni suddenly felt as if the sound of Rynn's voice was the only thing keeping the pain of his death at bay.

"I need to talk to Daniel," Rynn continued. "But before you resist, I think he might want to meet with me tonight. I understand the situation that Daniel is in, unable to truly mourn. I know he hasn't really had any way to say goodbye."

Toni felt tears threatening at the corners of her eyes, but said nothing.

Rynn went on. "You haven't told me if Patrick's parents knew about his relationship with Daniel." She paused, clearly waiting for an answer.

Toni swallowed against the tightness in her throat. "No, he never told them. In fact, they didn't accept that he was gay at all. He talked to them about that once, before he met Daniel, but they freaked out. They never spoke of it again, so far as I know. Then, with his father's ailing health and the need to keep their relationship a secret anyway, Patrick never forced the issue. I'm not even sure where his parents live now." She heard a slight noise on the other end of the call and pictured Rynn taking notes.

"They're in Florida. They're having Patrick's body flown down as soon as we release it from our investigative custody."

Toni waited, but Rynn was silent. She guessed what Rynn would not say. "They're taking him soon, aren't they?"

"Yes. We have no reason to hold Patrick's body any longer. Our medical examiner has finished her autopsy and assorted tests. There's not really anything else we can learn. We have no right to keep him here beyond that."

Toni nodded to herself. "So you have to release him."

"Yes," Rynn confirmed. "The family has a right to mourn him and lay him to rest according to whatever tradition they choose. We have no more authority unless we can make some claim related to the investigation, but I have no such reason." She hesitated. "I know that Daniel deserves to say goodbye. If he'll agree to an interview tonight, I'll arrange to let him pay his respects. Is that something he would want?"

Toni was touched by Rynn's concern. "Yes, I'm sure he'd be very grateful for the chance."

"Okay, then. As his attorney, you may come as well. Can you be here at nine o'clock?"

Toni agreed. Before the conversation ended, she said, "Thank you. I'm sure this will mean so much to Daniel." *I know it does to me*, she added silently.

"Toni?" Rynn caught her attention. Toni was surprised at the stir she felt when Rynn said her name. "Maybe your secretary could give me a trial period on the approved caller list. Until I can prove myself worthy of the VIP status."

Toni heard the click on the other end of the line. Rynn wouldn't have to worry about that. Even if it meant she had to deal with the media personally, she had no intention of letting another call from the detective be answered by anyone else.

CHAPTER NINE

At eight thirty that night, Rynn reviewed the Boden case file and thought back to her meeting with the lieutenant earlier that day. She almost laughed at the memory of his reaction to her update. She couldn't recall ever seeing him that surprised.

He'd shaken his head incredulously. "Hell, I watched the game last week. *I* can give Tommy Rocker an alibi."

Of course, the alibi alone didn't completely clear Daniel. She and the lieutenant discussed the possibility that Daniel had hired a hit. He certainly had the money, but considering the ME thought the murderer was likely inexperienced, the lieutenant thought it best to direct their resources elsewhere.

She had almost let the discussion end there, but her experience with Toni the day before had flashed in her mind. She'd wanted to clear Daniel from the suspect list, but convincing Daniel to come in for an interview seemed unlikely. Connecting it to the chance for Daniel to say his goodbyes would surely be persuasive, though. She had pitched her idea for incentive to the lieutenant, and he'd agreed.

The only other issue they'd discussed was whether or not to bring Pearson into the loop. Gruffly, the lieutenant had told her, "Talk to Rocker. If he checks out, especially with that alibi, there's no need to invade his privacy. If you have any reason to doubt him, than Pearson will know everything you know."

Now with about ten minutes left before Toni and Daniel were scheduled to arrive, Rynn set the case file to the side of her desk. She let her mind drift back to the warm laughter she and Toni had shared the day before on the way to the game, before all hell had broken loose because of Daniel's eye black. Toni had a great sense of humor. She loved the way her eyes sparkled when she laughed.

If Daniel wasn't a suspect, was there any reason she couldn't see Toni again?

The ringing phone suddenly broke the silence. Rynn answered, "Callahan."

"Hello, Detective. We're here," Toni said. "The front of the station still appears rather busy, and Daniel and I were wondering if there was any way we might avoid going through the lobby."

Rynn considered the request. Normally, they would be required to sign the visitors' log, but she decided she could record their visit without parading them through the crowded lobby. She replied, "See the side door? Should be tucked in the corner where the two branches of the station meet. I'll be there in a minute."

"All right," Toni answered.

Rynn ended the call, ducked out of her office, and headed to the side door. The hallways away from the front of the station were empty, but brightly lit. She considered the lights. *Good. If the halls were abandoned and dimly lit, I'd start to feel like I was in some spy movie.*

She came to the side door quickly and flipped an ID card in front of the scanner. She remembered how odd the security protocol had seemed when she'd started working here as a rookie cop. Everyone needed to scan to get out of the building, not just to get in. It made sense once someone explained it to her. The higher-ups needed to keep track of who left the station as much as who entered. A panic bar on the door would allow anyone out in case of an emergency, but an alarm would sound unless an ID card was used.

Rynn stepped out the door into the parking lot. Just a few seconds later, she heard a pair of car doors open and close, and two dark figures approached. *Perhaps there is a bit of spy movie feel.* She nodded at Toni and Daniel in greeting, and held the door open for them to enter the station.

"Hello." Rynn studied the man standing next to her. "You must be Daniel." She extended her hand. He took it, shaking firmly, and not saying a word. Even through his thin, dark jacket, Rynn saw the definition of his muscles, the strength of his body. At five feet eight inches, she wasn't short, but Daniel dwarfed her by six, maybe eight inches. Undoubtedly, this was a powerful man, but his physical strength was not what struck her. He exuded grief. He wore his broken heart on his sleeve, and her heart almost broke for him when she looked into his face.

In the fluorescent lighting, his gray eyes looked dulled, different than she'd noted on the television screen during the game. Where lightning had sparked in his gaze then, now there were only stormy clouds of pain.

Rynn nodded to acknowledge his sorrow but knew no words could comfort him. Instead, she turned again to Toni. "Let's duck into my office, rather than linger in the hall here." She turned quietly and led the way. Entering the office, she stepped around the desk and settled into her chair. "Please have a seat," she said, gesturing to the chairs opposite her. "I have a few questions before we go down to the morgue."

Daniel and Toni obliged, but she thought she saw suspicion flash across Toni's face.

She placed a small recording device on the desk and turned it on, watching her visitors closely. After each stated their identification for the record, she began the interview. "Where were you last Monday night?" she asked Daniel.

Toni immediately protested, "What? How dare y—"

"Relax, Toni." He cut her off. "She's just doing her job."

He answered the question as she expected, providing clear details of the football game that night and the travel itinerary. Rynn continued to interview him for nearly an hour. His answers and his body language both confirmed she was right to remove him from suspicion. Despite her focus on Daniel, she noticed Toni's demeanor grew ever colder as they spoke.

When she was finished, she rose from her seat. "Thank you. If you're ready, we'll go down to the morgue now."

Daniel nodded and stood, and Toni followed suit.

Rynn was glad Toni had come with Daniel. He would need a friend when he saw what she was about to show him. Still separated from them by her desk, she added, "Before we go, I need to be sure you understand the rules. I know you know that Patrick was murdered, but the nightly news never goes into any detail on an active investigation." Preparing family for viewing a body was usually done by a liaison officer, and she felt awkward in the face of Daniel's distress. She plowed on, "You should be ready. Patrick won't look like himself. His injuries and the postmortem…" Her voice trailed off.

Daniel's shoulders sagged and his gaze dropped to the floor. Toni wrapped her arm around his waist, offering him comfort. She glared at Rynn and shook her head as if to ask why this talk about Patrick was necessary.

In answer to the silent question, Rynn said, "I know this hurts. I can't imagine the pain you feel. But I need you to understand what you're about to see. I need to prepare you, because what you're going to see won't be the Patrick that you remember." She pulled a photo from the file and stepped around her desk. She touched his arm as she handed it to him. He looked at the photo taken after the autopsy and shuddered with grief. She continued, "Can you handle it? I'm sorry it won't be easier, but if you freak out or cause a scene, the investigation could be compromised. Then we may never be able to find out what happened or who killed him. Can you look without touching, see him without doing anything more?" She waited until he looked up and repeated softly, "Daniel. Are you sure you can do this?"

Resolve took shape on his features. Finally, he nodded. His deep voice cracked with emotion when he said, "I need to see him. I need to say goodbye."

Rynn took a deep breath. "All right. Let's go."

She led Daniel and Toni down a series of corridors, making her way to the back stairwell. Flipping through another key-card doorway and punching a code into the lab access pad, she finally motioned them through some offices and into the room with the morgue lockers.

Daniel kept his head bowed. Rynn turned to Toni, who nodded.

She moved to open one of the drawers. She slid the steel shelf out and folded back a sheet, exposing Patrick's lifeless face and shoulders. The cuts and coroner's incisions had been closed, but the damage was evident nonetheless. Hardly an inch of Patrick's face remained undamaged.

Rynn stepped back and returned to the doorway where Toni and Daniel stood. She heard Toni whisper something to her sorrow-stricken friend, but she wasn't able to make out the words. He shook his head and glanced up. After a moment's hesitation, he squared his shoulders and stepped forward alone.

Despite her professional distance, Rynn still hated each time she witnessed another person's grief. She'd been there countless times when family had been called on to identify a loved one taken brutally from them. It had gotten easier over the years, but she still empathized.

She stood back with Toni and watched Daniel. Caught in the turmoil of his grief, she also felt an impulse to be near Toni, to offer her comfort at this difficult time. She leaned nearer and whispered, "Are you okay?"

Toni shook her head. "No. But how could I be?"

"Do you think he wants a few moments alone?"

Toni nodded.

Rynn took Toni's hand to guide her back to the lab offices. From here, she could watch Daniel through the partition window without intruding on him. Once through the door, Toni immediately pulled her hand free.

Toni tried to mask her tears behind forced resentment. "You tricked me," she accused.

Yes, Rynn thought, but instead she said, "I had to clear him. Can you understand?"

"Yes. I just hated to see you put him through that." Toni's anger disappeared, overwhelmed by tears she couldn't hide any longer.

Rynn reached forward to console Toni. Words failed her, but she didn't need words right now. She simply wrapped Toni in a comforting hug. In that moment, her attraction didn't matter. In that moment, she was doing nothing more than comforting a hurting friend. Some small part of her mind questioned the depth of compassion she felt after having known Toni only four days, but she shrugged it off while they shared a silent embrace.

Sometime later—Rynn wasn't entirely sure how long—she saw Daniel turn toward them, so she released Toni and stepped back.

Daniel came through the doorway to join them. His face was tear-stained and his strong body appeared frail with grief, but once again, his expression was resolved. He turned to Rynn and uttered quietly, "Thank you."

She nodded and asked Toni, "Do you…" Her question died mid-sentence when Toni shook her head.

"No," Toni replied. "I'm here for Daniel. I can say my goodbyes another place, another time."

Rynn studied Toni a moment, reading her expression. She thought perhaps Toni might be afraid to view Patrick's mangled features, but she didn't see fear. Pain, yes. But more than that, there was compassion. Toni really was here solely to support Daniel.

After a deep breath, Rynn turned to reenter the other room. "Give me just a minute to secure things and I'll show you back out."

She slipped into the morgue to return the body exactly as she'd found it. When she returned, she found Toni and Daniel locked in a mournful embrace. Toni, though so much smaller than Daniel, held him close, clearly comforting him while he shook with tears. His face was buried in her neck. Her arms were wrapped tightly around his solid frame. He seemed to have shrunk two sizes. His entire body seemed limp and had collapsed in on itself in pain.

Rynn met Toni's gaze over Daniel's quivering shoulders. An understanding passed between them. She waited in patient silence for Daniel to be ready to go. At last, she took the pair to the side door and escorted them to the parking lot.

Once outside, Daniel turned to her. "Thank you, Detective, for allowing me that time to say goodbye. I…" His voice faltered, and he looked away.

Rynn touched his arm gently. "I understand. You love him. Love doesn't end with death. I just wish there was more I could do for you."

He stiffened with defiance. "There is. Catch the bastard, Detective. Bring Patrick justice. Nothing else matters anymore." Rynn was taken aback by the power of his conviction. He added, "I already owe you so much, but do that for me—for Patrick— and I'll be forever in your debt."

Rynn shook her head. "No, you owe me nothing. I'll do my best for you. I always do."

He nodded, whispering one more thanks before walking silently to his SUV.

Rynn watched him withdraw, trying to wrap her head around the clash of weakness and emotional strength he had shown her that evening. It took a lot for such a man to let himself be vulnerable in a stranger's presence and to put that much faith in a stranger's goodness. She hoped she would not disappoint him.

Toni stood beside her. She squeezed her arm and said, "Thank you. You have no idea what it means to him." She released her and turned to follow Daniel.

CHAPTER TEN

It had been four days since Toni last saw Rynn, and she couldn't get her out of her mind. She knew that Rynn had gone above and beyond in letting Daniel into the morgue to see Patrick one last time. She was struck by the compassion and sympathy she'd seen in Rynn's eyes that night.

Sighing, she pushed her lingering thoughts of Rynn from her mind and tried to focus on the computer screen in front of her. Work had calmed down, as much as her job ever did. Journalists had given up surprisingly quickly on gleaning further information about Daniel's eye black message. Perhaps her reputation preceded her there. Reporters had long since figured out that Davis Sports Consulting put their clients first, screw the media and the advertising dollars. If Daniel didn't want to talk, she would stand by his decision for better or for worse.

With the majority of the media off the scent, she'd had a day or two of normal business, haggling over contracts and trying to sell and negotiate endorsement deals for her various players. Daniel was no longer her sole focus, though like Rynn, he remained present at the back of her mind. Perhaps it was for the best that the team had left yesterday for their away game against the Dallas Cowboys. Maybe the distance would help Daniel cope. At least this time, he had warned her in advance that he planned to wear the eye black message again.

Toni pushed her chair back. Her mind wasn't on work today, and it was near enough to five o'clock for her to justify calling it quits. But she didn't rise from her desk. The week she'd had called for a Friday night out, not just returning to her condo alone as she did most nights. What should she do? A bar? No, besides being way too early in the evening, she wasn't in the mood for smoky, loud and dark. Something more calming, perhaps more intimate. Rynn's face flashed through her mind, and with it, the image of the two of them at Madeleine's the week before. That sounded like the perfect way to unwind after the chaos of her week.

Toni's hand moved tentatively toward the cell phone sitting on her desk. She could call Rynn, couldn't she? They'd shared a pleasant day together on Sunday, and she knew she could get lost in conversation with Rynn if they met for coffee. Something stopped her from dialing, a professional boundary between them she hesitated to cross. The reason they had met was painful. Until Patrick's murder was solved, maybe it wasn't appropriate to meet Rynn socially.

The interest she had in Rynn—was there any point denying it?—would have to wait. But a large chai tea and maybe some live music at Madeleine's sounded soothing nonetheless.

Traffic seemed to disagree with her plans since she was caught for nearly forty-five minutes in gridlock, the road resembling a parking lot more than a six-lane thoroughfare. She wondered if perhaps this wasn't a sign that she should just go home after all. Glancing across the grass median, she saw the lanes of cars flowing fine in the direction of her condo instead of north to Madeleine's.

By the time she got there, it was already past six o'clock and her stomach was rumbling. Entering the familiar coffee shop, she stepped right up to the counter.

Emma was working again. She smiled at her approach. "The usual again?"

Toni shook her head. "No, tonight I deserve a treat. Supersize my tea and toss some foam on top." She paused and perused the menu. "How's the minestrone?"

Emma replied, "Maddie's specialty."

"Okay, I'll have that as well."

Emma punched her order into the computer. She continued happily chatting while she ran her credit card. "You know, I was a little curious when your friend from last week showed up here without you a bit ago, but I guess it's just coincidence that you showed up, too, since you don't seem to be looking for her."

Toni's eyebrows shot up, and she spun around. Sure enough, there was Rynn, sitting in the same cushy armchairs they'd occupied the week before, a bemused smile on her face when their eyes met.

Toni offered a meek wave in greeting and broke the eye contact after a few seconds when she realized Emma was still talking. Turning to the counter, she was met with another amused look.

"Or maybe last week's coffee date did go well. You look a little flustered," Emma teased.

Toni rolled her eyes, trying to save face. "Isn't my drink ready yet?" She feigned annoyance, but Emma didn't flinch, instead passing her an oversized mug with a questioning glance. She grabbed the tea. "It's not a date, and it's none of your business."

Clearly, her pretend irritation wasn't even surface deep. Emma playfully gestured toward Rynn. "Well, then? What are you doing still standing over here with me?"

Chuckling, Toni turned and followed the barista's advice. What were the odds that Rynn would be here when that was exactly how she'd had wanted to spend her evening?

* * *

By Friday afternoon, Rynn and Pearson were scraping the bottom of the barrel for new leads. Frustrating didn't begin to describe the Patrick Boden homicide investigation, she thought. Every path she and her partner ran down quickly led to a dead end. Without a single idea left, she suggested to Pearson that they clock out half an hour early with the hope that fresh minds on Monday morning might bring some sort of welcome insight.

She left the station at the same time as Pearson, even walking with him to the parking lot. As he climbed into his blue Prius, she wished him a good weekend and headed toward her Tahoe.

She sat in her vehicle without starting the engine, realizing she didn't really want to go home. She didn't know what she wanted to do, but she did know who she wanted to do it with. She wasn't sure that calling on Toni socially was a good idea, though, so she decided to settle for a cup of quality hazelnut coffee instead. A little live music also sounded like a good way to unwind. She turned the key in the ignition.

Later, after pulling her Tahoe into Madeleine's parking lot, she paused long enough to ask herself if she was absolutely crazy. Either that or she must have fallen back to high school, hanging out at the cute girl's favorite café hoping to catch her eye. Shrugging, she hopped out of the car. Odds were, Toni wouldn't even be there anyway.

Rynn ordered the same drink she'd had last week, sorted through a magazine rack, and settled into the big chair by the window. A *Sports Illustrated* had jumped out at her, with Daniel's intense gaze staring off the cover. She had just finished reading the article when the bell on the door signaled a newcomer entering the shop.

She couldn't keep the grin off her face when she glanced up to see Toni making a beeline for the counter. She tried to find another article, tried not to stare while Toni chatted with the girl taking her order. Despite her efforts, she ended up letting her gaze run over Toni's stunning body.

The power suit fit her very well, but Rynn didn't like the tight twist trapping her sleek, dark hair. She'd worn her hair that way when she'd first come to the station a week ago, but at the game, she'd left it loose. The casual look seemed so much better for her.

Rynn could see herself running her fingers through Toni's hair. *What am I doing?* She forced herself to stop staring. *I don't know anything about this woman, and I'm...God, I'm fantasizing.* She shook her head. *Slow down, Rynn, she may not even be interested in talking to you.*

When Toni finally turned and met her gaze, she knew the interest was mutual. Although Toni seemed surprised to see her, it was a good surprise.

She and Toni spent the evening chatting, never once slipping into shop talk. Rynn was amazed how easy it was to talk to Toni. How much did she love it when Toni laughed?

Live music started at eight o'clock, same as the week before. The coffee shop crowd milled around them. A few times, Rynn found herself sitting close to Toni without either of them speaking a word, just taking in the music and relaxing in perfect company. She was surprised when the musicians began packing up their instruments. Glancing at her watch, she couldn't believe it was already after eleven o'clock. Had she really spent the last five hours with Toni?

Toni also seemed taken aback by how quickly the evening had gone. Rynn rose from her chair, and Toni walked with her out to the parking lot.

She felt a strong desire to take Toni's hand. Would it be a problem? Toni wasn't involved in the Boden case anymore. Still, she shoved her hands into her jacket pockets to keep from doing something stupid.

At Toni's Lexus, Rynn paused. She took a step forward, longing to close the distance between them. Toni's gaze flicked down to her mouth. Just when she might have given in to the desire to kiss the soft lips that were inches away, she was startled by the blaring of a car alarm.

She jumped back a step, the spell broken. Embarrassment set in when she realized how close she had come to crossing a line she probably shouldn't even be near. Grateful that Toni probably couldn't see her blush in the dark, she ran a nervous hand through her short hair and coughed to clear the huskiness out of her throat before speaking.

"Well, I guess this is good night." Rynn glanced behind Toni at the parking lot when the car alarm finally silenced.

"I guess so," Toni quietly replied.

Rynn felt her face flush with heat when she read the desire in Toni's expression. Desperate to make her escape before giving in to her body's wants, she took another step away from Toni. "I really enjoyed tonight. Maybe we could do it again sometime." She coughed again, afraid the rasp in her voice would give her away.

Toni smiled and stepped forward, shrinking the space between them. Her smile morphed into a playful and mischievous grin. She leaned closer. Rynn found herself unable to move when Toni's warm breath tickled her ear.

"I look forward to seeing more of you," Toni whispered.

Rynn's breath caught. Her mind went momentarily blank. Toni moved away, gave her a playful wink, and disappeared into the Lexus before she had a chance to start breathing again.

The sleek, black car darted out of the parking lot. She realized her heart was pounding. Still unable to form a coherent thought, she managed to turn and walk over to her Tahoe. Finally, a single word registered in her mind. *Damn.*

CHAPTER ELEVEN

"You seem different this morning," Pearson greeted Rynn when she entered the office the following Monday.

She shrugged, unsure how to respond.

He studied her a moment before a Cheshire cat grin oozed across his face. "Ooh, I recognize that look. All right, spill. Who is she?"

Rynn laughed. "I swear, Steve, you gossip more than a middle-aged church lady."

Pearson's eyes sparkled. "It's a product of being raised by three older sisters. But that doesn't let you off the hook. You met someone, didn't you?"

Rynn rolled her eyes and settled into her chair. She refused to be drawn into his gossip, trying to convince herself she could ignore Toni's effect on her.

Pearson pushed on. "Oh, come on, throw me a bone. Am I right?"

Rynn allowed herself a grin. Pearson was becoming so easy to talk to. They'd been partnered for two weeks, but the rapport that had formed between them felt like a bond of years.

"Well, I'll be. She must be something special to get that look on your ugly mug," Pearson said slyly.

Rynn blushed. She playfully threw a pen at him. "Who are you calling ugly? At least I'm not going gray at thirty."

He pouted. "Thirty-eight, if you must know, and I've been told I'm rather sexy." He ran his fingers through his salt-and-pepper hair and struck a pose.

Rynn laughed out loud. "I don't know, man, you're a little too good at that," she joked.

His expression turned serious, but he shrugged. "Amazing style comes naturally, I guess."

"Yeah, maybe you can give me some pointers sometime. Help me pick up the hot chicks."

"You bet. Not that it seems you need much help in that department. I still want to hear all about her."

Rynn made a show of turning to her computer and opening the top file on the stack on her desk. "Maybe if you're nice, I'll tell you later. For now, we'd better make some ground on the Boden homicide before the lieutenant chews our asses."

Pearson scrunched his face before turning to his own files with a sigh. "I don't know, partner, I've got nothing. All weekend, I've been trying to think of something we might have missed. But as far as we know, Patrick Boden was a ghost. He has a lemony fresh record, a perfect job where everyone loved him, and no social life to speak of. We haven't been able to figure out anything about him. No trace of any enemies. Plenty of valuables left in the house, so it wasn't just a random robbery." He shook his head.

Rynn added, "We knew from the start it wasn't a random break-in. No one beats and kills a victim like that without motive. Even serial killers have some reason for picking their victims."

She and Pearson spent the day going over everything they knew about the case, but by early afternoon, she had to admit they were out of ideas.

After Pearson left for the day, Rynn sat alone in her office a little while longer, frustrated by their lack of progress. There had been only a few major cases in seven years that she and Samson had been unable to solve. She hated every time she failed to bring justice.

In her mind, she recalled the fire in Daniel's expression when he asked her to find Patrick's killer. She shook her head and rose to go home. She wouldn't yet consider the possibility that she might not be able to do so.

* * *

Toni spent a typical Monday appeasing media interest in her players due to the weekend's games. She'd had a number of players with decent gameplay and no one who really played poorly, which was nice. Like most sports agents, she greatly preferred talking to journalists about her clients' successes over discussing their frustrations.

Of course, there were more questions about Daniel than any of the others. He'd worn his eye black message again, as he said he would, so there was still some media interest in cracking the mystery. For the most part, he'd returned to typical form on the field yesterday, leading a strong defense, but not single-handedly dominating the game as he had the week before.

She didn't have any players in the Monday night game tonight, so the desire to go home and put on football wasn't as pressing as in other weeks. Glancing at her desk clock, she was hardly surprised to see it was past seven o'clock already. The city outside her window twinkled to life with the setting of the sun.

She decided to call it a night, letting her mind drift to the world outside the office while she closed her notes and saved the open files on her computer. Like the past few days, her thoughts soon turned to Rynn and the teasing, almost-kiss she had left her with on Friday night.

She'd been disappointed that Rynn hadn't called over the weekend, but not really surprised. She didn't know the rules for detectives, but she suspected her job was the reason Rynn was so obviously resisting the mutual spark that had flared to life between them. Maybe she had to make the first move.

As she was shutting down things at the office, she was startled by her cell phone ringing. Tapping the screen, she raised the phone to her ear without paying attention to the caller ID.

"Hello, Toni." Daniel's sad voice sounded heavy across the line. He'd been calling more often than usual lately. She knew it was because he had no one else to talk to. No one else knew about Patrick.

"Hey, man. How are you today?" She knew her question was woefully underwhelming, but she also knew that there was nothing she could say to help him.

"You know. The same."

She and Daniel chatted for a bit. She struggled to think of some way to comfort him. Maybe it was best to talk to him about football. The subject had always served to ground him in the past. "You're having a good season. Are those local news flunkies still parked outside your house?" Any other time, she knew he would have laughed. "Occasionally. They seem to come and go. Sometimes, it's almost nice having the familiar faces outside. I suppose it breaks up the solitude."

For the first time, she heard loneliness in his voice nearly as strong as the grief. Without really thinking it through, she offered, "Do you want to come over for dinner tomorrow? Just to get out of your house?"

He was quiet for a moment. She wondered if he preferred to be alone for now. But he replied, "Yeah, that sounds nice. As long as I'm not imposing."

"Not at all." She and Daniel worked out a time and he ended the call.

Toni thought more about her invitation as she left the office. He clearly needed friends to comfort him. She was afraid she wasn't enough, but there was only one other person who knew about his situation. She slowed to a stop as an idea formed. Maybe Rynn would like to come to dinner. Thinking about that cold interview in the station still irritated her, but she knew talking to Daniel might help Rynn somehow. Even if that was fruitless, why shouldn't they be friends?

She resumed walking and pulled her phone from her purse before she could talk herself out of inviting her.

CHAPTER TWELVE

Rynn couldn't think of anyone else who put so much meaning into her job title. First, Toni had surprised her with the phone call and dinner invitation. The way she had whispered, "Good night, Detective," left her replaying the conversation in her mind long after it ended.

How did Toni have such an effect on her? How could she maintain any distance during their dinner date when her body's response was even stronger when Toni purred her given name? Then again, with no evident connection between Daniel and the murder, did she have to keep her distance? She wondered, unable to recall exactly why she was avoiding…whatever it was she was avoiding. More than that, how was she going to keep her cool around Pearson until this anxiety went away? She walked into the office, mulling over the problem.

Just as he had the morning before, Pearson called her on her agitation the moment he saw her. He practically sang, "Ooh, you must have talked to 'the Girl' again last night. Dude, you should see your face right now."

Rynn grinned, unsure if her good humor was due to her excitement over seeing Toni again, or if Pearson's goofing around was infectious. She found it hard to be around him and not feel happy, even with one of their cases proving difficult to solve.

Pearson nudged her. "So? When are you going to start sharing?"

Rynn shook her head. "I swear, Pearson, I've never met a guy who cared so much about my love life. Jack didn't even care this much when I was dating Gina."

Pearson laughed. "I figure without much else going on around here, I might as well live vicariously through you."

"No hot dates on your calendar?" she teased.

"Well, sure, but not until next summer. July in the Midwest is practically unbearable." Pearson dodged the pen she threw at him for his cheesy pun.

Rynn prodded him, hoping to deflect some of his attention away from herself. "Seriously, Steve, you harass me about my life outside the office, but you never say one word about yours. I'm a freaking detective and I haven't been able to figure out if you're married with six kids or a bed-hopping playboy. What gives?"

"Well," he replied, "playboy or monogamous, that doesn't mean I can't have six kids either way."

He practically danced back to his chair when she took a fake swing at him, muttering, "Men. Sometimes, I swear you're all pigs."

Pearson laughed again. "Well, wasn't it Churchill who said he liked pigs? I believe the quote was, 'Dogs look up to us. Cats look down at us. Pigs treat us as equals.' Now that's my kind of logic."

Rynn laughed at the absurd quote. "Where do you get stuff like that?"

He shrugged. "My mind is an endless sea of useless trivia."

She shook her head. "Your mind may be useless, I'll grant you that." It was her turn to dodge an office supply, but she and her partner eventually managed to get back to work.

Without me telling him about Toni, Rynn thought, which immediately pulled tonight's dinner date back to the front of her mind. *No, not a date*, she had to remind herself. She was just going to dinner.

* * *

Toni was nervous. No, nervous didn't begin to describe how she felt. She was agitated, practically crawling out of her skin while waiting for Rynn to arrive. *Good God, what is wrong with me? This isn't even a date and I'm fidgeting as if Sappho herself were coming to dinner.* She willed herself to calm down, wondering if it was too early to pop the cork on the bottle of wine in the fridge.

Rynn and Daniel were supposed to arrive around six o'clock. She took a deep breath and glanced at the clock for the umpteenth time. Five thirty-seven. How was it only two minutes later than the last time she'd checked?

Toni knew she hadn't been this tightly wound about meeting with someone in years. Maybe she was trying to steady her nerves the wrong way. If she admitted her attraction to Rynn, would it be easier to control? The first step to fixing a problem was admitting she had one.

Why did this attraction have to be classified as a problem anyway? Because Rynn was a detective? If they'd met randomly on the street—well, no one actually met randomly on the street, which she found either too fairytale-like or too creepy—but say they had met at Maddie's and hit it off there…why did this have to be different? *Because of Patrick's death.* She knew she shouldn't get involved with Rynn because of the investigation into Patrick's murder. But Rynn had conducted an interview with Daniel and nothing had come of it. Did that mean she was free to ask her out? Maybe she should still give it some time.

Toni surprised herself. Focusing on the situation and reasoning things out actually proved calming. She knew she could be patient, if waiting for Rynn to finish her job was what it took. But to pretend their magnetic attraction didn't exist? That was just foolish.

She was still pondering the possibilities when her phone rang. She jumped, startled by the sudden intrusion into her thoughts. She glanced at the caller ID and answered, "Hey, Daniel."

"Toni, I am so sorry, but I got caught up in stuff at practice. I'm gonna be late. Maybe an hour yet."

Meaning she and Rynn would be alone for a while. That wasn't so bad. "No problem, Daniel." The door chime interrupted her. "Sounds like Rynn's here, so I've got to go. See you soon."

As she walked through her condo to the door, Toni was somewhat relieved to realize her heart wasn't pounding like it had been half an hour ago. She could be patient, she told herself. Maybe the idea of this new, potential relationship with Rynn would open the door for some playful flirting without letting her slip back into a full-on fantasy mindset.

She flicked the deadbolt and pulled the door open. As expected, Rynn stood on the threshold, apparently having come straight from work since she still wore her pressed brown slacks, a casual, green button-down shirt and a light jacket. The green in her shirt brought out the stunning color in her eyes.

Toni smiled. *Flirt, don't drool.* She managed to maintain control and motioned Rynn inside.

Rynn flashed her a lopsided grin. After a brief glance around, she commented, "Nice place."

Toni gestured her further inside. "Can I get you a drink or anything? You can have a seat, or I can give you a tour of the place. There's not really a lot to see."

The condo was small, so Toni was able to cross the open floor plan and look in the fridge while Rynn lingered in the sitting area. Toni was glad for a moment with her back turned. She mentally smacked herself. A tour? That was a little personal, wasn't it? The only other rooms were a guest room, a bathroom, and her bedroom.

She quickly swallowed to keep her thoughts away from bedrooms. Playful flirting, okay. Sexual suggestions, not okay, she reminded herself. Hopefully, Rynn's mind had not already drifted to the same provocative place. If that happened, it would be a very long hour fighting against unspoken desire until Daniel arrived.

She glanced back at Rynn, who smiled and spoke with a playful sparkle in her eyes. "A drink sounds good. Maybe we can save a tour for some other time."

Toni refocused on the fridge, using the cold air pouring from inside to chill her heated thoughts. "Shall I open the wine?"

Rynn nodded. "Sounds great."

Toni poured two glasses and handed one to Rynn with a smile. "Daniel just called. He's running late. I had planned to eat around seven o'clock anyway, so we're okay there. Please, make yourself comfortable."

They moved from the kitchen to the living room, taking seats on the two leather couches.

Time flew by, and she fell into easy conversation with Rynn. At some point, she rose to check on the dinner she had cooking. During those few private moments turned away from Rynn, she laughed quietly to herself about what a nervous wreck she had been before Rynn's arrival. Talking with her was so natural. Sure, she was strongly attracted to her, but the attraction wasn't just physical. Rynn made her comfortable, made her laugh.

Shortly after seven o'clock, the chime rang. Toni hopped up to greet Daniel. Rynn rose from her place on the cushy couch, but remained at a distance, politely waiting for him to enter before stepping forward to say hello.

Toni watched as Rynn and Daniel greeted each other warmly, almost like old friends, though they'd only met once the week before and not under the best conditions.

Turning to Toni, Daniel wrapped her in a warm hug. She smiled at him and said, "You seem to be in good spirits tonight. That's refreshing to see."

He grinned, but the smile didn't quite reach his eyes. "Oh, I had a little fun shaking off the local news flunkie who was following me today. I think I may have succeeded in getting him to run a red light with a cop sitting right there. That's probably the highlight of my week."

Toni laughed. "I'm glad you enjoyed it. You're still getting tailed?"

"Sometimes. Less photos, though. I guess the paparazzi got tired of watching me do my grocery shopping and drive to and from the practice complex every day. That's really all I've been up to. Work, food and home." He released a deep sigh and murmured much more quietly so only she could hear him, "It's hard to get up the energy for much else. It's like part of me died with him, you know?"

Toni pulled Daniel into another hug, more comfort than greeting. "I know, hon, I know."

When he was ready, he stepped away and took his place at the table, seemingly ready to dig in to dinner.

Toni laughed. "As long as you've known me, you can't possibly expect to be served. Get up and help me in the kitchen." She smiled at Rynn, who had been hanging back a bit, apparently watching the interaction between her and Daniel.

Conversation progressed easily from there. She was a bit surprised at how readily Daniel spoke about his closeted life in the NFL. It seemed her instincts had been right. He needed an outlet to talk about his pain. Maybe he hadn't told these stories to her recently because she'd already heard them all, but with Rynn, he recapped most of his and Patrick's relationship.

"Sometimes, it was almost fun, you know?" he asked. "Like we were covert ops or something, sneaking off to mysterious international rendezvous."

Toni joined the story. "It was fun to help them get away, too. It didn't take a detective," she paused and playfully nudged Rynn sitting next to her, "to see that he and Patrick had something special."

Daniel agreed. "He could always read me. He just knew me better than anyone ever had. With his job, he could afford the travel, but he knew I loved giving him things like that. He let me play the hero, but really, he was the strong one." He choked up a bit, then, and Toni reached over and touched his arm to give comfort. Daniel took a minute to regain composure, offered a meek smile, and continued his stories.

Since she knew the history, Toni couldn't stop herself from letting her attention occasionally drift to Rynn as he talked. Something inside her felt warmer, almost more secure, in her presence. She was wonderful with Daniel tonight, engaged and listening thoughtfully while he talked.

The cynical part of Toni's mind wondered if Rynn was secretly in cop mode, but the interest in her eyes appeared to be simple, genuine empathy.

It felt good, sitting here with her best friend and this new acquaintance. Despite her near uniform attire, Rynn was relaxed.

Toni glanced briefly at her own loose-fitting blue jeans and snug long-sleeve Bears T-shirt, surprised she didn't feel self-conscious or underdressed. *Why should I?* After all, they were eating a simple dinner in the coziness of her condo. Still, she knew she had never been so comfortable with anyone else she'd felt so much attraction.

Rynn lingered behind briefly after Daniel left.

Toni had to fight the urge to fidget, amped up like a teenager hoping, waiting for a first kiss.

If Rynn shared her thoughts, though, she decided against it. She helped to clear the dishes from the table and thanked her again before leaving Toni undeniably disappointed. Despite that, she had greatly enjoyed the evening. Hopefully, this wouldn't be the last time.

CHAPTER THIRTEEN

The ringing phone interrupted Rynn as she shuffled through a stack of open cases. Another week had passed, and she and Pearson had been forced to admit they were still spinning their wheels on the Boden homicide. She answered the phone. "Callahan."

"Yes, Detective. I'm Lieutenant Jim Mueller up in Lake County."

"What can I do for you, Lieutenant?"

"We had a homicide victim in Zion early this morning. After running the details through VICAP, we think the profile matches one of yours, a Patrick Boden."

After speaking to Mueller a few more minutes, Rynn hung up the phone and said to Pearson, "I think we've got something."

Cooperating with another jurisdiction was never easy, but the Lake County murder proved just as gruesome as Patrick's, if not more so. According to the preliminary information shared by Mueller, the victim, Derek Quinn, had been brutally mutilated. His face and torso were similarly slashed multiple times, also with a nonserrated, commonly available blade. His knee was blown out, apparently a fresh injury. Their ME had also concluded that this was the work of an inexperienced attacker, though she suggested the varying depths and placement of the cuts indicated violent sadism more than anger or any loss of control on the killer's part.

Other aspects that had triggered a link in the Violent Criminal Apprehension Program included the details that both Boden and Quinn were in their midthirties and both lived alone. The locations of the crimes and the professions of the victims set them apart, and statements from friends and family painted stories of two very different men. While Boden was quiet and kept to himself, Quinn was known as an extremely sociable, boisterous man.

She and Pearson drove to Zion twice to meet with homicide detectives there, and were invited to observe interviews with Quinn's friends, family and co-workers. Unfortunately, there seemed as little to go on in the Quinn case as in Boden's.

On the drive home three days later, Rynn's mind raced while she considered recent developments. Beyond the usual aspects of the crime, she'd noticed Quinn had shown an affinity for the Packers. That brought Daniel's, and by extension, the Bears', connection to Boden to her mind. She wondered if a similar hidden relationship was possible.

She had observed interviews with three different women who had claimed recent relationships with Quinn, but was that enough to declare the victim straight and further separate him from Boden? Rynn had felt the lead was worth following up regardless of her feeling she might be grasping at straws.

Combing through various databases and even a typical Google search had yielded no possibilities of Packers players who might be gay. She'd considered calling Toni and talking to her about it, but she hadn't been quite sure how to broach the subject. Toni was a civilian, but she might be able to give her insight into the possibility of other closeted players, although

Rynn couldn't very well go into details about the Quinn homicide.

She was still debating when she arrived home and let herself in through the front door. The house was chilly. She realized with some reluctance that she would have to turn on the heat tonight, even though the first week of November was really too early for winter to arrive.

Rynn grabbed a glass of water and changed into her favorite sweats. After picking up her cell phone, she hesitated. She couldn't deny the quickening of her pulse when she thought about talking to Toni. *But this is a business call*, she reminded herself forcefully. She'd thought several times of calling Toni for other reasons, but so far had not worked up the courage. The possibility of getting information made it easier to make the call.

Taking a deep breath, Rynn flipped open the phone and dialed Toni's number.

* * *

Although it was Friday night, Toni settled on her couch to read a cheesy romance novel. Just as the two protagonists fell madly, hopelessly in love, her phone rang, nearly causing her to jump out of her seat. She grabbed the obnoxious noisemaker and glanced at the caller ID. She smiled when she saw the call was from Rynn. "Hello?"

"Hey, Toni, I hope I'm not calling too late." Rynn sounded tired.

Concern rose in Toni's chest. "No, it's fine. I was just reading a bit before bed. Is everything okay?"

"Yeah, of course."

Toni wondered what had happened in the days since they'd last talked. "What can I do for you tonight, Detective?" she asked.

After a second's silence, Rynn sighed, "This may seem like a random question, but I was just wondering if you represented anyone with the Packers."

What? The Packers? Toni hadn't been expecting a question about her business, but she kept her surprise to herself. "Yes, I do. Three players, actually. Why do you ask?"

Rynn fell silent again. Toni wondered why.

"Are you aware of any of them being gay?" Rynn finally asked.

Toni's shock at the unexpected inquiry bled through her reply. "Gay? What?" She had no idea what Rynn was talking about, or what had prompted this line of questioning.

"Do you know of any players on the Packers who are gay? Like Daniel."

Again, Toni was struck by the exhaustion in Rynn's voice. "I'm sorry. You've caught me off guard. Where are you coming from with these questions?"

"I wish I could say. It's not even anything solid, just trying to follow up on a hunch. Or better yet, eliminate one. Can you help me here?"

"I would if I could. The three guys I represent with the Pack are all straight. One's kind of a ladies' man, although he's calmed down since I began representing him. Worked some magic with endorsements, but I threatened to drop his ass if he didn't clean up his act. Surprisingly enough, he listened. The other two are happily married. And I've got no reason to think any of them are hiding anything. Again, why are you asking about the Packers?"

"Toni, I'm sorry, but I just can't say anything more."

Toni heard Rynn's frustration, and maybe even a tinge of regret at her admission. *She wants to be open with me, but something's holding her back.* She decided not to push, sensing the question had a connection to Rynn's job and probably Patrick's case. "Okay. Don't worry about it. You've certainly got me curious, but I understand."

"Thank you." Rynn paused before continuing quietly, "And thanks again for dinner last week. Have you talked to Daniel at all since then?"

"Yes, a little bit. He's doing about as well as can be expected, given everything he's going through."

"Okay. He's a good guy. I enjoyed spending time with him and you."

Toni shrugged. "He's great. I think sharing his history with Patrick really helped him grieve. It might not have come up directly at dinner, but he told me how badly he wants to do everything he can to help you. I know he's still blaming himself, wondering if he'd been publicly open about their relationship, he might have been able to protect Patrick."

"Please don't let him beat himself up. I doubt there's anything he could have done."

"Thank you." Toni was surprised at the emotion she felt. In the past few weeks, Rynn had really gotten to her, and they weren't even together. *At least, not yet.* She tried to ignore that last thought, focusing instead on the situation in front of them, but a little wanting-something-more feeling in the back of her mind wouldn't be completely suppressed.

Without consciously planning what she was doing, she suddenly blurted out, "Rynn? Are you busy tomorrow night?"

Rynn seemed taken aback by the unexpected question. "Um, no, not really."

Toni closed her eyes. *What am I doing here?* But the question was already out there, and she couldn't duck out of it now. She continued, "I was wondering if you'd be interested in attending an event with me."

She'd been thinking about asking Rynn. It was not an event she had been particularly looking forward to, but once the idea of going with Rynn had wiggled its way into her mind after dinner last week, the whole prospect of having to attend seemed better.

The silence from the other end of the line began to worry her. She wondered what Rynn thought of her invitation. "Rynn? You still there?"

"Yeah, I'm here. I…I don't know, Toni."

Even as her heart sank, Toni caught Rynn's frustration. Again, she spoke without thinking. "Well, it wouldn't necessarily be purely social. I was actually thinking that this might help you with Patrick's case. Although that may just be me making excuses for you to come…" She trailed off, unsure whether she had just made a fool of herself.

But it seemed Rynn's curiosity was piqued. "How would this event have anything to do with my case?"

Toni smiled. From Rynn's tone, the interest in spending time together was mutual. "Well, you see, it's a team event for the Bears. Every year, Vanessa Carter throws what she's cleverly dubbed the 'Bye Week Ball.' I personally think it's an excuse for her to act important as she mingles with the rich and famous, but I guess I've never been one for fame and fortune."

"Doesn't sound like you care for this Ms. Carter all that much," Rynn said.

Toni hadn't realized that her assessment of Vanessa wasn't entirely flattering until Rynn pointed it out. "No, I guess I don't. She's a little too rich glamour girl for me, I suppose."

"So who is she? And why is she throwing a team party that you feel compelled to attend?"

"She's the wife of one of the owners, Lawrence Carter. He bought into the team a few years back when the old family was feuding and selling off shares. He's got a relatively small chunk of ownership, but that doesn't stop Vanessa from acting like she personally owns the entire franchise." She briefly explained the politics of team ownership, trying not to be too disparaging.

"How might this party contribute to my investigation?"

"Do I really need to connect this to work to get you to come with me?"

Rynn's reply was playful. "No, not at all. I would have thought you knew by now that I want to see you outside of work, but I'm not really sure what to do. I certainly can't socialize with witnesses, but I'm not sure you qualify as such. It's a little hazy to me."

"I thought you cleared Daniel. Doesn't that remove me from involvement?"

"A minute ago, you were trying to sell me on this ball by connecting it to Daniel," Rynn teased. "But I think you're right. You're not part of my case. I don't want to screw anything up, though."

After a moment, Toni abruptly went on, "Well, if I have to convince you, fine. I thought this might give you an opportunity to go undercover, check out some of the people who have access to Daniel. Would that be a legitimate reason for you to attend the party with me?"

"You want me under covers, eh?"

Toni blushed, glad Rynn wasn't here to see her face turning bright shades of red. "That's not quite what I said would be on the evening's agenda."

"No, I suppose not. It would certainly add appeal, don't you think?"

Toni was shocked, but she couldn't deny she liked this side of Rynn. "Detective, I suspect you know exactly how I feel on the matter. I doubt my clues have been hard to follow."

"Perhaps not. But I pride myself on maintaining a professional façade, at least." Rynn's tone shifted with the statement, turning matter-of-fact. "What time are you picking me up?"

"Really? You'll come?"

Rynn laughed. "Yeah, I guess I will."

"Well, this isn't exactly one of those parties with a defined start and end time. It is black-tie, so I hope you don't mind. Might take us a little bit of a drive to get to their mansion in North Shore. I'm sure the event will be well catered, but would you like to meet for a quieter dinner first and then head over afterward?"

Rynn took time to consider the offer. "Sure, I guess that sounds good."

"Any requests?"

"How about I let you surprise me. I'm pretty flexible."

Toni wasn't sure how much flirtation was intended behind those words, but she immediately caught her mind wandering to places it probably shouldn't be. *Flexible?*

Before she could open her mouth and embarrass herself, Rynn continued, "You're between my house and North Shore, so why don't I come to your condo and we'll leave from there?"

"You already know where I live. I guess that makes sense. Can you be here at seven o'clock?"

"Sure, I can do that."

"Okay, it's a date."

A pause on the other line held a hint of promise. Rynn replied, "Indeed it is."

They said their goodbyes. After the call ended, Toni sat on the couch, musing about the conversation with Rynn. Sure, she'd couched the invitation in a tale about helping investigate Daniel's acquaintances, but surely neither of them really believed that excuse. Rynn had understood what she was really asking, and she had accepted anyway.

Toni grinned at the thought.

CHAPTER FOURTEEN

Toni checked her appearance in the mirror again. She was a bit surprised that her nerves weren't on edge yet. Perhaps they were just waiting for Rynn to arrive, she thought, which should happen any minute now.

When the doorbell rang at exactly seven o'clock, Toni's heartbeat jumped a little. She pulled the door open, pleased to catch a glimpse of smoldering desire on Rynn's face as the woman's stunning green gaze flicked up and down her body, taking in the tiny, black cocktail dress that clung to her figure in all the right places and accentuated her best features.

Rynn entered the apartment silently. Toni wondered if she'd been struck temporarily speechless. God knew her own words had been swept away by her first glance at Rynn, who looked absolutely dashing in a jet-black suit complete with pressed white shirt and silver vest that suited her strong figure perfectly.

Toni smiled. She liked what she saw and wasn't afraid to show it.

Rynn finally spoke the first words of the evening, a barely audible, "Hey."

Toni's breath was almost stolen by Rynn's smile, but somehow, she managed to return the greeting with a playful, "Hey, yourself." She motioned Rynn further into the room. "I'm just about ready to go, but just let me double-check myself in the mirror one more time."

Without glancing away from her, Rynn replied, "Trust me, you look amazing. I don't think you need to double-check anything."

Toni felt a slight blush heat her face, but she simply nodded, reached for her coat, and led the way outside.

As they climbed into Toni's Lexus, Rynn asked, "Where are you taking me?"

"How do you feel about Modern French cuisine?" Toni checked Rynn's expression before putting the car in gear.

The slightest frown touched Rynn's lower lip before a nonchalant smile returned. "Don't know much about it, actually, but I'll give anything a try." She made a casual shrug.

Toni smiled to herself. She hadn't missed the momentary hesitation. Maybe she was stereotyping, but she would have been surprised if Rynn had been excited by that particular proposition. "Well, in that case, I'll have to take you to Marcello's sometime. He emigrated here after being classically trained in the Basque region and his food is unbelievable."

Confusion wrinkled Rynn's brow.

"Not knowing your food preferences, I thought we'd be safe with Italian," Toni went on, amused. "As far as I know, everyone likes that. I'm taking you to Francesca's. Best Italian I've found in the greater Chicago area."

Rynn nodded and smiled. "Italian sounds delicious."

* * *

Later at Francesca's, Rynn was pretty sure the meal had been the best Italian food she'd ever eaten. She didn't think she had any room left for dessert, but Toni insisted on ordering the tiramisu. Taking the first bite, she couldn't stop a slight moan from escaping her lips. No, *this* was the best Italian food ever.

Toni's amused smile at her reaction prompted her to say, "Sorry, but this is amazing. I don't think I've ever tasted anything so light and…I don't even know how to describe it. I'm going to give away my lack of culinary knowledge if I keep talking." She blushed slightly.

"Don't worry about it. I'm just glad you like the tiramisu. I told you we couldn't leave without ordering their *pièce de résistance*."

Rynn had to resist the urge to melt at Toni's warm smile. The time spent with Toni was rapidly turning into one of the best evenings she'd had in a long time. Oh, how easy it would be to surrender to those dark, chocolate-brown eyes! Trying desperately to hang on to reality, she nudged the conversation forward. "Do you know all the best restaurants around here?"

"I know a fair few," Toni answered. "I generally try to avoid big chain restaurants—it just seems like they rarely have any soul. I end up going to business dinners quite often with clients I need to impress or with company reps from whom I'm trying to win endorsement deals. It leads to a fairly robust knowledge of the available food selection."

Rynn nodded. "Makes sense. Sounds to me like great food might be a pretty good perk of your career field."

Toni laughed lightly. "Yes, I suppose so. It does mean I have to work out twice as often to keep myself looking decent. Especially dining with the athletes, some of whom I swear eat their own weight in steak every day."

You look incredible. Rynn mentally smacked herself. She let her eyes wander a little lower. Toni's little black dress didn't leave much to imagination. Her breath caught. She coughed and sipped from the glass of sparkling water. After the cool liquid calmed the tightness in her throat, she took another stab at civil conversation. "It sounds like you really enjoy what you do. What led you to become a sports agent?"

"I guess it's because of my dad," Toni said thoughtfully. "I think I mentioned before that he's been in this business for decades. He got his start in New York and eventually, he and my mom moved to California. Growing up, I can't tell you how often I watched sports with my dad. We always had to keep an eye on his guys." Her face glowed with fond memories.

"He worked with a couple different sports," Toni went on. "The business was different back then, the players were different. Nothing like the multimillion-dollar deals we have today. He had to represent a variety of guys year-round to make ends meet at first, but as the players' salaries started to grow, so did the agents' cuts. Anyway, he represented some baseball guys in the spring and summer, and a hockey or basketball player here or there. But his favorites were always the football players. I think it was his love of the game that led him to stay as close to sports as he could. He never had the physical skills to play competitively, although he still talks fondly of his days in the Pop Warner leagues. Coaching back then was hardly a career at anything below the top levels. Without playing himself, it was hard to break into that.

"But being an agent? That he could do. Even my grandpa was okay with that, since my dad went to college and got a degree in business management to facilitate his career dreams."

Rynn felt captivated by Toni's story, amazed by the passion she wore on her sleeve. *Well, not her sleeve.* The spaghetti straps on the dress only showed off perfect skin. Toni might be talking about her father's love of the game, but her own affinity was obvious.

Toni continued to talk about her father's business and the intricacies of contracts and finances. Mentioning the public perception of her career and her clients, she chuckled. "I mean, how often do you hear about an offensive lineman holding out for an extra million? No, most pro athletes are reasonable and the few who aren't just give a bad name to their teammates. Dad learned early on that those few were the ones he didn't want to waste his time on. He realized he could make as much money with far less stress by representing a handful of good guys than by hitting a homerun with one delusional diva.

"He used to take me to the office in the summers, and sometimes his office was a ballpark or a stadium. I used to wonder if he would have taken me so freely if I'd had a brother, but that's just one of those things I'll never know. My little sister was my mom's beauty queen, and I was my dad's sports buddy. He shared his love of the game with me. When the time came for me to pick a career, following in my dad's footsteps was a no-brainer."

Toni smiled, turned her head, and looked at Rynn. "You know, it's not often I get to talk about myself," she said. "Most of the time, I'm talking about my clients and what I can do for them. Daniel is one of the few who made that jump to friend as well as client. I work so much that sometimes, it seems like I don't have time for friends outside the office."

Rynn heard no remorse in Toni's tone. More telling, there was no sadness in Toni's eyes. She understood that Toni really did love her work and had no regrets about a stunted social life.

In that moment, Rynn felt an alarming kinship with Toni, an attraction so strong that she had to look away for a second to control herself. She shook her head slightly and met Toni's concerned gaze. Did Toni have any idea how she affected her?

Her dessert finished, Rynn listened while Toni chatted a while longer. She was surprised to learn that Toni had left the California sunshine for the misty weather of New England after graduating high school.

Toni laughed when Rynn asked about it. "Why not?" She continued thoughtfully, "Honestly? I was afraid to come out to my parents. I didn't know how they'd take it. And I wanted to get far enough away to figure out what was going on with me. I knew I was gay, but I didn't really know what that meant. When I was trying to figure out my future, there were two places known nationally for gay culture. San Francisco was too close to home, so I chose Boston."

Rynn nodded. She hadn't really considered leaving the place where she'd grown up, but she thought if a person was looking for space to find herself, going clear across the country was probably a good way to do it. "So where did you end up? Harvard?"

"Why? You're not a Yale girl, are you?"

Rynn shook her head quickly. "No, no. I was actually just thinking that I don't believe I have any friends from an Ivy League school. Do you get the honor of being my first?"

Toni shrugged, but her eyes sparkled with good humor and a look showing she was debating whether or not to say something suggestive. Rynn found herself slightly disappointed when Toni evidently decided against it, answering instead, "We're not all that special. And I didn't go to Harvard for undergrad, just law school."

Impressed by Toni's credentials, Rynn said, "Harvard Law sounds pretty special to me."

Toni smiled and slid to the edge of their booth. "Perhaps."

Rising from her own seat, Rynn offered Toni her hand. "Shall we?" she asked, grinning.

Toni matched her expression and accepted her outstretched hand. "I'd love to."

CHAPTER FIFTEEN

They arrived at the party, and Toni pulled her car up to the valet. "There will be a coat check, but it might be easier if we leave our top coats in the car." Rynn nodded and followed Toni's lead at the car and into the house. Just inside, they were approached by a pair of massive men. She felt an amused smile tug at her lips when she sensed Rynn's discomfort and almost imperceptible shift to a more defensive stance. *Must be the cop in her.*

She knew the two giants were no threat, and greeted them warmly. "Malakai! Ziggy! Fancy seeing you here." Turning to Rynn, she made introductions. "Rynn, these are two of the players that I represent with the Bears. Malakai Johnson, an offensive tackle, and one of his linemates, Frank Ziggler. Guys, meet my date, Rynn Smith."

Both guys warmly shook Rynn's hand. Toni considered the instructions she'd been given during their car ride. She'd learned that knowledge of Rynn's profession sometimes led to unwanted curiosity and scrutiny. Rynn had suggested a complete name change, but that might be too difficult to remember.

With that in mind, they'd compromised. Tonight, her date was Rynn Smith, bank manager at a Bank of America branch in Bartlett. If anyone asked, they'd met when she stopped in to make a routine deposit. She had protested the extremely boring story but been told that was exactly the point. She still didn't see how Rynn could possibly be forgettable.

She and Rynn exchanged small talk with Malakai and Ziggy for a few moments before moving further into the mansion. She was impressed by how natural Rynn acted with the crowd after her initial unease. As they worked their way around the room, she frequently introduced Rynn to players and other sports royalty.

Eventually, a familiar man appeared. Toni found herself wrapped in a massive bear hug. "Tommy Rocker! Hey there." She couldn't help an almost girlish squeal when she was lifted from the ground. "Okay, okay, it's good to see you too. Now put me down, you big lug. This dress isn't meant for that kind of greeting." She laughed when he returned her feet to the floor.

"Hello, beautiful. My, don't you look stunning this evening." Daniel smiled.

It had been almost a month since Patrick's sudden death. Daniel looked better now, Toni thought. His smile almost reached his eyes, but he still seemed to lack his old spark.

Daniel touched her arm affectionately and turned to Rynn. With a goofy grin, he asked, "And who is this lovely lady?"

He'd clearly gotten the short text message she'd sent him from the car, explaining he should act as if he'd never met Rynn before. "Tommy, allow me to introduce you to my date for the evening, Rynn Smith."

Daniel smiled and played the complete gentleman, bowing slightly and kissing the back of Rynn's hand.

Toni found Rynn's surprised look and the slight blush tinting her cheeks amusing. "Hey now, buddy, no flirting. She's my date." She punched his arm playfully and echoed his laugh.

She stood with Rynn while Daniel talked casually about his teammates. Suddenly, their group was approached by a tall, elegant woman. Spotting the newcomer, she tensed.

"Well, if it isn't Tommy Rocker. And how are you this evening?" the woman crooned, pushing her way into their small circle and paying little attention to Rynn or Toni.

Toni noticed Daniel react with a similar distaste, but he remained polite. "I'm quite well, Vanessa, but how could I not be at this splendid affair?"

Vanessa laughed gaily. Toni wondered if she missed or simply ignored the hint of sarcasm in Daniel's tone. After her forced laughter died down, Daniel continued, "Vanessa Carter, I believe you've met my agent, Toni Davis. This is Rynn Smith." He gestured to each of them in turn.

Vanessa barely glanced over her before turning a shrewd gaze on Rynn, who met the unmannered appraisal head-on and offered a critiquing look of her own. Her calm confidence didn't seem shaken by the appearance of the party's hostess.

Toni smiled, feeling her muscles uncoil. This coolness under pressure was just one more reason to like Rynn.

Vanessa failed to extend a welcoming hand to Toni or Rynn. Instead, she turned to fawn over Daniel. "Oh, Tommy, I didn't know you were bringing a date. I had rather hoped that we might spend some time together. You know, since we got cut short last time."

Toni thought Daniel shuddered at the blatant flirting. Shrugging off Vanessa's touch, he offered some clarification. "Miss Smith isn't my date. We've only just met."

Vanessa cast another appraising look at Rynn, perhaps slightly more interested in the object of her evaluation. "Then forgive me, Miss Smith, but who have you come with tonight?"

Toni stepped in to answer the question. "Rynn is my date tonight, actually. I thought I might introduce her to all the glamour and gore of sports management."

Vanessa finally looked at her. The assessing gaze took on an almost glaring quality, but in the blink of an eye, once again she became the showy, magnanimous hostess, whose fifty-thousand-dollar-smile threatened to blind anyone who looked directly at it. "Your date? Well, isn't that splendid." Turning back to Rynn, who had not spoken a word, she offered a limp wave. "Miss Smith, I do hope you enjoy your brief brush with fame and fortune. I'm sure I'll see you around." She glided away, having apparently decided none of them were worth her time.

Toni shook her head in disgust and shared an exasperated smile with Daniel. Returning her gaze to Rynn, she found her staring after the departing Vanessa Carter.

After a moment's silence, Rynn spoke. "I think I can see why you don't like her much, Toni. She's not quite…well, it doesn't seem you two would have much in common." Her statement caused Toni to laugh. She turned to Daniel. "What did Mrs. Carter mean when she said you were cut short last time?"

He shrugged. "She managed to sneak her way into the locker room after practice a few weeks back and tried hitting on me. I wasn't very receptive for obvious reasons beyond my own tastes. I actually find her to be a repulsive example of all that is wrong with football."

Rynn's raised brow made Toni's pulse quicken slightly. "You seem to have as favorable an opinion of her as Toni shared with me the other day."

Daniel snarled. "Vanessa's an ex-cheerleader and a gold-digging slut, if you ask me."

"Wow, even I wasn't that harsh," Toni commented.

"Maybe not, but I think the sentiment was about the same," Rynn said. She continued to Daniel, "But you even say ex-cheerleader as if it's an insult."

He launched into a discussion about the merits—or lack thereof—of NFL cheerleaders while Rynn politely listened. Toni smiled. She'd heard Daniel's cheerleader rant before. Now Rynn was forced to be the captive audience of his opinion. *Better her than me.*

Rynn's face suddenly erupted in a devilish grin. "Were you the star football player who dated that head cheerleader in high school?" she asked Daniel, who blushed.

"No. Fortunately for me, I wasn't the quarterback so I didn't have to." He leaned in closer to keep their conversation private. "But I do have firsthand knowledge of those collegiate cheer men I was talking about." He shifted back with a smile.

Rynn laughed.

Toni studied Daniel. Was that a hint of a long absent sparkle in his eyes? Maybe, just maybe, Rynn was good for him.

* * *

The rest of the party seemed to fly by. Rynn managed to keep half her mind on people-watching, but her scrutiny of the other partygoers was hindered slightly by the absolutely stunning brunette at her side. When she wasn't asking discreet questions or observing Daniel's interactions with other guests, she couldn't help sneaking frequent looks at her companion. Toni's black dress excited an electricity inside her entirely different than the static cling of brushing elbows with so many others.

Apparently unaffected by the heat or the crowd, Toni remained composed and charming as she greeted and introduced countless new faces. Rynn was hard-pressed to keep up. By the time they were ready to leave, she found herself looking forward to escaping the bustle.

While they waited for the valet to bring Toni's car around, Rynn noticed the cold night air bring a shiver to Toni's elegant frame. She offered her suit jacket as further protection from the chill.

Toni smiled at the gallant effort but refused to accept. When Rynn protested, Toni laughed. "And if I let you give me yours, what would happen? You'd stand out here freezing for five minutes and I'll still be thawing you out by the time we make it back to my condo."

Rynn shrugged. "Mmm, and what might that involve?" She sent a flirtatious glance Toni's way, pulled off her jacket, and stepped behind the shivering woman to wrap the warm garment around her shoulders.

Toni whispered, "That last shiver had nothing to do with the temperature, you know."

Those few, purred words drove heat through Rynn's body. She hardly even felt the cold while they waited. She didn't move far from her position behind Toni, keeping an arm draped loosely around her waist.

When the valet roared the powerful Lexus up the drive, a startled Rynn was disappointed to have her contact with Toni broken. For a moment, Toni seemed almost shaken by the experience, stepping out of her light embrace and returning her jacket before stepping forward to tip the driver. She must have been colder than she let on, though, as she pulled her coat from the backseat then slipped behind the wheel.

Rynn glared at the young man, who did a double take. *He probably got a kick out of cock-blocking me, thinking I was some guy sweet-talking a beautiful woman.* Annoyed, she accepted her moment with Toni was gone and rounded the car to climb into the passenger seat.

Toni navigated the Lexus away from the Carter estate without speaking. Fearful she might be embarrassed about their brief connection, Rynn chanced a quick glance in Toni's direction, but saw nothing in the neutral expression that indicated discomfort.

Toni appeared simply focused on the road ahead, but a hint of her true feelings was revealed by the tiniest upturn at the corner of her full lips. Rynn bit her own lip as thoughts of kissing Toni's lush mouth raced into her mind. When she realized she was staring, she quickly turned to face forward again, hoping Toni hadn't noticed.

After a minute more, Toni broke the silence. "You know, we spent most of dinner talking about me and about how I ended up where I am in life. We've got a good forty-five minute drive home, so I think it's your turn to share."

Rynn glanced at Toni. She wasn't sure whether to be relieved she hadn't been caught or doubly nervous at being asked to open up. Toni's relaxed smile brought a warm calm to the car's atmosphere. After a brief hesitation, she responded. "I don't tend to talk about myself all that much, really. Honestly, I'd rather hear more about you."

"Oh, no, Detective, you're not getting away that easily. Come on, tell me something. I hardly know anything about you," Toni chided.

Tonight, the way Toni said her title was full of affection. Rynn suspected Toni didn't even know she was doing it. "I don't know what to say. I tend to ask questions, listen and watch body cues. I guess I'm not used to being the topic of conversation," she admitted.

"Oh, come on, Rynn, I'm not asking for your deepest, darkest secrets." Toni paused and threw a brief glance at her. "That comes later."

Rynn was glad for the darkness that hid her face. "Okay, I'll talk, but you have to help me. Ask me something specific. What do you want to know?"

"You realize that could be a dangerous offer."

Rynn smiled. In any other situation, with any other person, Toni might be right. But here and now, she felt completely safe and didn't have a need to hide. When no question came, she teased, "I wouldn't wait too long over there, Toni. This could be a limited-time deal."

"I had rather hoped that time might be on my side." Toni's mischievous grin struck Rynn speechless. After a pause, Toni finally said, "Just tell me about yourself, about what makes you *you*. Why don't you start by painting a setting for me? Have you always lived in Chicagoland?"

The question's specific focus drew Rynn out. "Different suburbs over the years, but yes. My dad managed to work his way up in the management of a retail chain. As his job situation improved, he was able to move me and my mom to a nicer area. Where we moved in Elgin, it's really nice. Got a small lake out back. I still like to just sit and look out over the water. I guess I've always found the lake view calming. I've lived in that house for almost fifteen years, except the few years I was on my own after high school and at the academy."

Toni frowned. "Wait, back up. You still live with your parents?"

Rynn chuckled. "Yes and no. Yes, I live in my parents' house, but no, I'm not the sketchy, basement-dwelling, thirty-something kid who still lives with my parents. They—"

"Wait, you're thirty-something?" Toni asked in mock horror.

Rynn wondered if Toni was trying to change the subject. She didn't want to leave her with the impression that she didn't support herself. She went on. "Yes. Do you want me to explain my living conditions or not? A minute ago, you seemed appalled by the thought that I still lived with my parents."

Toni shrugged. Her dark profile remained pointed toward the road. "You said you didn't. And even if you did, why should that matter to me?"

"If at my age, or even five years younger, I were still living with my parents, I'd hope there was a good reason for it. The concept doesn't exactly scream maturity and independence."

"Perhaps not, but you could be caring for them or you could be supporting them. The economy hasn't been great, and plenty of mature college grads have been forced to move back in with their folks. But rather than continuing with all this speculative banter, why don't you tell me how it is that you live in your parents' house, but not with your parents?"

Toni sounded understanding, not the least bit judgmental. Rynn really believed if things were different, Toni would actually sympathize with an unusual living arrangement. That didn't mean a highly successful business woman would be okay with the basement-dwelling image she'd painted, but the attitude did speak to the strength of her compassion.

"I live in my parents' house, but not with my parents, because I inherited it," Rynn said. "You see, I'm an only child, so that made me sole beneficiary of my parents' belongings, the house included...when they died." She paused, her gaze falling to her lap.

The car slowed slightly. Out of the corner of her eyes, she saw Toni turn to look at her. An unexpected flood of sadness left her unable to meet Toni's questioning glance. Plenty of people knew her parents were dead, including her co-workers at the station. But it had been years since she'd really talked about her mother and father or about losing them. She wanted to share with Toni, but she wasn't sure she was ready.

"Oh, Rynn, I'm sorry," Toni said quietly. "I didn't know they were…you don't have to tell me anything else if you don't want to."

"No, talking to you feels right, I guess. I haven't talked much about their deaths in so long."

Toni reached across the car seat and took Rynn's hand in her warm, comforting grasp. "In that case, what happened?" she asked.

"Car accident. Six years ago. They were driving back from the grocery store one afternoon and a trucker had fallen asleep at the wheel. The collision was head-on, happened when the truck drifted into their lane. Left my parents' car completely smashed." Rynn fell silent, nightmare images flashing through her mind for the first time in years. "The police told me that it would have happened so fast, there was nothing my dad could have done to get out of the way. He and Mom would have been killed almost immediately, no suffering at least, and may not even have known what was happening."

Toni squeezed her hand gently, offering solace and strength.

"The truck driver lived, but barely," Rynn went on. "He was in a coma for three days, and then intensive care for weeks. You know, at first, I was so angry at him. But when he recovered enough to learn what had happened and to speak, the first person he wanted to see was me." The memory blazed into her mind. "I didn't want to. I hated him. Hated the fact that he survived when both of my parents were taken. When the nurse called me from the hospital to ask if I would come visit him, I was so shocked and angry I could barely respond, and I pretty much hung up on her after making it clear that I wanted nothing to do with him. Afterward, I felt terrible. I called back to apologize to her—it wasn't her fault, after all—but she didn't hold it against me. She just asked me to reconsider.

"Maybe it was guilt for that outburst that took me back to the hospital. Either way, I did visit him, and by that time my rage had burnt itself out. I felt hollow with grief and gutted by my spent anger. But going to see him...I've never seen a stranger cry harder. That man had beaten himself up so badly over the accident, I no longer felt it my place to hold a grudge. I didn't say anything to him. I couldn't. But before I left, I think some understanding of forgiveness passed between us. He whispered, 'thank you' as I left, and his daughter still sends me a card every year on the anniversary of my parents' deaths."

A few heavy miles ticked by in silence. Rynn didn't need Toni to say anything. Somehow, Toni understood. No one, not even Samson, knew about that hospital visit. She had never talked about it in detail before, always focusing solely on the raw facts of her parents' loss. Why had she shared as much now? She wasn't sure, but it felt right.

Toni continued to hold her hand, her thumb rubbing comforting circles on the skin.

After the shock of the memory lessened, Rynn was able to go on, sharing a few more stories about her parents and her childhood until they arrived at Toni's condo. These memories were more cheerful, lightening the mood considerably.

Toni seemed relaxed when she pulled the Lexus into the empty space next to the Tahoe. She turned off the engine and twisted in her seat to face Rynn. A moment passed between them, a contentment that invited lingering without the necessity of words. When the night chill seeped into the car, Toni squeezed her hand, released it, and opened the door.

Rynn followed Toni's lead, climbing out into the cold night air. Mid-November wasn't usually quite this brisk, but it had gotten to be quite late in the evening. The best advantage of the cold, she thought, was that it gave a clear view of the bright stars overhead.

She paused by the back of the car, reluctant to bring the night to a close despite the time. As she looked up at the bright stars, she felt Toni take a place beside her, so near their shoulders practically touched. She let her gaze drop from the stars to the sparkle in Toni's eyes. She met Toni's glance for a second and looked away, smiling.

"Toni," she said, "thank you. For everything tonight. The party was…"

Toni laughed quietly and leaned against the Lexus's trunk. "I don't know about you, but the party was probably the least interesting part of the evening."

Rynn nodded. "You're right. But everything was great. Dinner, just talking with you, and yes, even the party." Despite her misgivings, she moved closer to Toni and turned to face her. Their heavy coats brushed together. "I also need to thank you for the ride home. I didn't know how much I needed to share that part of my past, and I don't think I could have spoken with anyone but you. I haven't been able to talk about my parents before. Not like that."

Toni's hands slipped around Rynn's waist, pulling her into a hug that offered nothing but comfort and sympathy for her loss.

Rynn allowed herself to be taken in by Toni's warm strength and the soothing embrace. She rested her head on Toni's shoulder, her face buried against the skin at Toni's neck. When she felt Toni's hands shift higher on her back, a different emotion coursed through her body. She raised her head, her face barely inches away from the stars sparkling in Toni's eyes. She lowered her mouth just enough to find Toni's lips.

The kiss was both tender and strong. It lasted a few seconds, but in that brief time, Toni responded with every ounce of the same desire that Rynn felt.

Rynn let her eyes fall closed at the taste of Toni's sweet mouth. The kiss ended. For a moment, neither of them moved. Opening her eyes, she was met by Toni's calm smile. Whatever uncertainty she'd had about professional distance no longer seemed to matter. There was no turning back from this moment.

She moved first, her lips coming within a hairbreadth to Toni's ear. "Thank you," she whispered, giving another quick kiss to Toni's lips before forcing herself to break the embrace.

She stepped back and stopped, realizing her fingers were entwined with Toni's. She had no idea when they'd grasped hands. She released her grip and turned toward her Tahoe.

Toni nodded and started walking to her condo.

Rynn watched Toni disappear into the building. For a moment longer, she was reluctant to leave, but finally, the cold made itself known. She climbed into the car, started the engine, and drove home, still smiling.

CHAPTER SIXTEEN

Rynn didn't normally watch Sunday football. If she watched football at all, it was college. Today, though, she settled onto the couch with her burger and plate of fries and flipped through channels until she found a game. She knew it was because the NFL was now linked with Toni in her mind. She hadn't been able to stop thinking about their date the night before. In truth, she didn't want to stop.

The game started—Packers versus Vikings. As the first quarter progressed, she found herself wondering more about the inner working of the league. The television coverage zeroed in on some starting players, practically ignoring others. Obviously, the quarterbacks were media centerpieces, and there were two or three defenders that seemed to attract the camera. After listening to Toni talk about the divas and the workhorses, she was curious how much influence agents and endorsements had on which players the commentators chose to discuss. That was certainly something she could research online, but why not go straight to the source? Smiling, she decided to call Toni.

As the talking heads on TV rambled on, she picked up her cell phone and dialed Toni's number. To her disappointment, the call went to voice mail. *Damn it.* She considered hanging up–after all, everyone checked the caller ID these days—but when the beep sounded, she blurted, "Hey Toni. It's me. Rynn. I, uh, I've been thinking about you today and just thought I'd give you a ring. A call, I mean. Also, I've got a bit of a football question and I was wondering if you could help me out. So call me back when you get a minute. Hopefully, I'll see you soon."

Rynn ended the call. She didn't get nervous easily, but that little beep had thrown her off. She reflected on the jumbled and anxious message she'd just left. She stared at the phone in her hand, trying to blame it for her uneasiness. Oh, well. Hopefully Toni would think she was cute instead of awkward. There certainly wasn't anything she could do about it now.

She shoved the phone back in her pocket. Almost immediately, it rang with an incoming call. Pulling the phone out, she smiled when she saw Toni's name on the screen. She flipped the phone open and offered a friendly, "Hello."

"Hi." Toni greeted her. "Did you call? I was just getting out of the shower and didn't quite make it to the phone."

The shower? Rynn had to blink away a stunning mental image before responding. "Yeah, that was me. Did you listen to the voice mail I left you?"

"No, not yet."

"Good. Don't."

"What? Why not?"

Rynn grinned. "Because I hate talking to machines and it wasn't one of my finer moments. So please, spare my pride and just delete that one."

Toni chuckled. "Well, I think your explanation makes me want to listen to it more."

"Oh, come on. You wouldn't do that to me, would you?" Rynn playfully pleaded. She wasn't embarrassed talking to Toni, although she'd practically stuttered her message.

"You bet your cute ass I would," Toni teased.

"Cute? How d'you know my ass is cute?"

"Trust me, I checked. You pass with flying colors."

Rynn blushed. "Mmm, well, if you keep up the flattery, I guess I could survive you hearing that mess of a message."

"You're easy to flatter, Detective. Keeping that up shouldn't be too hard."

"Really? Because I've been told before that I can be a bit rough around the edges."

"Oh, you are," Toni agreed matter-of-factly.

Rynn responded with an indignant, "Hey, now!"

Toni chuckled and added, "But that's part of what makes you so adorable."

"Are you just being nice because I'm such a great kisser? If I had known it was so easy to get these compliments rolling, I would have kissed you weeks ago."

"I would have welcomed that. So what kept you?"

"It certainly wasn't for lack of desire, but I think you know that. I couldn't resist you anymore," Rynn admitted.

"Good. Because you were killing me, holding out like that. I hope you won't keep me waiting quite so long for a second kiss."

Toni's sultry tone made Rynn glad she was sitting down. Damn, the woman could flirt. She'd known the attraction was mutual, but Toni wasn't holding herself back today.

"Well, after last evening, I think I owe you dinner, at least. Maybe some night this week?" It had been a while since Rynn had asked someone out on a date, but she was surprised by the butterflies roiling in her stomach while she waited for Toni's reply.

"Okay. I'd like that." Toni paused, "Does this mean I'm going to have to wait for dinner in a few days to see you again?"

Rynn grinned. "Why, Toni, you're not the impatient type, are you?"

"Maybe, maybe not." Toni laughed. "I think I'm more willing to wait for some things than for others. But you got an avalanche rolling last night. Are you really going to keep me waiting?"

On impulse, Rynn said mischievously, "I don't know about any avalanche. It was a short, simple, good night kiss."

"If you're trying to tell me it gets better, you sure as hell better not be making me wait."

Rynn laughed. "Oh, it gets better."

"I'm not coming on too strong, am I, Detective?" Toni asked.

"Not at all. How does seven o'clock Wednesday sound?"

"Okay. Fancy or casual?"

"Let's go with casual this time. I can't top Francesca's, so I'll go for a different angle."

Toni laughed. "Fair enough. I played my best cards there, so I hope it's not so easily topped."

Rynn talked with Toni a while longer before saying her goodbyes. It was only after her attention returned to the TV that she realized she'd completely forgotten to ask Toni about business.

CHAPTER SEVENTEEN

Rynn pulled into her parking space at the station the next morning with an unfamiliar feeling in her gut. Dread was far too strong a word, but she had a feeling Pearson would demand to know the identity of the "lucky lady" again.

She hadn't even made it to the bullpen when a voice behind her called, "Well, well, looks like someone had a good weekend." Pearson sidled up next to her, grinning from ear to ear.

Rynn shook her head. "You know, I was stressed about you getting on my case. There have to be frown wrinkles all over my face. What makes you think I had a good weekend?"

Pearson shrugged. "I'm just that good."

She punched him on the arm. "No, really. I'm curious. I consider myself pretty good at reading people, so I want to learn your technique."

"Ah, bowing before the master. Come, my young padawan, and I will teach you." The response earned him another punch to the arm, but he blocked her blow and swung his arm over her shoulder. "You glow," he said.

She looked at him and raised a single, skeptical brow. "Excuse me?"

"You glow. When you're happy. I think you do it even more when you're trying to hide that you're happy. It's a sparkle in your eyes."

Rynn studied him, debating whether he was teasing her, but he seemed sincere. Furthermore, his smile was completely genuine. "Thank you, I think," she finally responded.

"Are you ever going to tell me who she is?"

"Okay, I'll buy that I glow when I'm happy, but how could you possibly know I'm happy because of a woman?"

"Now that one, I just know. And I'm right, aren't I?" Pearson grinned again.

Rynn let out a big sigh. "Yes, you're right." She retreated to her own desk.

Pearson pulled his chair right up next to her and plopped down to attentively await details.

"Oh, come on, man!" Rynn shoved him away, chair and all. "Give me some space, at least."

"Fine," Pearson agreed, but didn't move his chair any farther from her desk. He leaned back and continued his concentrated scrutiny.

Rynn turned on her computer, determined to ignore him. "What?" she demanded after a minute, putting more irritation into the question than she felt.

"I'm waiting."

"Don't you have something more important to do?"

"Perhaps. But I'm guessing our dead guy isn't going anywhere, and last I heard, we didn't have any particularly hot leads to follow up on. Your situation, on the other hand, has promise of some heat," he teased.

She glanced away from him, embarrassed but amused, and let her hair fall into her eyes while she debated what to say. Finally she looked up and met his gaze. "I don't kiss and tell." She grinned, feeling devilish.

"Oh, no, no, no." He leaned forward in his seat, shaking his head. "You can't do that to me! No way you're going to tell me there was kissing and not say anything else! That's just cruel." He laughed as he complained.

Rynn kept her gaze steady.

When she didn't offer a response, Pearson pushed one more time. "Oh, come on, Rynn. Throw me a bone. Give me something. A name. Just tell me her name." He adopted a pleading expression that made her laugh at his persistence.

"Why do you care so much?" she asked.

He flopped back in his chair. "Three reasons. One, I'm a hopeless romantic, and I can see it written all over your face that this girl is someone special. That, combined with being a natural detective, makes me want to know everything about it." He stopped.

Rynn waited for him to continue. When he didn't, she prodded, "What's number two?"

He pushed the chair to his own desk. Had he really given up? she wondered.

"Two is that I have no love life of my own. I'm starving to at least live vicariously through someone. Listening to you tell stories about hot chicks works as well as anything," he said. "As you're the person I spend the most time around, and you seem to have a blossoming love life that fits my dramatic personality, that makes you a perfect candidate."

She chuckled. "Oh, gee, thanks. Should I be honored?"

He nodded firmly. "Indeed you should. Hopeless romantics such as myself require strong candidates for vicarious living. You should be flattered that you make the grade."

Rynn chuckled at his odd sense of humor.

Pearson started his computer and appeared to focus on it intently. He didn't give any indication that he had anything more to say, and finally her curiosity got the better of her.

"Well? What's number three?" she asked.

He looked up with a serious expression that took her back a moment. "Wait, wait, wait. Now you want me to talk? You want details? How's it feel to have the shoe on the other foot, eh, Rynn?" He gave her a cocky grin.

The need to know nagged at her. She threw a pen at him and tried to return to work without letting him distract her. There probably wasn't a number three anyway, she told herself.

By midafternoon, Rynn felt the need to clear her head. She stepped outside and breathed in the chilly afternoon air. The sun was bright and the sky clear, so these few minutes away from her desk were beneficial in lightening her spirits. She was just about to head back inside when her phone buzzed at her hip. Checking the caller ID, she felt a familiar affection steal over her.

A young deputy walked past as she flipped the phone open, so she tried to tone down her smile and answered with a touch of formality. "Callahan."

"Mmm. Callahan. You sound so official." Toni's sweet voice immediately sent a warm jolt through Rynn's body.

The deputy lingered a few feet away, lighting a cigarette. Rynn wished he would disappear. "Hello, Miss Davis. How are you?"

"You're someplace where you're being overheard. At work, I expect. This could be fun."

"I'm well, thank you. What can I do for you today?" Rynn struggled to maintain formality, but the annoying deputy wasn't making things any easier.

In fact, he gave her a little nod of hello, which she deliberately failed to return. Despite her snub, he wouldn't take the hint and didn't seem inclined to grant her any privacy whatsoever.

"I imagine there's quite a lot that you could do for me. Or perhaps to me. And I suspect that I might enjoy it. What do you think?" Toni's voice slipped into a coy, sultry tone.

Rynn couldn't stop the heat coloring her face. She gave up on keeping a professional façade and turned her back on the deputy. Realizing that Toni might drive her over the edge if she wasn't free to respond, she decided to finish the conversation from the privacy of her Tahoe.

Taking a few steps away, she whispered into the phone. "You're cruel, you know that?" She sounded a bit husky, hardly surprising since Toni easily stirred desire in her.

"Aw, you've moved somewhere more private, haven't you? Sad. I could have had a good deal more fun."

"I already owe you for trying to embarrass me. I'm just lucky Pearson wasn't here to see my reaction when you started flirting with me."

"I caused a reaction? Good." Toni chuckled.

Safely inside her car, Rynn started afresh. "You never answered me. How are you?"

"I'm doing all right. Better now that I'm talking to you."

"Better? I hope you haven't been having a rough day."

"Nothing unusual for a Monday. My Texans had a good weekend, so there's some call for press for them. And I've got a guy on the Chargers. They play tonight, so there's a little pre-game agent prep work. That's routine, usually a Friday task I can do on autopilot." She hesitated. "Actually, I'm calling about Wednesday. I have to cancel."

Immediately, Rynn's mood dropped. "Is everything okay?"

"Yes. I mean, I wish I could make dinner. Maybe I can get a rain check? I just had to schedule a business meeting out of town, that's all."

"Oh." In her disappointment, Rynn struggled to think of something better to say.

After a beat of silence, Toni asked, "Will you come over to dinner? I'll cook tonight to make up for bailing on you."

"You don't have to do that," Rynn replied.

"I know. I want to."

Her good cheer returned quickly. "Sure. I'd love to come for dinner."

"Great! Do you think you could pick up a bottle of wine?"

"No problem. Is six o'clock good?"

"Perfect. I'll see you later."

Rynn flipped her phone closed and smiled. *Today just got a lot better,* she thought as she abandoned her Tahoe and returned to work.

By the time she arrived at Toni's, she was eight minutes late, having gotten caught in traffic on her way over. Sure, she'd called to let Toni know, but she still hated being late to anything.

Rushing into the building, she had to duck around a mountain-sized man in a charcoal-gray down jacket and skullcap leaning against the doorframe. Perhaps because she was already in a bad mood, she found herself annoyed with the guy and his failure to move so she could easily pass. She hurried down the hall, trying to forget the man's leering brown eyes and oversized clothing. She needed to relax before crashing on Toni with the stresses of her day. Seeing Toni again promised a good end to what had otherwise been an exasperating afternoon.

Rynn took a deep breath for calm before ringing the doorbell. A few seconds later, Toni opened the door with a smile. That glowing countenance did more to soothe her nerves than a thousand deep breaths.

"Hey." Rynn stepped through the door.

"Hey, yourself," Toni replied. "You're late."

Rynn apologized, but she could see by Toni's smile that she was kidding. She felt some of her tension bleed away. "Thanks." She lightly kissed Toni's lips.

Toni returned her kiss and backed away, leading her into the room. "For what?"

Rynn shrugged. "Just being you, I guess."

Toni turned and studied her. "Correct me if I'm wrong, but if I had to guess, I'd say you've had a rough day."

"Not as bad as some, but not the best. Am I that obvious?"

"Yes, you are. You're wearing frustration on your sleeve."

Rynn perched on the arm of the couch with a sigh. Toni stepped close and embraced her. Her breath caught, and she was unable to speak.

"Maybe I can help you with that later," Toni whispered, close enough that Rynn felt warm breath against her cheek. Toni closed the gap and softly kissed her. When she returned the kiss, a wave of desire rushed through her body. She leaned into Toni's embrace, deepening the kiss as her arms snaked around Toni's slender waist.

All too quickly, Toni pulled back until their lips just parted. Toni touched their foreheads together. Rynn heard the heaviness in her breath. *Don't stop*, she pleaded silently, not wanting the kiss to end. She pushed forward to capture Toni's mouth again, but Toni moved a little farther away, smiled, and shook her head slightly.

"Slow down, Detective. If you don't let me keep my senses enough to check on dinner, you might end up with burnt lasagna."

Rynn nudged forward again anyway. "I'm sure it's delicious, but that's not what I'm hungry for." She succeeded in meeting Toni's mouth once more, getting lost in a second kiss.

Abruptly, Toni broke the kiss with a laugh and stepped out of her embrace. "You're dangerous, Rynn. I'm going to have to be careful around you."

Toni's hands still lingered around her neck. Strong fingers flexed in a few massaging squeezes before Toni walked off.

Rynn melted at Toni's touch, the stress flowing from her shoulders during the brief rub. "Oh, you're cruel. First, you deny me your kiss, and then you tease me with that hint of a massage? That's just not right." She let her eyes fall closed, opened them a few seconds later, and rose to follow Toni into the kitchen.

* * *

By the time she and Rynn finished their meal, the second quarter was already half over and the Chargers were driving the ball, Toni saw, finally paying some attention to the game. Rynn had settled on the couch next to her, a choice of seating that made her smile. She shifted just enough so that their thighs touched slightly.

Rynn caught her movement and called her out on it with a single eyebrow flicked upward.

Giving up any pretense of subtlety, Toni moved again, this time twisting in her seat and turning Rynn as well, so the woman faced away from her. Ignoring the confused grunt, she pulled Rynn more closely between her knees and worked her hands firmly over the muscled curves in Rynn's back.

Rynn moaned in pleasure. "Oh, my God. Marry me now."

Toni laughed as Rynn completely melted under her touch. *Marry you?* She smiled at the comment. More than ten minutes later, when she still hadn't succeeded in kneading out all the knots tensing Rynn's back, she commented, "Either you are really, really stressed, or you're distantly related to Quasimodo."

Rynn shifted away from her hands. She rolled her shoulders once or twice and stretched out. "No French in me that I'm aware, so I guess I have to admit to stress. That massage made it go away, though, if only for a minute." She twisted around, raising her gaze to meet Toni's. "Thank you."

Toni leaned in, kissing her gently. "It was my pleasure," she said, nestling back into the couch with Rynn still between her knees.

Rynn smiled and rested a hand on her leg.

Toni forced her attention back to the ongoing football game.

* * *

It was late. The game had been over at least half an hour, but Rynn hadn't noticed. She and Toni were on the couch, lost in kisses. She tangled her hands in Toni's dark hair and relished the small sounds Toni made when her lips traced a line down her slender neck.

She took another sweet taste of Toni's mouth, tugging on the lower lip and grazing it gently with her teeth. She was rewarded when Toni pressed closer. She felt Toni's hands sneak under her shirt and slowly work their way up her sides. Longing desperately for Toni to find her breasts, she was equally afraid of what might happen if she did.

When Toni captured her breast, her thumb circling the firm nipple through the obstructing fabric of her bra, Rynn let her head fall back, wanting more. "God, Toni," she whispered. "Do you have any idea what you're doing to me?"

She felt Toni smile against her neck. Kisses peppered her jawline. "Only as much as you're doing to me, sweetheart."

A surge of pleasure overtook her as Toni sucked an earlobe into her mouth. She feared she would lose control completely if she didn't regain it right now. With a force of will she didn't want to invoke, she pulled her fingers from Toni's hair and caught the strong hands at her chest.

"Toni, please." Rynn could barely speak, her breathing heavy. Holding Toni's hands with one of hers, she raised the other to tenderly cup Toni's jaw. "I want you. I want you so badly that it's driving me mad. But we can't do this. Not this way, not this fast." She paused, afraid she would hurt Toni's feelings. "I don't want to fuck this up with a quickie. You deserve better."

She needn't have worried, as she saw Toni's expressive eyes blaze with understanding as much as desire. Toni let out a heavy sigh. "I know. You're right. But can you really blame me?"

Rynn wanted nothing more than to give in to the craving she felt for Toni. "I don't. But trust me, everything will be worth the wait." She barely brushed Toni's mouth with her lips.

Toni's eyes fell closed. She leaned her forehead against Rynn's. After a minute more in their embrace, she moved away. "Does this mean you're leaving?"

"I should. We both have to work tomorrow," Rynn replied, tugging her shirt into place.

Toni ran her fingers through her thick hair, smoothing some of the evidence of their activities.

Rynn smiled, admiring the way Toni stretched her arms over her head to display her stunning figure.

Toni reached a gentle hand forward and smoothed her hair as well.

Rynn responded to the touch, nuzzling into Toni's fingers as her hand lingered for a moment, tenderly caressing her face. She turned against Toni's palm, placing a gentle kiss on the center.

Together, as if by mutual consent, they rose from the couch. Rynn grabbed her jacket and stepped to the door. She struggled not to take Toni into another lingering embrace. Instead, she simply kissed her quickly and crossed the threshold.

Halfway down the hall, Rynn turned back. "Hey Toni?"

Toni paused with the door partly closed.

"Who won the game?" Rynn flashed a devilish grin.

Toni laughed and went inside her condo without answering.

Rynn chuckled and headed to her car.

CHAPTER EIGHTEEN

Rynn needed coffee. Her alarm had screamed at her far too early that morning, and the snooze button just didn't help. Pearson would badger her whether or not she was coherent, so she might as well let caffeine give her a boost.

She ducked through a Starbucks drive-through on her way to the office. Unsure whether as a gesture of kindness or a bribe, she decided to pick up something for Pearson too. If she were being honest, she'd admit to the latter motive. Maybe if she plied him with fancy coffee, he wouldn't press her about why she looked so happily exhausted.

After arriving at the station five minutes later than usual, and bearing gifts at that, she recognized the look of suspicion in Pearson's eyes. She slumped into her chair without a word and turned to her computer.

"Is this to buy me off so I don't ask where you were last night?" Pearson interrogated her immediately.

Rynn smiled and shook her head. "I don't know what you're talking about."

"Uh-huh. Well, since you managed to get one of my favorite blends, I guess I won't ask about her today. Because I'm not stupid enough to think you weren't out late with your girl."

Rynn neither confirmed nor denied, just kept her attention on the computer. Glancing up a moment later to verify that Pearson was focused on his work, she allowed herself another small smile. *My girl, huh? I like the sound of that.*

Rynn didn't have time to dwell on that thought. Her lieutenant rounded the corner into the bullpen and barked her and Pearson's names. He disappeared as quickly as he arrived. She sprang from her seat and followed, Pearson on her heels.

The lieutenant barely waited for them to get inside his office and close the door before starting the impromptu meeting. "This Quinn murder up in Zion—is it related to ours?"

Pearson glanced at Rynn. She replied. "Don't know yet, sir. The method of attack appears quite similar, though not identical. We've been observing the investigation, but the connections are looking pretty weak."

"Lieutenant Mueller called. His guys have a few more interviews lined up today. He's invited you two up to follow along."

Rynn looked at her partner, but he was focused on the lieutenant. "Sir," she began, "I'm not certain there's much benefit to us going up there again. The two cases don't have enough tying them together to merit us watching over their shoulders."

He studied her first, and then Pearson. "What do you think?"

"I agree with Detective Callahan, sir."

The lieutenant nodded. "Very well. I'll request that they forward us interview transcripts and anything else they come up with, but I agree you're better off here, focusing on our cases." He dismissed them.

When the report came back from Zion on Thursday afternoon, Rynn and Pearson filed into the lieutenant's office once more.

"This is the final report on their case," he said, passing out copies.

"They solved it?" Rynn asked, hoping it wasn't too good to be true.

"Nope. Shelved it. They're chalking it up to hate crime with no further leads."

"Hate crime?" Pearson's question told Rynn he was just as surprised as she.

"Apparently Quinn was gay."

Rynn flipped through the report. "That doesn't match with the interviews we observed. The detectives up there had multiple women on record claiming to be recently romantically involved with the victim."

"Fine. He was bisexual, then." The lieutenant was always gruff, but now his tone was harsher than normal.

Rynn glanced up from the report. She knew better than to waste the lieutenant's time perusing it here. "Is there anything else, sir?" she asked.

"No. Look through this, figure out if there's anything we can use on the Boden case. There's got to be a lead you two haven't found yet, so get on it."

Pearson led the way out of the small office.

Rynn closed the door behind her. "Can you believe this?" she asked, holding up the report.

"Should make for an interesting read. I'm gonna grab some coffee." He turned away and walked halfway down the hall before she recovered from being so brusquely brushed aside.

That was odd. She watched after him for a moment before returning to her desk.

An hour later, she was back at the lieutenant's door. "A word, please, sir?" When he waved her in, she quickly took a seat. Setting the report on the desk in front of her, she asked, "Sir, did you read this?"

"Yes."

"Then you know how many holes there are. There's no way this case should be shelved. It looks like they stopped caring about five minutes after they realized Quinn was bisexual." Rynn tried to keep her temper in check, but the report they'd received from Lieutenant Mueller's office disgusted her. "Surely, there's more to investigate here."

He settled back in his chair and gave her a stern look. "Yes. But it's not our case."

She took a deep breath. "It could help with our case."

He was silent. Rynn wondered if pushing the issue was wise. After a moment's hesitation, she decided she couldn't in good conscience let it go. "Especially considering Quinn shares the characteristic of being a sexual minority with Boden. If anything, this links the cases, not separates them."

"I thought you said you had nothing to tie Boden's or Rocker's sexuality to the crime."

"I don't. That's why the Quinn connection could be more important now than it was before. No one knows about Boden's relationship, so the two cases sharing that trait might not be coincidence."

"It sounds like you're making a case that the detectives up north are right. Hate crime." He sounded like he was losing patience, but Rynn pressed on.

"If they had even half done their jobs, these detectives might be able to find a lead that could help us with the Boden case. There are so many loose ends here, it's ridiculous."

"Yes, but it's not our case," he repeated.

She heard the ice slipping into his tone. "Sir, there has to be more we can do. If I could follow up on—"

"No, you can't."

She shut up. Despite her outrage at the poor work the other detectives had done on the Quinn case, she knew better than to challenge a direct order from her lieutenant. She stiffened, coming to attention as much as was possible while still seated, and waited for instructions.

"You and Pearson are investigating the Boden case. Are we clear, Detective Callahan?"

"Yes, sir." Rynn rose from her chair and left the office without another word. She stopped in the bullpen long enough to ask Pearson to join her outside for a moment.

"Can you believe this?" She struggled to keep her voice low, although they were in the far side of the parking lot. "He just wants me to drop it when there's so much left undone!"

Pearson watched her pace, letting her vent her anger. "It's not our case, Rynn."

She spun on him, "No shit, Sherlock. But it could help our case."

"How? Quinn and Boden have nearly nothing in common. I'll grant you, the way they were murdered is unusual enough to link them, but there are no other similarities."

She looked away. For a moment, she'd forgotten that he didn't know Boden was gay. *I could tell him now.* But what difference would it make? They had nothing to go on in their case, and she'd been explicitly ordered not to pursue the other one. "It's not right. You know they aren't doing their jobs with the Quinn case."

"That doesn't make it our job. Why do you care so much?"

She couldn't believe what she was hearing. "Why don't you?"

He glared at her a moment. "It's not our job to solve every hard-luck, sob story out there. So the establishment is turning a blind eye to an antigay hate crime. Are you really surprised?"

He turned and walked away, leaving Rynn stunned and standing alone in the cold.

What the fuck just happened?

CHAPTER NINETEEN

Toni smiled when she saw the caller ID. "Hello?"

"Hey."

Just hearing Rynn's voice shouldn't make her this happy. She waited a moment, but Rynn didn't say anything else. "You still there?"

"Yeah," Rynn sounded exhausted. "Sorry. I was just…" A few more beats of silenced passed. "I was just wondering if you were back from your business trip."

"Yes. My flight got in a few hours ago and I decided to put off going back to the office until tomorrow. Is everything okay?"

"Yeah, it's fine. I just had a kind of shitty day, but maybe I shouldn't be bothering you with that."

Toni rolled her eyes. "Don't be silly. You're not bothering me."

"In that case, what if I pick up a pizza and come over for dinner?"

Toni enjoyed the warmth from knowing Rynn had turned to her. Before she could answer, Rynn added in a rush, "I mean, if you're not busy or anything."

Toni had to bite back a chuckle at Rynn's nerves. "That sounds great. I'd like to see you too."

When Rynn arrived a little while later with the pizza, Toni could see the frustration that had been so clear in her voice earlier. She looked harried, obviously agitated. She pulled her inside, took the pizza and set it aside, and kissed her strongly.

After they broke apart, she asked, "Rough day?"

Rynn took a deep breath, as if she were trying to breathe in the good and exhale the bad. "It sucked. But kiss me again, and it might not be so bad after all."

Toni shook her head. "Maybe later. Go sit on the couch while I grab some cold beers."

A minute later, when Toni slid into the space next to her, Rynn had already pulled out a slice of pizza. "I hope you like Meat Lover's."

"I could make a crack about lesbian stereotypes, but the food smells too good to wait."

Rynn nearly choked on her pizza. Her eyebrow shot up. She didn't say anything though, so Toni chewed innocently on her dinner.

After a quiet moment, she asked, "What was so crappy about your day?"

Rynn slowly set her pizza down and took a sip of beer. "Work was just unusually trying."

"Can you tell me about it?"

Rynn looked away.

Toni could see that Rynn wanted to share and wondered if she often struggled with keeping her work life separate from her personal life.

Apparently deciding to talk, Rynn said, "There's a case we've been looking at that deserves more attention, but my lieutenant told me to give it a rest. I hate feeling like my hands are tied."

Toni immediately thought of Daniel. "Is it Patrick?"

Rynn didn't answer right away, making her fear bad news. "No. Another case."

The hesitation made Toni wonder, but she didn't push it. "Is that the end, then? You can't…well, I'm trying to imagine what I would do if I disagreed with my boss. I suppose I would take my complaint to his boss. Do investigations work like that?"

"No. If I thought my lieutenant was doing something unethical, I could go to the captain, but it's nothing like that. I just disagree with his assessment of the situation. It's not the first time and won't be the last time."

"It must be hard though."

"Yeah." Rynn chewed thoughtfully on another bite of pizza. "Maybe what makes it more frustrating is that my partner was acting weird about it too. My old partner, Samson, always had my back when I got pissed off at the lieutenant. Pearson just shut me out."

"Pearson's your partner now?"

"Yeah, and I have no idea what was up with him today. We usually get along so well."

"I'm sorry, sweetheart. Maybe things will be better tomorrow."

Rynn tossed the crust of her pizza back in the box. "It's already better." She leaned over and Toni met her kiss.

After she broke away, Toni got up and put the leftovers in the kitchen. Coming back to the sitting area, she offered, "Tell you what, why don't we put on a movie, and you can just relax and forget about your shitty day."

Rynn smiled. "Is there snuggling involved?"

"I think we can definitely work something out." She settled in the corner of the couch and pulled Rynn closer, back to front so they could both see the TV. "How's this?"

"Perfect." Rynn paused. "I'm sorry for crashing in on you and venting all my frustrations."

Toni pressed a kiss into her hair. "Don't apologize. I like having you here."

* * *

Arriving at work the next morning, Rynn wasn't sure if she wanted Pearson to harass her about her glow from seeing Toni the night before, or if she wanted to hash out his problem.

When she took her seat at the desk opposite his, he looked up. They regarded each other silently for a moment before he spoke. "You know, you really can't hide your feelings for shit. How do you ever pull off interviews?"

She didn't answer. He'd apparently gone the route of pretending the argument between them hadn't happened. She wasn't sure she was okay with that.

He got the message. "Look, I'm sorry about yesterday. I was pissed about it too, and I handled myself poorly."

"Yeah, you did."

He nodded. "I deserve that."

She didn't want to forgive him so easily, but he put on such a sad pout, she couldn't help letting him off the hook. She shook her head. "Whatever, man. Next time, though, try to remember we're partners."

"Deal."

She and Pearson settled down to work, focusing the whole day on files that had taken a backseat to the Boden case and, indirectly, the Quinn case. Rynn was frustrated that they seemed to have hit a wall with the Boden murder, but they simply didn't have any other leads. She wouldn't forget it as easily as the other detectives had shelved Quinn's. There had to be something more she could do to find justice for both victims.

When Rynn saw Toni's name on her caller ID after lunch, she didn't even have a chance to answer before Pearson put on his shit-eating grin. She immediately shot him down. "No. Your harassment privileges are suspended." She flipped open her phone as she walked away. "Callahan," she answered.

"The official tone is kind of a turn-on. Don't suppose I get to have fun with it today, do I?"

Rynn laughed. "Nope. I'm not falling for that twice."

"Sad. Well, in that case, I'll make this call quick. I forgot to mention last night that I'm going out of town again this weekend. I've got some business in New England, and then I'm sticking around for their Monday night game. Before I leave, I was wondering if we could schedule that rain check?"

"You mean pizza last night doesn't count?"

"Nice try, but no."

"All right, I guess I can still take you out. When would you like to go?"

"I get back on Tuesday, so how does next Wednesday night sound?"

Rynn mentally flipped through her calendar. "Sounds great. I'll pick you up at seven o'clock."

"Wonderful. Hey, is work going any better today?"

Toni's concern made Rynn smile. "Yeah, it's better. I seem to have made peace with my partner anyway. That's a relief."

"Oh, good. I'm glad you worked that out. I don't want to keep you from work, so I'll say goodbye. See you next week."

Rynn said goodbye and closed the phone. Back inside the station, she sat down at her desk and ignored her nosy partner. When he made a playful whimper, she refused to glance away from her computer screen. "Don't even start."

CHAPTER TWENTY

Wednesday night couldn't come fast enough. Toni was surprised how much she had missed Rynn over her business trip. When the doorbell finally rang, she felt warmth spread through her as she walked over to answer it.

Rynn stepped out of the cold and into her arms, brushing her lips with a soft greeting kiss. "Hey, you."

"Hey, yourself," Toni replied. She gave the door a little shove closed and guided Rynn further into the condo. She wrapped her in another hug, paused, and took a step back. "I feel like I'm hugging a giant teddy bear with that massive coat you're wearing." She suggestively tugged on the zipper, Rynn made that face she loved by arching an eyebrow. She continued, "Why don't you let me help you with that?"

Rynn obediently held her arms wide so Toni could take the thick coat off her.

Tossing the garment aside, she pulled Rynn close. They kissed again. Smiling, she observed, "You're early tonight."

"I thought I'd make up for being late last week," Rynn replied.

"Oh, and here I was hoping it was just because you couldn't wait to see me again." Toni loved the way Rynn's eyes sparkled in response to her teasing.

"Well, that too."

Rynn pulled Toni close again, giving her another kiss.

Toni accepted happily, but gestured toward the couch. "I was just taking care of a few things in my guest room-slash-study. Wait here. Let me finish that up and we can head out."

She wasn't really surprised or displeased when Rynn followed her instead of sitting on the couch. She slipped into the chair at her desk. Rynn took a seat on the guest bed.

"Are you always this bad at following directions?" Toni questioned playfully.

"When it comes to staying away from you, yes, it seems I am," Rynn retorted.

Toni faced her. "Oh, really? And who has been directing you to stay away from me?"

"Just me. I've been telling myself not to get involved with you from the very first day I saw you. I didn't want to mix work and…and pleasure. But it seems I was ultimately unable to resist your wily charms." Rynn shrugged.

"Hmm. Well, to ease your fears, I will try not to be as seductive in the future." Toni laughed when Rynn feigned shock and dismay.

Shaking her head, she turned to save her document and shut down her computer before leading Rynn downstairs to the parking lot. After a moment's debate, they hopped into her Lexus and were off to dinner.

Two hours later, Toni was still laughing. Rynn's dry sense of humor came through most when she told stories about her days in the police academy. Having taken a more traditional undergraduate degree immediately followed by the law school route, she was especially entertained by these stories, so different from her own educational experiences.

Toni chuckled as Rynn told another story and enjoyed a spoonful of fried ice cream. Rynn's eyes sparkled when she was happy. Toni liked the look. The grin Rynn wore made her wonder if she'd thought about the funny moments in her academy days in recent years.

When Rynn set her spoon down, Toni realized she'd gotten a bit of chocolate sauce on her lip. Leaning forward, she whispered, "You've got a little something…right there." Guiding Rynn's mouth to hers with a gentle finger on her strong jaw, she removed the chocolate with a kiss and a nibble on Rynn's lower lip. She returned to her seat, seeing the sparkle in Rynn's eyes change, seeming to darken with desire. "Do you want to get out of here?" she asked.

"Yes." Rynn's reply was barely audible.

"Good, but I think we need to pay first." Toni enjoyed the effect she had on Rynn, whose need mirrored the feelings racing through her body. For the moment, she was in control.

"Check. Right. I should do that." Rynn gestured to a passing waiter.

Toni was amused by how thoroughly Rynn had come unwound with one small kiss.

Having taken care of the bill, she and Rynn walked arm in arm to her Lexus. Once inside with the engine started for warmth, she was pleasantly surprised when Rynn leaned across the front seat and captured her mouth. Rynn's sweet breath filled her senses.

Toni felt Rynn slip a hand inside her coat to pull her closer as they kissed. Every nerve in her body sprang to life. She wanted nothing more than to take Rynn home. Right. Now. Finally, she broke away for air. She breathed heavily, leaning against her door and the icy window glass. "Rynn, we're in a parking lot," she pointed out. "We need to go home."

"I can't help it. I want you. So much. Please tell me you want me half as badly."

Toni smiled. "You know I do. More than half. But you have to wait at least till we get home."

"I don't know if I can wait that long," Rynn purred, pulling at Toni's coat and trying to draw her closer.

Toni resisted. "Yes, you can. What was it you said to me last Monday? Oh, yes. 'Trust me, it will be worth the wait.'"

Rynn's emerald eyes slid closed. Toni could only imagine the delicious thoughts streaking through her mind. "Then what are we still doing here?"

"I have no idea," Toni laughed. She pulled on her seat belt and shifted the sports car into gear. Backing out of the space, she was startled when a horn blared and a navy blue pickup barreled through the parking lot behind them. "Okay. Definitely need to focus on driving for a minute. You stay over there," she ordered.

Rynn smiled. "Yes, ma'am."

The Lexus made it out of the parking lot without further incident. Toni drove toward her condo. After a few minutes driving on the nearly empty roads, she asked, "Where is everyone tonight? I haven't seen the roads this deserted in ages."

Out of the corner of her eye, she saw Rynn shrug. "I heard we might get the first snow of the season tonight. Maybe people are just trying to avoid it as long as possible."

"Maybe we'll get snowed in and you'll have to spend the night," Toni suggested.

"Aren't you supposed to be paying attention to your driving?" Rynn asked.

Toni glanced from the road long enough to see Rynn chewing her lower lip. Cute, but it made her want to drive a little bit faster.

Instead, she was forced to slow when the Lexus approached a red light at an otherwise empty intersection. She secretly hoped the light would stay red long enough to sneak a kiss, but her wish wasn't granted. The light turned green just before she brought the car to a full stop. She let the car coast through the intersection and moved her foot back to the gas.

In an instant, lights blinded her from the left. She had no time to react as something large and dark plowed into her car, and everything went black.

CHAPTER TWENTY-ONE

"You asshole! You were supposed to hit the front of the car! From the other direction! Mess up the axle and set off the airbag or something. Maybe even take out the girlfriend, what do we care? But not hit the agent. The boss is gonna be pissed if you killed her. We're supposed to bring her back alive and kicking."

"Shut the hell up, man. I know what I'm supposed to do, and if you'd leave me alone for three seconds, I'd do it!"

"Man, you fuckin' cut my arm knocking the windshield glass everywhere."

"I didn't knock the damn glass anywhere, you're the idiot who wasn't wearing his seat belt and had to save his face with his arm. I can't believe you fucked up my windshield. You'd be more careful if you knew how bad an injury can fuck your career."

"Yeah, an injury like wrecking your knee jumping off a balcony 'cause you're drunk at the fuckin' after-party for the Rose Bowl! You're such an asshole."

"At least I wasn't so stupid that I blew it after I made it into the league."

"Shut up! I made it once, I'll make it again. The boss is gonna get us our break after all this shit is done."

"Just one tryout and I know I'll make the league. Killing fruitcake boyfriends should be a nice warm-up to blowing up some defenses. Let's get to it."

"Yeah, whatever. Wait, fuck, man! Are we gonna be able to drive your truck now?"

"Yeah, I think so. It rides so much higher than this stupid little sports car, I'm sure she'll be just fine. Nah, she barely has any damage on her. At least, she wouldn't have if you'd been wearing your damn seat belt."

"All right, all right. Let's just grab the girl and get out of here before another car comes along. What do we do with the banker?"

"I don't care. The boss said to get rid of her. So shoot her, stab her, break her neck. I don't give a damn. I'd play with her, but we don't have time for that. Let's just do this thing."

"You're a sick bastard, you know that?"

"What? Haven't you ever taken a woman? It's a rush, man. It's a rush."

"Seriously. If the boss would let me, I'd shoot you myself. That's just sick. It's bad enough you like torturing those faggots and bustin' up their knees just 'cause you fucked up your own."

"Fine, whatever, go take care of the girlfriend, I'll get the dyke agent."

Who was speaking? What banker? Dyke agent? Rynn shook her head, trying to bring her vision into focus. She saw shadows, heard something that sounded like fizzing—was that the engine?—and the unmistakable sound of a revolver cocking. She saw a dark figure in front of the car. Another figure at the driver's door. *Toni!* The sound of twisting metal rent the air when the crushed door was yanked open.

Processing what she'd heard just enough to know that Toni was in serious danger, she pulled her gun and fired at the person in the huge gray jacket grabbing at Toni's limp body. *Oh, God, please don't take her from me. Don't let them take her from me!* She heard a scream.

"It's the fucking girlfriend! She fucking shot me!"

The second shadow crossed in front of the windshield. "You gonna die, man?"

"No, you fucker, but I'm gonna kill that bitch with my bare hands!"

Rynn fired a second shot. Her eyes still wouldn't focus properly. She moved, trying to free herself, trying to protect Toni. She felt something wet on her face, swiped at it instinctively, and looked uncomprehendingly at the blood smeared across her hand.

"Cutter! Fuck, man, Cutter!" the second voice shouted. His cries were joined by a siren.

An ambulance? Had someone seen the accident? she wondered.

"Shit!"

Rynn saw a flash of red. The second guy panicked and ran. She heard his footsteps race down the empty road. The threat gone, she weakly dropped her gun in the footwell. She finally found the seat belt latch and freed herself. Trying to get to Toni, she moved too quickly. Her head swam. She leaned across the seat.

"Toni? Toni, God, wake up." Rynn could barely speak, could barely move, but every thought was focused on an unresponsive Toni. Her vision swirled. She heard another vehicle's tires squealing as it pulled up to the accident scene. Emergency lights flashed.

Rynn wrapped her arms around Toni, careful not to jar her, and prayed. *Please God, let her be okay.* With that thought, she passed out.

CHAPTER TWENTY-TWO

Beep. Beep. Beep. Beep. Rynn woke up to the steady tones of a vital signs monitor. The room was dimly lit. She didn't know where she was or how she'd gotten there. Her head throbbed. Raising her fingers to her brow, she discovered a bandage near her right eye.

In fact, now that she thought about it, she realized her eye was swollen nearly shut. How? She sat up and looked around the room, ignoring the vertigo. A hospital? Why was she...car accident...*Toni!* In a flash, memories overwhelmed her.

She slid out of bed and immediately fell to her knees. *Okay, so moving fast is a bad idea. But I need to find Toni. Oh, God, let her be all right.* With difficulty, she tried to rise. Instead, she was hit with a swell of nausea.

Suddenly, a nurse appeared at her side with a plastic basin. Once she stopped vomiting, the nurse said, "You really shouldn't have done that. Now you're going to have bruises on your knees to match the one on your head." Her voice was soft but her hands strong as she helped Rynn back to bed. "Sit. Don't move. You've suffered an acute concussion and you lost a bit of blood."

Rynn wiped at her mouth and stubbornly tried to get up.

"Oh, please, you're not going anywhere. Stay put and tell me what you want," the nurse commanded, holding her firmly in place on the bed.

Rynn's mouth was dry. Her vision was still blurry, but things were starting to come into focus. She closed her good eye, needing to speak more than see. She thought she tasted blood. After a momentary struggle, she found her voice. "Toni Davis."

"You're looking for the other person injured in the accident. I'm sorry, I should have realized."

Rynn's senses were slowly returning and with them came another wave of nausea.

"Ms. Davis is stable. She's banged up pretty badly, but she'll recover," explained the nurse.

Relief and exhaustion hit Rynn with overpowering force. She started to slump. The nurse caught her and gently propped her up on a pillow. She tried to breathe, but it was more challenging than it should have been. She tried her voice again. "See her?"

"No, I'm afraid you can't see her now. She's in surgery. The doctors need to fix her up first."

"How long?"

The nurse smiled. "Right now, you just need to rest and get your own strength back. I'm sure you'll be the first to know when Ms. Davis is able to have visitors."

Rynn fought the pounding in her head, barely able to form complete thoughts. She knew one thing: the hospital did not have to let her see Toni at all. She wasn't a relative. "Promise?"

"Yes. I promise. I'll let you know myself as soon as you can see her. In the meantime, there's an officer here to speak to you."

Rynn knew the nurse was lying about visiting Toni to pacify her. Despite that knowledge, she felt calmed. She glanced toward the door, noticing for the first time the other person in the room. Had the strange woman been there the whole time?

Apparently satisfied that Rynn would stay in her bed, the nurse left them alone.

"Detective Callahan." The visitor approached the bed and offered her hand.

Rynn didn't have the strength to meet it. She nodded weakly and leaned back into her pillows.

The woman appraised her before continuing. "I'm Detective Sanders. I'm not sure we've met before. I work in Internal Affairs. You've given us quite a puzzle to solve."

Rynn closed her eyes, trying to stop the room from spinning around Sanders. Memories burst back into her consciousness and faded just as quickly. She was having a hard time recalling exactly how she had gotten here, but what she could remember explained this interview. "Where's my lieutenant? My partner?" she asked.

"You'll get to talk to them after you talk to me." Sanders seemed reasonable.

Rynn didn't have the strength to argue. "You want to know what I know. Fine." She recapped as much as she could, pausing more than once when she was unable to make sense of her memories. She'd been talking for ten minutes before she realized Sanders had taken out a tape recorder and was scribbling notes. *Good. Maybe she'll be able to remind me of what I'm saying later.* Her head throbbed again, as did her stomach. She reached for the clean basin the nurse had left. This time, the vomiting spell left her so weak, she almost dropped the basin off the side of the bed.

Sanders had apparently signaled the nurse, who replaced the soiled basin and left the room again.

"I'm not sure what else to tell you. I...I don't remember anything after that." Rynn tried to sit up straighter, needing to ensure that Sanders understood the urgency of the request she had to make. "Toni...Toni Davis needs to be protected. They tried to grab her. They could come back."

Sanders nodded. "I agree. I'll have a couple uniforms posted outside her door for now. She'll have to decide what sort of protection she wants after she's discharged."

With that reassurance, Rynn fell back onto the pillows, unable to fight her exhaustion much longer. "Thank you."

Sometime later, she woke again, with no idea how much time had passed since she'd first woken up or how long since the accident. Xander...no, Sanders was gone. Her head was marginally clearer now. When she opened her left eye—her right eye was still badly swollen—her vision came into focus after a few seconds.

Her room remained dimly lit, but she realized that was because curtains were drawn at the window. She saw daylight peeking out from under the edge. Eventually, her gaze found a clock on the wall. Eight twenty. The calendar next to the clock told her it must be the morning after the wreck. When had she and Toni left the restaurant? Around ten o'clock, ten thirty at the latest.

Rynn scooted to the edge of the bed and carefully tested her legs. She felt sore and stiff, but didn't seem seriously injured. If she moved too fast, her head pounded and vertigo threatened. She felt a swell of nausea but managed not to vomit again. She sat there a moment, unsure what to do. More than anything, she wanted to see Toni, to find out how badly she was injured. To tell her she was safe now.

The memories jumbled into her mind, but they didn't make much sense. She couldn't think clearly. She tried to focus. Two men's voices, the horrible things they had said, the threats, conspiracy, kidnapping and murder. The accident was no accident. Toni had been targeted. But why? Had the men talked about motive? She couldn't remember. There was something else, something she should have considered. What had she told Sanders? Had she told her enough to make sense of what investigators must have discovered at the scene? Maybe she could amend her statement if she could make sense of these memories.

She tried to go through it all in her mind. She remembered one man running away. What about his accomplice? She'd shot him, but what had happened to him afterward? Suddenly the weight of everything she didn't know crashed in on her. Sanders had told her nothing. She closed her eyes, trying to regain some sense of stability.

Answers. She needed answers, which meant first, she needed to find someone to question. Where was her partner? She thought she had asked for him. But then, maybe she hadn't. Pearson would surely have heard something. However, last night's attack could wait. Toni's condition was more important. She had to find out if Toni was okay. The nurse, she decided. She needed to find the nurse.

She rose shakily to her feet. *Okay, so far, so good.* She stood still, making sure her balance was steady enough to walk. Her head throbbed, but her feet seemed willing to obey. She turned and walked slowly out of her room. Fortunately, the nurses' station was only about thirty feet down the hall. When she reached the desk, her balance failed her, but she was able to catch herself.

The woman seated there looked up, startled. "What do you think you're doing?" She jumped up and rushed to her side. "You're not supposed to be out here."

Rynn accepted the support, but refused to turn around when the nurse tried to steer her back to her room. "I need to know what's going on."

The nurse took a step back to assess her. After a moment's scrutiny, she relented. "All right, fine. Sit down and I'll call Nurse Moore."

Rynn agreed and settled on a bench in the hallway.

A minute later, a young blonde nurse walked over. "You know, you could have waited in your room instead of exploring the hospital."

Rynn glanced up at the comment. The voice was familiar from last night, but she had no memory of a face. "You're Nurse Moore?" she asked.

"Yes. And you're Kathrynn Callahan." Her response was a statement, not a question.

Rynn simply nodded.

"Why don't we go back to your room?" Moore suggested.

"No," Rynn said. "Nothing in my room. Where's Toni?"

Moore smiled. "I figured you'd be asking for her. Ms. Davis is okay."

Rynn remained seated. "You promised I could see her. Can I now?"

The nurse studied her. "For as hard as you hit your head last night, you've got a good memory."

Rynn frowned. Her memory was shaky at best right now, and that hadn't answered her question. She tried again. "Can I see her?"

Moore sighed. "You're a persistent one." She paused. "Fine. Ms. Davis was awake and asking for you too, but you're not walking with your concussion. Let me go get a wheelchair and I'll take you over."

Rynn nodded, grateful. She doubted she would have been able to walk very far. After the nurse disappeared down the hall, she closed her eyes and tried to focus on her memories of last night. She struggled to hear the conversation in her mind and recall what images she could.

She mentally replayed the voices. She could recall the words but couldn't picture the participants. The men had come for Toni, referred to a boss, and planned to leave her dead. They'd mentioned torturing gay men, specifically the victims' shattered knees, so these guys were definitely involved in the Boden and Quinn murders. Which unmistakably meant that Toni was now deeply involved too.

Rynn's mind raced. What did all of this mean? She needed time to think, but didn't feel like she had any. Her head swirled again, whether from thought overload or her apparent concussion, she wasn't sure.

"Hey, you still all right?" Nurse Moore had returned with a wheelchair.

"Yeah, I'm fine. Just trying to remember last night," she explained, opening her eyes.

Moore nodded and helped Rynn switch from the bench to the wheelchair.

"What happened to the other driver? By the time the ambulance came, were the other guys still there?" Rynn asked.

This time, Moore squatted down to meet her gaze. "How much do you remember?"

Rynn shook her head. "I'm not sure."

"Do you remember shooting a man?"

Rynn didn't respond. She needed to talk to the police again, not answer some nosy nurse's questions.

Apparently, Moore took her silence as a confirmation. "Why?" she asked.

"Is he still alive?" When Moore didn't respond, Rynn tried a different approach. "If you know I shot at him, then you must have found him. How is he?"

"Why did you shoot him?" the nurse persisted.

Rynn sighed, frustrated, not wanting to talk to a nurse and needing answers. For the first time, she looked down at herself and realized she was in a hospital gown. "If you took my clothes and found my ID, then you must have found my badge."

Moore nodded.

"Okay. So there's something big going on here, and I'd really appreciate it if you just helped me out."

Rynn saw Moore wanted to know more, but fortunately for them both, the nurse relented. "Fine. He was DOA."

Rynn took a deep breath, processing the news that she'd killed a man last night. "Can you take me to Toni, now?"

Moore agreed and began to wheel Rynn down the corridor. "Before we get there, you should know that she's pretty badly bruised up. Doesn't quite have the black eye to match yours, but she's got some new colors."

Rynn touched her face tenderly. She had a black eye? *I guess with the throbbing headache and bandage there, I shouldn't be surprised.*

Finally, they stopped in front of another room. Rynn felt relief at the sight of two uniformed officers sitting within ten feet of the door. The nurse instructed, "Now, I don't need to explain to you how much she needs her rest. Don't make me regret bringing you over here."

Rynn nodded. "I promise you I would never do anything to hurt her."

Moore helped Rynn to her feet. She'd had half an hour's rest on the bench and now felt twice as steady. She entered the room, as dimly lit as hers had been.

Toni opened her eyes when they walked in, and a faint smile appeared when she saw Rynn. Moore followed and moved a chair to the right side of Toni's bed. After performing a quick check of Toni's monitors, she silently turned and left the room.

As soon as Moore left, Toni's eyes fell closed again.

Rynn sat in the chair. "Hey. Are you okay?"

Toni nodded weakly. "Tired."

Rynn had a good view of most of Toni's injuries. Toni was bruised, but not as badly as she had feared. Her hospital bed had been inclined upward, so that she was positioned in a half-sitting, half-lying position. She had a plain, white cast on her left foot up to the knee, propped on a stack of pillows. A thin sheet covered her to her waist.

Rynn gently reached forward, brushing her fingertips along Toni's soft cheek. She could barely hear her when Toni asked, "You okay?"

"Yeah, I'm fine." She was scared by how weak and drowsy Toni seemed, and glanced at the IV drip in her arm. God only knew what the doctors had her on, but maybe that was why she was so out of it. While she watched over her, Toni's breathing slowed and evened out, signaling that she'd fallen asleep.

Rynn's hand was still at Toni's cheek. She traced delicately along her neck, finding bandages on her shoulder below her hospital gown. She pulled her fingers back, afraid to touch, but wanting to share contact. She leaned closer, daring to place the gentlest kiss on Toni's barely parted lips. She brushed her dark hair away from Toni's eyes and kissed her once more, this time on the forehead, then she sank down into the chair behind her, the exhaustion flowing up again, threatening to drag her under like a rip tide.

She grasped Toni's right hand in both her own. Looking tenderly at Toni's sleeping form, she whispered, "Hey, you. I'm here now, okay? You're going to be just fine. I…I'm sorry. I should have figured this case out by now." She gazed at her sleeping companion. With some surprise, she felt a tear track down her cheek. "Toni, don't leave me, okay? I...I think I'm falling for you. Come back to me, okay?"

Rynn held lightly onto Toni's hand and shifted so she could rest her head at Toni's side. Lying down like that, she let sleep claim her again.

* * *

Her sleep was dreamless. For that, Rynn felt grateful. She hadn't known what memories of the attack might leak into her subconscious, and she was in no hurry to find out. Stirring softly, she became aware of her surroundings, but she didn't want to open her eyes just yet.

A comforting, gentle touch stroked through her hair. She realized Toni was also awake. Smiling, she raised her head and met Toni's gaze. "Hey."

"Hey, yourself," Toni whispered, her fingers still entangled in Rynn's short hair.

"How do you feel?" Rynn asked.

"Not so bad with you here. I've been better, though."

Rynn's happiness at seeing Toni faltered when memories of last night slammed into her mind. "I...I'm sorry. This is my fault." If she'd been able to figure out Boden's murder, Toni never would have been put in danger.

Toni rolled her eyes. "Don't be ridiculous. Nothing is your fault. It was a car accident and I was driving. If there's anyone to blame, it's me."

Rynn studied Toni. In her eyes, she saw tenderness and strength tainted with pain and exhaustion. "No, not you." She paused. Did Toni know it hadn't been an accident?

She didn't want to face that conversation yet. She wanted to forget about the world waiting for them outside. She knew reality would come crashing down on them sooner rather than later, but she wanted just a few seconds to feel Toni's touch and ignore the rest.

Toni touched her shoulder. She lifted Toni's hand to her mouth, placing a kiss on her palm. Toni's fingertips brushed her jaw, a gentle touch seeming to pull her pain away.

Rynn let her eyes fall closed, gathering strength for the words she needed to say. Exhaling, she opened her eyes and looked at Toni, hesitating.

"That was a big sigh," Toni observed.

Rynn nodded. She grasped Toni's hand in hers, bringing it down to rest on the bed, and held her gaze steady. "Toni," she started, "how much do you remember about last night?"

Toni seemed confused for a moment, struggling to remember. "Just the blinding lights from the oncoming car, a jolt of impact, and then…nothing. Nothing until I woke up this morning in the hospital."

Another sigh escaped Rynn. She'd thought as much. She posed a second question. "Have you talked with any of the nurses, or doctors or anyone else yet?"

Toni shook her head. "I think…I talked to some doctors. There was a cop in here too, asking me questions. It's kind of fuzzy. I didn't know what to tell him. I was only awake a minute or two before you woke up just now." With a smile, she added, "It was like you knew I was here, waiting for you."

Rynn tried to return the smile, but Toni's situation was too acute.

Toni detected her dismay immediately. "What is it?"

"There's just so much I need to explain. I—"

Nurse Moore entered the room, interrupting them. "Well, well, well, look's who's awake again." She raised the lights slightly and made her way over to Toni's monitors. "Both of you. Good to see that you're up and chatting." She looked at the screens and made a few notes. "First, Ms. Davis, how are you feeling?"

Toni started to shrug, but winced in pain when she moved her shoulder. With a sharp intake of breath, she answered, this time choosing words over body language. "I'm all right."

The nurse looked at her skeptically. "No, you're not. But you're well enough to be brave, so that's a good sign." She turned to Rynn, "And you. How's your head?"

Rynn stared at her. She didn't want to talk about herself and really wanted to finish her conversation with Toni in private. "It hurts, but it's no big deal."

Moore shook her head. "So you're both stubborn. Given you suffered a concussion, Ms. Callahan, I'm guessing your head hurts quite a bit, but your tolerance for pain is your decision. Now, I've got a very agitated police officer who has been pacing my waiting room."

Rynn closed her eyes. "My lieutenant?"

"Didn't introduce himself as a lieutenant, but I don't know," Moore replied.

"I really don't want to leave Toni just yet," Rynn insisted.

Moore considered her. "I'm not surprised. But I don't have the authority to keep the police from speaking to you. As long as you were asleep, I could keep him out. He wants answers. We've got a dead body and far too much excitement, so come on, you're coming with me to go see him."

Rynn felt Toni start. Her grip tightened. Her expression turned panicked. "Dead body? Someone was killed in the accident? Oh, God!"

"You don't remember anything?" Moore asked.

"No, she doesn't," Rynn replied. "I'd like a private moment with Toni, please."

Moore looked skeptical, but said, "I'm not going to interfere with law enforcement. Ms. Davis appears well enough to handle another visitor, so if Detective Pearson wants to speak to you both, I will not stand in the way."

"Wait." Rynn paused. "It's Pearson down there?"

"Yes."

"Well, that changes things. I thought my lieutenant would be here. Pearson can come up."

Nurse Moore shook her head and left the room.

"There's a lot going on here, more than you know yet. Last night was not just some accident." Rynn saw Toni's confusion and frustration deepen. "It's all connected, but I still don't know how. I need to explain what I know to Steve as much as to you, so I'm going to tell you together."

Toni frowned. "Not an accident? All connected? What are you talking about?"

"Everything," Rynn replied. "All of it. The car wreck, you, Daniel, the murders…all of it."

"Wait, murders? As in, more than one? What does this have to do with me or last night?"

"Yes, more than one murder. I'll explain everything to you, sweetheart. No more secrets. You are part of this now."

Toni looked frightened.

"I didn't know what was going on," Rynn said. "I still don't know, really. I'm sorry. I should have figured it out faster. But I promise I will protect you. This won't happen again." She squeezed Toni's hand, leaned forward and placed a comforting kiss on her brow.

Toni reclined on the bed without moving or speaking, clearly in shock.

Rynn tried to offer what strength she could, but when her agitated partner came bowling into the room, any chance of peace or calm was instantly chased away.

"Rynn Callahan, I swear, if you weren't so beat up already I'd wring your neck with my bare hands," Pearson said.

"Detective Pearson!" A low rebuke came from immediately behind him. "May I remind you that you are in a hospital? Keep your voice down, and try to avoid threatening my patients!" Moore entered the room around him.

Pearson blushed. "Sorry. Of course."

"You keep the excitement levels down. There are other patients on this floor who don't need to be disturbed by your drama, and for that matter, neither do Ms. Davis and Ms. Callahan." Moore checked Toni's monitors and bustled out of the room.

Toni broke the silence after a startled moment. "I think my nurse is rather intense."

Rynn chuckled. "Yeah, she sure seems that way."

Pearson added, "She's been on my case to calm down all morning. Wouldn't let me see you or tell me anything about you, other than you were sleeping and you'd be fine."

Rynn's gaze was drawn back to Toni, who considered Pearson with some curiosity. The interest appeared mutual.

"So this is your girl, eh?" Pearson asked her.

Rynn felt a flush heat her face. "Yeah. This is my girl." Despite everything, she laughed at the amused suspicion on Toni's face. She explained, "Pearson has been harassing me about you for weeks. Apparently, I...well, I look different after I've been around you."

Toni smiled and turned her attention back to Pearson. "I take it you're her partner?"

He nodded. "Yup. Steve Pearson. As you see, Callahan's very bad at introductions. I've been looking forward to meeting you, though I must admit I had envisioned different circumstances." He stepped forward and tentatively held out a hand.

Rynn was reluctant to release Toni's hand, but she relented after getting a look from her. Once freed, Toni reached out and shook his hand.

"Okay, you can have her hand back now," he teased Rynn, releasing Toni. He pulled up a chair and took a seat next to her.

"Thank you." Rynn threaded her fingers with Toni's. Facing Pearson, she said, "You know, I'm surprised to see you here, actually. With everything the first responders must have found at the scene, I expected to be interrogated by the lieutenant himself."

Pearson studied her. "You must have hit your head pretty hard if you forgot he's on vacation in Hawaii all this week and next. I'm sure he's been in touch with Internal Affairs, though. You might still get a phone call."

Rynn blinked, surprised that she had indeed forgotten the lieutenant was away. She wondered what else she might have forgotten, but Pearson was anxious to advance the conversation.

"I need you to tell me what the hell happened. The ambulance responds to a call on a car accident, and arrives to find the two of you unconscious and one guy shot dead."

Toni jumped and stared at Rynn, panic returning to her expression. "Shot?"

Pearson looked from Toni to Rynn, and back to Toni. "Yes, shot," he confirmed. "One hit to the shoulder and another through his chest."

Rynn took a deep breath and gave Toni's hand a light squeeze. "I told you, it's a big mess, and it's all connected." Addressing them both, she continued, "Look, there's a lot going on, and you both have been kept out of loops. Pearson, Toni was targeted last night by two men, one of whom is the dead guy. The other ran off. I never got a good look at him."

Toni shivered.

"It's okay, I'm here. I'll keep you safe now," Rynn leaned forward and whispered. She turned back to Pearson. "This is tied to Boden's murder. And Quinn's, too."

Pearson's eyes grew wide. "What? How?"

Rynn paused, trying to gather her thoughts. Her head throbbed, and she feared that she might vomit again. After a moment, she was able to push the pain and nausea aside. "Let me back up. Okay. I met Toni the week of Boden's murder. She came to the station, wanting to discuss something that she thought might be relevant to the case."

She saw Pearson bristle. "Why are you only telling me about this now? If you let a crush on a witness interfere with our investigation, you are not the detective I thought you were."

Rynn went rigid, feeling as if he'd slapped her with those words. But she also knew that she'd be pissed too, if she found out her partner had withheld information. "Our relationship has nothing to do with it. I talked with the lieutenant when Toni came to me. We decided that her information wasn't pertinent and therefore you didn't need to know. That's changed now."

Pearson glared at Toni, as if the secrecy were her fault. Without taking his eyes off Toni, he demanded, "Rynn. Explain. Now."

Rynn looked at Toni, wanting to shield her from Pearson's anger, no matter how justified it might be. Instead, she found Toni holding up against it just fine, studying Pearson as his gaze burned into her. Before she could say anything, Toni spoke. "Rynn, you never told me your partner was like us."

It was Rynn's turn to be confused. "Like us?"

Toni's eyes flicked to Rynn. She laughed. "Maybe I'm wrong. But I suspect he'll understand Daniel's situation in a minute."

Rynn looked at her incredulously. "Wait, you think Pearson is...he never...I don't know about that."

Toni shrugged, a knowing smile curling her lips. "Rynn, you should probably start explaining things before Steve really loses it."

"Yeah, that would be a good idea," Pearson growled.

Rynn considered Pearson in a new light, wondering if Toni could possibly be right. But she didn't have time to worry about that now. "Okay. Short version. Toni is a sports agent, and one of her clients, Tommy Rocker of the Chicago Bears, was the longtime boyfriend of Patrick Boden. She came to me, unsure if that information impacted our investigation and asking for my discretion so as not to out Rocker. I'm sure you could imagine what that would mean to an NFL star."

While she spoke, she watched Pearson's face transition from anger, to skepticism, to outright shock. "Tommy Rocker? Gay?"

"Yes. I was as surprised as you when I first heard. I was also sympathetic to Toni's request since I know what it's like to be outed. When Rocker's alibi checked out, his relationship with Boden offered no leads on the case."

"Wait." Pearson interrupted her. "Toni, when you said just now that I was like you and Rynn, and that I would understand, did you mean to say you think I'm gay?"

Rynn noted Pearson's incredulous expression and turned to Toni to see her response. Toni simply nodded, with a slight smile.

"But how? How did you know? I haven't told anyone, dated anyone, since I moved to Illinois." Pearson's question was quiet, unbelieving.

Rynn was completely floored. "Wait, she's right? But you never—why didn't you ever tell me?"

"I didn't know how you'd react. I didn't want another incident like in Cleveland."

"Steve, I've been out to you since day one. How could you think I would have any problem with the fact that you're gay too?" Rynn asked, surprised by the mix of hurt and anger she suddenly felt.

"It's funny. People see lesbians as stronger, fiercer than straight women. But gay men? We're weaker, more emotional, unstable. I know plenty of cops who are fine with lesbians—even getting into spitting matches to prove who is more macho—but these same guys freak out at the idea of working with a gay man. As I got to know you better, I thought you'd be okay. But even if you were, who's to say the rest of the station would be? I came out in Cleveland and it didn't end well. I didn't want to go through that again."

Rynn stared, unable to process this confession on top of everything else swirling through her mind.

Pearson was still focused on Toni. "How did you know? We've only just met, and you figured it out in what, ten seconds?"

She smiled. "I've just got really good gaydar. I work all the time with strong men who are afraid to come out because of what it might do to their careers. You're in the same situation. I've learned to recognize it."

"Right." Pearson nodded. "NFL players. So Rocker's not your only gay client?"

Toni hesitated. "No. He's not."

Rynn was taken aback. "He's not? You didn't tell me that."

"You never asked," Toni said defiantly.

She was right, but Rynn was agitated by this new knowledge nonetheless. She took a deep breath. *Okay, calm down. Focus on getting everyone on the same page.* She steadied her nerves and began to go through what she knew, speaking the facts aloud.

"I was ordered to forget the Quinn case. I shouldn't have given it up so easily, though. If I could have found a link between Quinn and Boden, or even anyone connected to the NFL, I would have known right away you might be in danger." Rynn dropped her head, ashamed and angry. "I should have known. I should have seen it. I should have protected you." Her voice was so quiet, she doubted Pearson heard her.

Toni heard. She pulled her fingers free and gently touched Rynn's chin. "Rynn, look at me. You didn't know. This isn't your fault." Her eyes shone with emotion.

Rynn swallowed back her tears. Toni had been hurt and she might have prevented it if she'd only figured things out sooner.

Toni whispered, "Do you hear me? This is not your fault." She tried to lean closer, but flinched in pain. "Damn it. Come here. I can't move."

Despite her misgivings, Rynn obeyed Toni's orders and shifted closer.

"I can see it in your eyes that you don't believe me," Toni said. "But I need you to protect me, so snap out of it. No guilt. Now kiss me, and get on with the story."

Rynn was startled by the tone of Toni's command, and actually smiled. Toni was not one to mince words. She kissed her and settled back into her seat.

Pearson made mock gagging noises. "You two are so cute it makes me sick. Can we just get back to the detective work and spare me the mush?"

Rynn shook her head. "With that kind of sensitivity, how could you ever tell that he's gay?" she asked Toni, who smiled.

"He used the word cute. Straight men think lesbians are hot," Toni explained. "Gay men think romance is cute."

Rynn raised her brows. "Maybe you should have been a detective, too."

"No, I leave that in your capable hands." Toni looked at Pearson. "Both of you."

"Okay, now we have two homicide victims, one of whom was dating Toni's NFL client," Pearson recapped.

Rynn nodded and filled them both in on the rest of what she knew.

Pearson took a deep breath. "So how did you end up unconscious in a hospital?"

Toni started to mumble her own summary. Rynn suspected she had to search her memory to rebuild connections. "We went out, had dinner. We were just heading home when we got hit. I don't know what else happened. I woke up this morning, spoke to an officer about the accident, then Rynn got here. The next thing I know, people are talking about someone getting shot. I...I don't understand."

Rynn sympathized with her confusion. "I'm going to explain. You don't have to remember. In fact, maybe it's better you didn't wake up last night." She paused while smoky scenes from her memory flashed through her mind's eye. "I was knocked unconscious by the impact as well, but I woke up quickly. I don't know how much time passed. I could see shadows, hear two men's voices. They were talking about you, about kidnapping you and taking you to their boss. They mentioned the NFL and torturing...torturing fa—torturing gay men, and were trying to decide who would kill me and who would grab you."

"Oh, my God." Toni gasped, shock and fear welling in her eyes.

"My vision was blurry. I was disoriented, but when I heard them saying they would hurt you, I couldn't let that happen. I heard the sound of a revolver cocking. One of them opened the door to pull you out. I'm not sure how, but I managed to draw my weapon and fire. The guy screamed, so I knew I hit him. I think the other guy, the one who was coming for me, went back over to him. I saw more movement and fired again." Rynn struggled to remember. "I heard sirens, and someone running away. Then...then it's all black until I woke up in the hospital last night."

The room fell silent. Rynn shook off her nightmares. She noticed Toni had silent tears streaming down her face. She hated that her words had caused such distress. She hated even more that someone had dared put Toni in danger. She lifted a hand to wipe away Toni's tears, while Toni breathed heavily to regain control.

Pearson stared into space, his expression angry. Rynn suspected he was mostly focused on the fact that someone had harmed her. Good partners were usually protective of each other. In light of her recent discovery that he was gay, she wondered for the first time how these two murders—the murders of gay men—sat with him.

"The first responders only found one other person," Pearson said. "The guy you shot. Like I mentioned earlier, he took two bullets, one to the left shoulder and one through the chest. So disoriented or not, you're a good shot. We found no sign of anyone else, except there was blood on the broken windshield in the truck on the passenger side. The dead man didn't seem to have any injuries apart from the gunshot wounds that killed him. I assume his accomplice must have been the passenger during the collision. We now have DNA tying him to scene, provided we get a hit in CODIS," he added, mentioning the DNA database.

Rynn nodded. "Do we know who he is? The one I killed." She felt Toni squeeze her hand and was surprised by the comforting gesture. This was not the first person she had been forced to kill in the line of duty, but still, she hated the idea. No regrets, though. She would never regret stopping someone from hurting Toni, no matter what she had to do to protect her.

Pearson flipped open a small notepad. "Torian Michaels, age twenty-four. He's got a California driver's license with an old address. Landlord there says he hasn't seen him in two years. Beyond that, we haven't figured out much else about him yet. Basic searches resulted in dozens of men with that name."

Rynn heard Toni mutter quietly. "Torian Michaels…I know that name." She seemed confused. Her expression changed as if she was focused on turning over an old memory. A flicker of recognition crossed her face. "You don't mean Cutter Michaels, that USC running back from, I don't know, four or five years ago?" she asked.

"Cutter?" Rynn blurted. "I heard that name last night. After my second shot, the other guy was screaming that name."

Pearson scribbled notes in his pad. "Toni, you just told us more than we've been able to figure out on Michaels all morning. Thank you, I'll follow up immediately."

Toni looked as if she wanted to shrug. "If it's him, he's got a surgically repaired knee. Blew it out at a party after—"

"—after the Rose Bowl. Yeah, he and the other man were talking about that last night," Rynn interjected. "They were talking about making it in the league, and how someone—they just kept saying 'the boss'—was going to get them both into the league when they finished this job."

"They're both doing someone's dirty work in exchange for a shot at the NFL?" Pearson asked after a pause.

Rynn nodded. "That's what it sounded like. They've murdered two innocent men that we know of, but they're just working for a promise. So who's really running this operation? How far are they going to go? And why are they doing it in the first place?"

Toni shuddered. "Why did they come after me? I'm not dating an NFL player. And if just having ties to them is all it takes, there would be hundreds of people—boyfriends, girlfriends, parents, agents—in danger. I don't understand what I have to do with this."

"I'm not sure either," Rynn admitted.

"I'm going to get back to the station and put some wheels in motion," Pearson said. "We'll push for the lab to get us DNA results on the mystery passenger, too. See if that gives us anything. And I'll see if CSI got any fingerprints from the truck as well."

Rynn nodded. "Okay. Call me if you learn anything." She patted her hospital gown, searching for her cell phone until she realized she had no pockets. "Actually, I need to track down that nurse. I don't know what happened to my stuff."

Pearson looked at her skeptically. "I don't think you're allowed to leave the hospital yet. And you're definitely not coming back to work so soon."

"You're kidding me, right?" Rynn glared at him. "You think I'm going to let this go without hunting these guys down as fast as possible? No, I want to end it."

Pearson stared back at her. "You've got a concussion. You need to rest and relax, not chase bad guys."

Rynn bristled. "You think there's any way I could relax, knowing Toni might still be in danger? Hell, no. Screw my headache, I'm going to work this out," she snapped.

"No," Pearson countered. "*We're* going to work it out. But for now, you're going to rest until the doctors clear you. Even then, you know damn well you'll have to go through evaluations at work. You shot a man. You'll be on desk duty—if not on leave—for at least a week. So calm down and stay with Toni. I assume she'll be more comfortable having you around than the uniforms posted at her door."

Rynn settled down. She wanted to do everything in her power to protect Toni. Pearson was right. She wouldn't be allowed to return to work anyway. Maybe he could handle the investigation from the office, and she could stay at Toni's side. "Okay. I'll accept that." Actually, she should have thought of it herself. Maybe her head was a little off.

"Good," Pearson said. "Because I'd hate to have to get that nurse to sedate you."

As he spoke, Nurse Moore returned. "I'm half tempted to sedate her regardless. I can hear you two arguing halfway down the hall."

Pearson apologized. "I'm sure she'll be quiet now that I'm leaving. Nurse Moore, can you return Detective Callahan's possessions? I need to be able to contact her at all times."

The nurse nodded. "I can get her things in a few minutes. We discourage the use of cell phones in the hospital, so if you need to reach her, please call the room phone." She scribbled numbers on a pad drawn from her pocket. "This first one is the number for her room, but as I doubt she'll let me keep her there, I've also given you the number for Ms. Davis's room." She handed the note to Pearson.

Pearson accepted the paper and turned to leave the room. Stopping at the door, he said over his shoulder, "It was nice to finally meet you, Toni. Take care of Callahan for me. She can be difficult sometimes." He disappeared into the corridor.

Rynn smiled at Toni. "I hope I'm not too difficult."

Toni chuckled and closed her eyes. "You're doing all right, so far."

CHAPTER TWENTY-THREE

Toni sat in the dim hospital room, her eyes closed, just listening to the quiet around her. Rynn had been taken for a checkup, leaving her alone with her thoughts. The beeping of monitoring equipment had ceased to be annoying, shifting instead to a metronome keeping the beat of her meditation. Nurse Moore had offered to silence the machines, but she didn't really mind the sound. It was constant and simple, two qualities the rest of her life currently lacked.

She was unable to fall asleep with too many thoughts racing through her mind. Beyond that, she had a hard time getting comfortable. Her leg felt weird, though not painful, trapped in its plaster prison. Her shoulder felt worse, although her doctor assured her that should heal very quickly. Apparently, she'd dislocated it and would need to keep her arm in a sling for a few days. Small movements were acceptable as long as she was careful. The doctor didn't seem to think it very likely that she might reinjure the joint with everyday activities.

Toni really wanted Rynn to come back. She'd been alone almost two hours, and she wasn't entirely sure what was keeping her. Nurse Moore would only say Rynn would return when she was done with her medical examination. So she was left alone, trying to be patient.

Despite her meditation efforts, she couldn't get her mind to slow down enough to focus on what they had discussed. Patrick's murder was something she had accepted weeks ago. But a second murder? And the men involved were now after her for some reason? As Rynn had pointed out, she didn't even know Derek Quinn, so why would someone want to harm her?

It was a lot to process. She wondered if the painkillers prevented her from really focusing. She wasn't sure that was a bad thing, but it would be nice to wrap her head around the situation.

"Hey." A quiet voice came from near the foot of her bed.

Toni smiled. "Hey, yourself," she answered, opening her eyes. She met Rynn's concerned gaze and felt warmth flow through her body, as often happened when she saw her. "They changed your bandage."

Rynn stepped around the bed, coming to her right side. Toni patted the mattress, inviting Rynn to sit closer rather than take the uncomfortable looking hospital chair she'd occupied all morning.

Rynn accepted the invitation, seating herself carefully, no doubt trying to avoid bouncing or jarring her in any way. "Yeah, they took another look at my head. Cleaned up the cut I've got there and checked my stitches. There's not really much else they can do for a concussion, apparently, so I'm simply under strict orders not to stress myself for at least two weeks." She shrugged, as if she had no intention of disrupting her usual lifestyle.

Toni decided she would have to force Rynn to take it easy. She lifted a hand to Rynn's face, careful to avoid her black eye, one of the best she had ever seen. The skin was puffy and she was afraid to touch it, so she traced her fingertips along Rynn's jaw instead. "Does that hurt?"

"What? My eye? No, but it probably would if they hadn't given me painkillers." Rynn smiled mischievously. "My head hurts more than my face, but I guess that's to be expected."

"You also changed your clothes." Toni gently grazed her fingers down the soft fabric of Rynn's black, long-sleeved T-shirt. Eventually her hand came to rest on Rynn's denim-clad thigh.

"Yeah, Pearson brought me the spares I keep in the locker room at the station. I've been cleared to go home, actually."

Toni marveled at the clarity of Rynn's emerald eyes. Cleared to go home or not, she did not for one second doubt that Rynn would stay by her side.

Rynn reached over and brushed a few strands of hair away from her face. "How are you feeling?"

It had taken several painful reminders, but Toni had managed to stop trying to shrug when people asked her that question. "I'm okay. Sore, but like you, on painkillers."

"Have they given you any indication of how long you'll be here?"

Toni grimaced. "The doc wants me to stay till tomorrow, but honestly, I'm not sure why. They've got my shoulder wrapped up, and I'm actually allowed to walk already, as long as I use a crutch and don't put any weight on my foot. I guess they gave me a special kind of walking cast." She sighed. "Really, I'd prefer to go home. I think I'd be much more comfortable there. And it's unnerving here, too sterile. I don't like hospitals."

Rynn took her hand. Toni liked the gentle gesture. She entwined their fingers together and let her eyes drift closed. "Besides," she added, "I could be closer with you if we weren't here."

"I don't know about that," Rynn said, squeezing her hand. "I think snuggling and making out might be a no-no until you heal up a bit."

Toni opened her eyes and made a face. "Screw that attitude. You'd better be doing more than snuggling the first opportunity you get."

Rynn's eyebrow shot up. "Oh, really?"

Toni's confident nod made Rynn laugh and flush slightly. She smiled. For the most part, she was teasing, lightening the mood and shifting the focus. She certainly wanted Rynn as much as she had before, if not more, but she knew her body wasn't currently capable of lovemaking. "For now, I'd be content with snuggling," she said. "You can do that much for me, can't you?"

Her heart skipped a beat when Rynn smiled and said, "Yeah, I think I can handle that." She shifted around on the hospital bed to take a place at her side, sitting slightly higher and wrapping an arm around her shoulders, being very careful not to jar her injury.

Toni was able to move her left arm just enough to pull Rynn's right arm across her stomach. She was rewarded with a gentle hug and a kiss on her forehead. She rested her head against Rynn's chest, wondering if Rynn wore a bra or not. She wished she could raise her hand enough to caress the soft breasts she snuggled against. "Mmm. Good pillows," she commented, grinning.

Rynn chuckled. "Why, thank you. I grew them myself."

Toni laughed, enjoying Rynn's closeness. She felt secure and safe for the first time since waking up that morning. Within minutes, she drifted to sleep.

CHAPTER TWENTY-FOUR

Late in the afternoon on Friday, the air was cold and the skies dark with a threatening storm. Rynn opened the front door of her house, motioning Toni inside. It seemed like forever since she'd been here, though it had actually been two days. So much had happened in those two days…

Once she was discharged from the hospital, she had left Toni's side only long enough to go with Pearson to Toni's condo, collect some things, and leave in her Tahoe. As her memory cleared, she'd realized she might have seen the men who tried to grab Toni. She couldn't be sure, and she wasn't about to risk letting Toni go back to the condo alone. Pearson agreed. The department had approved keeping two officers on a protection detail for Toni and offered to put her in a hotel or safe house, but she'd balked at the idea. She had also refused the officers guarding her at all times. In the end, the only protection she would accept was Rynn. It had been decided that Toni would stay with her until the case was resolved.

She and Toni crossed the threshold together. Rynn quickly closed the door behind them.

Toni hobbled immediately to a couch and sank down in the center. Rynn was amazed she could move so well, managing to hop around on her walking cast with the aid of a crutch under her right arm. Movement would have been easier with two crutches, but for now, Toni's left shoulder was still too sore. Toni had reassured her the shoulder was healing surprisingly quickly, and in a day or two, a second crutch might be useful.

Rynn studied Toni while she looked around her new surroundings. The living room was fairly simple, with an older, cozy feel. She had left much of the decor her mother had chosen, although it was now six years removed from her parents' deaths. She tossed her coat and Toni's bag near the stairs and took a seat on the couch. "Here, let me help you with your coat."

She scooted closer to Toni and gently lifted the coat from around her shoulders. Toni winced slightly, but the improvement was remarkable. The doctor said she would have limited mobility for a little while and shouldn't overdo it.

"Are you warm enough?" Rynn asked, rising to hang both coats in the small closet by the door.

Toni smiled. "Yes, I'm fine."

Rynn wanted to do everything possible to help Toni feel at home. "You hungry? Can I get you something to eat? Or a drink, maybe?"

"No." Toni chuckled. "You can come back and sit down. I just want to be with you for now."

Rynn nodded and obeyed, taking a seat at the end of the couch. "You sure there's nothing I can get for you?"

"Yes, I'm sure." Toni studied her. "Why are you so nervous? I'm not going to bite." She paused and grinned. "Well, not if you keep sitting that far away, anyway."

Rynn moved closer. "Better?"

Toni nodded. "Much." She stayed quiet for a few minutes before sighing. "Do you think we can try to forget about things for tonight? You've got a decent TV there. Why don't you put on a movie and come relax with me. I don't want to think about car wrecks, attempted abductions or horrible murders. I just want to be here. With you. Just us."

Rynn considered Toni's request and nodded. "Okay, deal."

A little while later, after some negotiating of Toni's cast, she found herself snuggled with Toni on the couch. She stretched out, her upper body leaning in the corner, while Toni nestled between her legs, curled against her chest. While they watched the movie, she idly stroked Toni's long, dark hair. In another world, this might have been a perfect evening. No worries, no outside commitments, just the two of them fitting together so perfectly.

Rynn's mind drifted. Reclining here with Toni felt better than anything she had experienced in a long time. They didn't have to talk, they didn't have to fill the time, they didn't have to work at enjoying each other's company. They could be together and be comfortable. She couldn't remember another relationship where that was true, where she and her lover had gotten past the infatuation stage. Maybe that was why her dating life had slowly thinned and faded. Nothing else had ever felt so right. She felt like there was so much more with Toni.

There were moments she wanted Toni so badly, she thought the need would kill her. She longed to touch Toni, to have Toni touch her, in ways she knew would shake her to the core. She felt herself getting aroused by these visions of what might be. She didn't have a memory to conjure, she thought, and Toni was already the best lover she'd ever had.

Even before making that physical connection, she considered Toni more a lover than anyone else in her past. Was that possible? she asked herself. What about love? It was a terrifying prospect. She realized while leaning her cheek against the top of Toni's head that not finding Toni, not finding love, would be far worse.

* * *

Toni listened to Rynn's heartbeat as the movie credits rolled. Neither of them had spoken in the past hour and a half, but that was okay. She loved the sensation of Rynn stroking her hair and holding her close. No words were required.

When the DVD jumped back to the selection screen, Rynn moved just enough to aim the remote at the TV and turn it off. For a moment, they sat together in the dark.

Toni heard Rynn's soft voice at her ear. "Baby? You still awake?"

She nodded, barely moving her head against Rynn's chest. She felt Rynn place another soft kiss on the top of her head and ask, "How are you feeling?"

"I'm fine," Toni sighed. "Comfortable. How about you?"

She felt Rynn's nod. "I'm good. What do you want to do now? It's got to be after seven o'clock. Do you want something for dinner?"

Toni didn't want to move at all, but at the mention of food, her stomach grumbled. "Yeah, that's probably a good idea."

Rynn hesitated. "If you want me to get you something, you're going to have to sit up and let me get to the kitchen."

"No," Toni replied.

Rynn chuckled, causing Toni's head to bounce slightly against her chest. "No? What do you mean 'no?'"

"I mean, I don't want to move, nor do I want you to move. Food can wait. Just sit with me a little longer."

Rynn tightened her embrace a little. Toni smiled at the affectionate squeeze and was completely satisfied when Rynn agreed to stay put.

"Well, if you're not going to let me get up just yet," Rynn said, "can we at least figure out what I'm getting once you do?"

"Food," Toni replied simply.

Again, Rynn chuckled. "You're in a good mood tonight, aren't you?"

Toni didn't say anything.

"I know I'm getting you food, but what kind?" Rynn asked.

"I don't care. What do you have?"

"Honestly, probably not much. I need to hit the grocery store." Rynn sounded distracted.

Toni figured she was probably running a mental inventory. "Not tonight," she insisted. "No shopping, grocery or otherwise. I don't want you to leave me."

Rynn gave her another gentle squeeze. "Sweetheart, I'm not going anywhere. I'm all yours tonight." She paused and then suggested, "How about we order in?"

"Okay," Toni agreed. "Pizza?"

"Sure. Lucky for you, I can reach my phone, so that means I won't have to get up until the delivery guy gets here."

Toni heard the smile in Rynn's voice. Rynn seemed happy snuggling with her on the couch, which she found comforting.

After they haggled about toppings and Rynn placed the order, the TV was turned back on. Rynn switched to cable. The channel was already on some crime show Toni didn't really recognize. Rynn didn't change to another channel, so she tried to pick up on what was happening. The program seemed to be some sort of alphabet soup agency with sexy detectives and a big case to solve in only an hour of screen time.

My detective is sexier. The thought flitted through Toni's head. She grinned.

Rynn must have felt the movement. "What?"

Toni shook her head slightly. "Nothing. Just thought it's interesting that you watch these shows, what with seeing this stuff in real life every day."

Rynn shrugged. "I don't watch them a lot. Actually, this channel is probably on from the spy show reruns I was watching the other night. The chick on that one likes to blow things up and I get a kick out of that. Why, what kind of TV shows do you watch?"

"Sports, actually. I guess it's a good thing I'm so passionate about my job."

Rynn nodded, her chin moving against the top of Toni's head. "Yeah. But don't you ever like to escape from it?"

"You come home from work and watch detective shows, and you're surprised that I come home and watch sports?"

"Touché," Rynn conceded.

Time flew past while they chatted on about the entertainment options.

When the doorbell rang, Toni reluctantly moved enough to let Rynn answer it. She was alarmed when Rynn took a sharp breath as she rose to her feet. "You okay?" she asked anxiously.

"Yeah. I'm fine. My leg has been asleep for about an hour, that's all, so walking is shooting that tingly feeling all up my body."

Toni chuckled. "Why didn't you say something? I could have moved."

Rynn turned to look at her. "Why on earth would I have wanted you to move? You were perfect exactly the way you were."

She went to the door and settled with the pizza delivery guy, acting like they were just another couple staying in on a Friday night. Toni saw the way the kid stared at Rynn's black eye, though, and she was reminded of the threat against her. She still didn't want to think about it, but she knew there was no escaping the danger until the whole thing was over.

CHAPTER TWENTY-FIVE

After she and Toni finished eating, Rynn cleaned up and popped in another movie, a romantic comedy chosen by Toni. As she watched the two leads shift from laughable hate to serendipitous love, she couldn't believe she held such an amazing woman. She loved the feel of Toni snuggled against her, safe in her protective embrace.

When the screen characters shared another deep kiss, Rynn wanted to raise Toni up in her arms and follow their lead. Instead, she contented herself with another gentle kiss to the top of Toni's head and tenderly stroked her satin hair.

"Rynn?" Toni murmured.

"Hmm?"

"Do you believe in that?"

"In what, sweetheart?" Rynn wasn't sure what Toni was talking about. Neither of them had said much in the past hour. Her mind tracked back to their last topic of conversation. They'd just been casually chatting, but about what?

"Love like that. These two characters," Toni explained. "They seem so sure of things, but they met what, a week ago? Heck, there's probably a wedding scene as the end credits roll. And they hated each other at first!"

Oh, Toni was talking about the movie. Rynn chuckled. "I don't know what I believe. I guess I think anything is possible and everyone is different."

"That's a cop-out answer," Toni accused.

Rynn shrugged. "Well, I *am* a cop. Why? What do you believe?"

Toni was quiet for a moment. She sighed. "I used to think that love takes time. My parents dated for five years before they wed and now, almost forty years later, they're still making it work. I've just seen so many couples, friends even, date briefly and jump into marriage claiming love, only to be divorced within six months of tying the knot. It just seems like you should take the time to be sure."

Was Toni trying to tell her something? Rynn might have agreed except for the feelings that welled from deep inside her after barely more than a month of knowing Toni. It wasn't love, but she knew it could be in time.

Toni sighed. "But now? I'm not so sure."

Rynn couldn't help smiling. Yes, Toni was telling her something. "Why not?" she asked, praying she was right about the answer.

Toni suddenly squirmed in her arms, twisting so they were face-to-face. She still lay between her legs, practically on top of her. "You know why."

Rynn was captivated by what she saw in Toni's stunning dark eyes. Her breath caught. She found herself unable to respond.

Toni smiled and leaned in, closing the little distance remaining between them, and kissed Rynn deeply.

She returned her passion, opening her mouth to invite Toni's tongue inside. She felt her heart pound as Toni's tongue explored her mouth. The kiss broke apart. She let out a small gasp when Toni worked those sweet, soft lips along her neck.

"God, Toni," she moaned in pleasure, her heat and desire building.

She wanted to feel Toni's skin. Obeying the impulse, she reached under the thin cotton sweatshirt. As Toni continued to nibble her neck, she curved her hands around Toni's slender waist, her fingertips following the line of her lower ribs. Toni shifted to find her mouth. Their kiss was hungry, full of need.

Rynn moved her hands higher, boldly shoving the fabric of Toni's bra aside and capturing her breasts. She heard Toni gasp. A shudder of pleasure rippled through Toni's body. She felt heat concentrating just below the point where Toni's hips met hers.

Toni's left arm was held in the sling tight at her side, but her right hand worked through Rynn's short hair, settling at the back of her neck and pulling her deeper into their kiss. "Rynn..." she breathed after a moment. "I want to feel you against my skin. Help me."

Rynn smiled at Toni's need, her impatience. "Slow down, baby, I've got it," she replied.

Toni raised herself up, slipping into a half-seated position, and lifted her good arm.

Drinking in the desire she sensed in Toni, Rynn grinned. She drew her hands away from Toni's soft skin long enough to quickly unclasp the sling and toss it aside. She found her way back to Toni's skin under the sweatshirt, her fingertips lingering there. The motion was slow, deliberately teasing.

Toni rolled her head back. "God, you're killing me, Rynn. Please. I want you." She whispered her protest, her eyes shining with intense heat.

Rynn resisted the urge to hurry, pulling the sweatshirt carefully over Toni's injured shoulder, still bandaged to prevent jarring. Despite her caution, the fabric caught and pulled at the injury.

Toni gasped, this time clearly not from pleasure. She closed her eyes, grimacing.

Rynn stopped, afraid to move. "Toni, are you okay?" she asked.

Toni clenched her jaw. Tears glistened. She choked out, "Damn it. I'm fine."

Rynn knew she'd caused Toni pain. "Maybe we should stop," she suggested reluctantly.

"No, Rynn, please don't. I can do this. I want this," Toni pleaded.

Rynn couldn't ignore the tear clinging to Toni's delicate eyelashes. She shook her head. "Toni, you know I want this too. You know how much I want you. But not if it's going to hurt you. I never want to hurt you, in any way." She carefully slipped the sweatshirt back into place.

"No, please," Toni whispered.

"Soon, baby. But not yet." Rynn sat forward and kissed Toni softly, regretting their passion had been stolen by a flash of pain.

Toni released a heavy sigh and sank back onto the couch, kicking her casted leg out in frustration, which only made her wince in pain again. "Damn it," she repeated.

Rynn moved closer and touched her forehead to Toni's. After a few seconds, she pulled away to see tears tracking down Toni's cheek. She delicately brushed them away. "Oh, sweetheart, don't cry. Does it hurt that bad?"

"Yes and no," Toni answered. "It's not because my shoulder hurts, it's because I can't be with you. I want so much to be with you, to touch you." She paused, her frustration and pain clear. "Rynn, I want you to love me. To make love to me."

Rynn's breath caught. Her heart pounded. She couldn't speak.

Toni went on. "And I *hate* that those fuckers have stopped that by smashing up my car with us in it." Her whispered words were wracked with pain, tinged with anger.

Rynn held Toni and took her hand. "No, not stopped. Only slowed. I want to make love to you. I *will* make love to you. They can't stop this thing between us. It's too strong. We'll get there, it's just going to take a little longer than either of us want."

Toni sighed again. "I know." She flicked a stray tear away from her cheek with an abruptness that spoke of lingering irritation.

Rynn suddenly realized their movie had started over and was halfway through playing a second time. When had it gotten so late? "Maybe we should call it a night, get you ready for bed," she said.

Toni nodded, but didn't show any intention of moving. She held Rynn's hand.

They sat quietly together for a moment longer before Rynn helped Toni to her feet, handed her the crutch, and led her upstairs to the bedroom.

CHAPTER TWENTY-SIX

Toni woke the next morning wrapped in Rynn's arms. She didn't move, just enjoyed the feeling of Rynn's warm body at her back and the breath tickling the nape of her neck. They lay together, a perfect fit. She nestled a little closer. In her sleep, Rynn responded to the movement by tightening the arm wrapped around her waist. She used Rynn's other arm as a pillow.

She loved the intimacy of waking up in another's arms and thought it had to be one of the best experiences in the world. In the comfort of Rynn's embrace, she drifted in and out of sleep. She stirred again sometime later, roused by a kiss on the back on her neck. *Mmm, Rynn is awake.* She smiled and twisted her head to give Rynn easier access to her skin.

Rynn's kisses were soft, tracing a slow line along her collarbone. Fingers tugged at the neck of the oversized T-shirt she slept in. Pulling the fabric down a little lower, the trail of kisses continued until they reached her bandage.

"Good morning, sweetheart," Rynn whispered in her ear. "Did you sleep all right?"

Toni smiled. "Mmm-hmm. Best I've slept in…oh, probably in years. You?"

She felt Rynn nod behind her. "Yeah, me too."

She turned in Rynn's arms and lay on her back. Rynn pushed herself up on an elbow, hovering over her. One of Rynn's legs fell between hers. Their thighs brushed under the sheets. Rynn lowered her head and kissed her.

Toni kissed Rynn back, but pulled away after a moment and scrunched up her face. "Don't kiss me yet, I probably have morning breath."

Rynn chuckled. "Yeah, and your cast is kind of itchy too."

When Rynn rubbed her leg against hers, Toni realized with some disappointment that she couldn't feel the touch below her knee. The brush at her thigh, though, was enough to send a shiver of desire through her body.

"Do *not* get any ideas," Rynn commanded, apparently catching the glint in her eye. Before she could protest, Rynn gave her another quick peck on the cheek and rolled away from her.

"No, wait! Come back!" Toni pleaded.

Rynn stretched beside her, just out of her reach.

She was unable to turn onto her left side without putting weight on her injured shoulder. Instead, she pouted and made a futile attempt to reach across her body to pull Rynn back. She scooted into a reclined sitting position and weakly reached for Rynn with her left hand, but her shoulder wouldn't give her much range. She was getting frustrated.

Rynn, however, seemed content to play hard-to-get because she wiggled lower on the bed, still keeping just out of reach, and stretched again.

From her new higher vantage point, Toni was afforded an amazing view of Rynn's perfect body. As Rynn rolled over, her eyes traced along the stunning curves revealed by an oversized T-shirt similar to her own. The ridge of Rynn's hip against the twisted sheet gave way to just a hint of skin barely visible above the band of her boxers.

Moving upward along Rynn's body, Toni's gaze lingered at her breasts, the shadow of her nipples straining against the thin fabric of the old shirt. She had to swallow her desire, knowing she could not yet touch.

"Ahem."

Toni started when Rynn cleared her throat. Her face flushed at having been caught staring, but when she raised her eyes to meet Rynn's gaze, she found the woman sporting an amused grin.

"Can I help you?" Rynn teased.

"Yes. Come closer and let me have my way with you," Toni replied matter-of-factly.

"Ah, a morning person. I'll have to remember that." Rynn showed no indication of moving any closer.

"Damn it, Rynn, at least switch over to my right side so I can reach you!" she pleaded.

Rynn looked away, seemingly considering the request. Without warning, she rolled back over Toni's body, holding herself off by inches, just hovering above her. Their faces, their lips were barely separated.

Toni was so surprised, so aroused, she stopped breathing.

Rynn's intense gaze held her stunned. Toni fell hard into the depths. She and Rynn stayed still, neither one moving, neither one breathing, for no time and for eternity. Her heart pounded.

With another grin and another sudden movement, Rynn finished her roll over Toni's body and lay on her side, propped up on an elbow, watching her.

A few seconds later, Toni realized she needed air. "God, Rynn, you are cruel," she gasped.

Rynn just smiled at her.

Toni turned onto her side, mirroring Rynn. Her shoulder chose to be merciful, and she was able to move her left arm enough to reach Rynn's side. Her fingers danced slowly along Rynn's ribs, trying to tug the shirt up enough to find skin, but Rynn pulled her T-shirt down, keeping it in place.

"Not yet, sweetheart," Rynn said, shaking her head. "And if you touch me, I will not be able to control myself."

Toni begrudgingly accepted, but her hand remained at Rynn's side. She lay quietly, just watching Rynn, keeping a light touch on her and sharing a tender smile. Again, she was struck by the comfortable silence they shared.

Eventually, the silence was broken by Rynn's phone. She grumbled as she rolled to retrieve it. Toni shared the disappointment in their morning being interrupted.

"Callahan."

Toni smiled at hearing the gruff greeting. Direct, to the point, but not at all reflective of the depth and complexity of its speaker. Not wanting to eavesdrop, she wiggled into a sitting position and looked around for some indication of time. She was surprised when she discovered the alarm clock next to the bed read after nine o'clock. She knew Rynn had been joking when she accused her of being a morning person, but it was true. She hadn't slept past seven o'clock since college unless she was sick or jet-lagged, neither of which was the case this morning. Could it be she was just that comfortable with Rynn?

Knowing she'd slept in for the first time in years, and with Rynn occupied on the phone, she decided it was time to get up. She climbed out of the queen-sized bed and tugged her T-shirt into place while she hopped on her good foot, pleasantly surprised to realize her shoulder didn't hurt as badly as it had yesterday. She was able to pull on her sling and grab her crutch without help.

Rynn had also risen from the bed to pace slowly by the window as she talked on the phone. Toni watched for a minute, smiling at Rynn's lean form outlined by bright sunlight beyond the thin drapes. Rynn personified strength and stability. She wondered if that stunning physical fitness was a result of being a cop, or if she was purely self-motivated. Thinking about the number of chubby cops who'd given her speeding tickets, she decided it was most likely something Rynn did independent of her job.

Making her way to the kitchen, Toni paused to consider that she had no idea where Rynn kept anything. Would it be rude to rummage through the cabinets looking for breakfast? She decided if she took something in to Rynn, the intrusion would hopefully be forgiven. She opened a cupboard in search of coffee and maybe some bread for toast.

She got lucky, finding a small two-cup coffeepot and some grounds in a cabinet by the fridge, in the same place as the toaster. Pulling out the supplies with only one hand was challenging, but she managed to get things going quickly enough. Waiting for the brew and toast, she tried to figure out how she was supposed to take more than a single plate or cup into the other room. She was still standing in the kitchen, staring at the counter when Rynn snuck up behind her, brushed her long hair out of the way, and placed a gentle kiss on the side of her neck.

"Something smells good. Where did you find coffee?" Rynn asked.

Toni laughed. "What do you mean, where'd I find it? This is your house."

Rynn shrugged. "Well, yeah, but I didn't know I had any coffee. It's been awhile since I made myself any."

"It was right next to the coffeemaker and the toaster, actually. It seems you were somewhat organized once upon a time," Toni teased. "I was going to bring breakfast in to you, since you were on the phone, but I kind of got stuck at the transportation phase of my plan."

Rynn smiled. "Why don't you go sit at the table and let me take care of that?"

She agreed and limped over to the large oak dining set. "This table is gorgeous. Seems so big for just one person," she observed, taking a seat in a smooth, high-backed chair.

Rynn carried over two coffee mugs and a single plate piled with buttered toast. "My parents loved this table. They liked to host dinner parties, always said that conversation and food were the keys to lasting friendships. I think, out of everything in the house, this table was probably Dad's favorite possession."

Toni hesitated, unsure if she'd touched on a sensitive memory. She saw sadness in Rynn's expression, but it was undercut with a smile.

"They would have been pleased that you like it," Rynn added.

Toni smiled and took Rynn's hand. She didn't have anything to say and simply shared the quiet moment until Rynn's stomach growled. She laughed and pushed over the plate of toast. They both munched their breakfasts and sipped their coffees, enjoying the quiet morning.

"Pearson's coming by in a bit," Rynn commented after a few minutes. "We need to go over some things on this case, but I didn't want to leave you here alone."

"Thank you," Toni said. "I take it that's who was on the phone?"

"Yeah."

"When is he coming over?"

Rynn took a big bite of toast before answering. "He was at the station, and with the snow last night, he might be delayed. But probably in an hour or so."

Toni glanced out the kitchen window. She hadn't even realized it had snowed, but that would explain the extra brightness that had lit up Rynn's profile earlier. Looking outside now, she saw the yard was covered with three or four inches of pure white powder, and the lake beyond had ice rimming its banks. "It's beautiful. I love early snow, right at the beginning of winter."

Peering at Rynn out of the corner of her eye, Toni could tell she had not followed her gaze and was instead watching her from across the table. She smiled and turned face Rynn. "So is this crutch enough to get me out of shoveling snow?" she asked playfully.

Rynn chuckled and nodded. "Yeah, I guess so. But I should go do that for Pearson." She gathered up the empty dishes and returned to the kitchen. "Do you want any more coffee?" she called. "There's about half a cup left."

"No, it's all yours." She remained sitting at the table.

After a moment, Rynn returned. "I've got to go find my snow shovel in the garage. You'll be okay in here for a little bit?" she asked.

"Yes," Toni replied. "I'll be fine. I'll probably limp my way over to the shower and freshen up, if you don't mind." She threw a flirty wink toward Rynn and saw her quirk her brow.

"That's not fair," Rynn grumbled.

"Mmm, just a thought to keep you warm." She smiled and climbed to her feet. She would have been better able to make a suggestive getaway without the walking cast, but considering how much the doctors had rebuilt her foot, she reminded herself to be glad that she was up at all.

Rynn mumbled a few more complaints behind her.

Toni grinned as she left the room.

* * *

Smiling as she shoveled snow, Rynn mused on the fact that the task didn't seem quite the annoying chore she knew it would become by February and March. For now, it was actually rather pleasant, tossing the crisp white blanket away from the sidewalk. The sun shone and the sky was clear, adding to her generally good mood.

Of course, the biggest factor to her mood was most likely the image drifting through her head. Toni had known exactly what she was doing, hinting she needed something to "keep her warm" while she shoveled. Despite the suggestion, her mind actually wasn't focused so much on thoughts of Toni's stunning body steaming in the shower with warm water flowing over her.

Well, maybe just a little. But more than that, she was warmed by the thought of Toni snuggled deep in her arms when they'd woken up together that morning. She smiled again at the memory and flipped another shovelful of snow into the yard.

"You didn't have to shovel just for me," Pearson called from the edge of the driveway, still ten feet from the path she was clearing. "But since you are, think you could make your way over here?"

"You got here faster than I expected," she replied. Instead of continuing to clear the entire width of sidewalk, she carved out a single shovel-wide lane to the drive.

"How are you?" Pearson asked, concern in his eyes.

Rynn suspected that in addition to the soreness and stiff neck she'd complained about the day before, he wondered about her emotional health with the case. "I'm doing all right. My head still hurts, but I haven't vomited since the hospital. Even my black eye is fading." She tugged the hood of her sweatshirt away from her face so he could see the healing injury. The gesture bought her a few more seconds while she considered how best to answer the implied second half of his inquiry.

Pearson nodded. "That is looking better. More yellowy-green than purply-black, so that's progress."

She laughed. "Yeah, I'm trying to get the whole rainbow on my face at some point."

"When do you get those couple of stitches out?" he asked.

She reached up and touched the area above her eye. "I'll swing by the doctor sometime next week and get them taken care of."

He nodded. "And what about the rest?"

She sighed, her breath visible in the icy air. "I'm fine, Steve."

He studied her a moment. "Good enough for me. Have you scheduled your psych eval yet?"

Rynn consciously unclenched her jaw. She hated going through the standard evaluations that occurred after an officer was involved in a shooting. "No. I spoke to the lieutenant yesterday, but he wants me to stay home for a few days."

"I'm not surprised. He hasn't called to tell me you were off the case, though, so why don't we go talk about what you know?"

He reached out to take the shovel from her, but she pulled it back. "I'll take care of the rest later. Let's head inside."

She turned to walk back to the front door of the house. Propping the shovel against the corner of the porch, she stomped snow off her boots and entered the house. Pearson followed suit. She realized this was the first time he'd been to visit her.

He looked around, much as Toni had done the night before.

"Do you mind hanging your own coat?" Rynn asked. "There's a closet just behind you." Having gone out in only a sweatshirt, she didn't have anything to put away. She gestured to the closet door and kicked her boots onto a mat in front of it. "Can I get you something warm to drink? I can put on a pot of coffee or something."

"Yeah, I found her long lost bean stash this morning." Toni's voice came from across the room.

Rynn looked up to find Toni standing in the hallway that led to the kitchen. Her hair was darker than usual, almost jet-black, still glistening from her shower. There was a slight curl that fell out when her locks were dry, and she liked the way Toni's hair framed her face.

Toni wore a loose T-shirt and sweatpants that Rynn immediately recognized as her own, navy blue with gold and white stripes up the side and a small Notre Dame leprechaun on the thigh. Her dad had given her those sweats when she was still in high school. She smiled to think that somehow Toni had managed to find her favorite old pair.

Toni followed her gaze. "I didn't know where you put my bag. I hope you don't mind that I helped myself."

Rynn grinned. "No worries. Actually, I'm not sure I thought of getting sweats for you, so you might be stuck with mine for a few days." *Damn, she even looks amazing in sweats. My sweats.* She had trouble taking her eyes away from Toni, but behind her, Pearson closed the coat closet door, unknowingly preventing her from giving in to the desire to take Toni in her arms.

"No coffee needed. At least not yet," he said, answering the question Rynn had almost forgotten she'd posed. He continued, "Toni, it's nice to see you up and around. How are you feeling?"

She broke her gaze from Rynn and smiled at him. "Surprisingly well, actually. Thanks for asking. I seem to be a quick healer."

He nodded. "I'm surprised to see you walking. How's your shoulder?"

She moved her left arm a little, apparently trying to show the injury wasn't as bad as it looked. "It's coming along. A lot better every day. I could probably ditch the sling if I had to, but I'm trying to be careful."

Rynn moved into the room, Pearson following behind her. He set a soft leather briefcase on her coffee table and took a seat on the couch. She walked over to Toni, wanting to check to make sure there was nothing she needed. Toni assured her she was fine and slipped back into the kitchen.

Rynn sat in a recliner near the corner of the coffee table. "Have there been any developments?" she asked.

Pearson pulled some papers out of his briefcase. "We confirmed the identity of Torian Michaels. Toni was right, seems he was a washed-up star athlete out of Southern Cal. After he wrecked his knee at that party, no one wanted to touch him in the draft. Not sure if he'd heal for one, and there were some serious character concerns not just limited to how he'd gotten injured in the first place." He shuffled more papers. "Here's something that might interest you. Beyond what you heard that night, we now have concrete evidence tying Michaels to Boden's murder. Apparently, some of the unidentified fibers from the crime scene are a match."

"Good. What else have you got for me?"

He flipped through his files and notes. "How does an ID on mystery guy number two sound?"

Rynn straightened up in her seat. "Sounds promising. Keep talking."

He laughed. "We got a partial match on some prints in the truck that hit you Wednesday. The CSI techs still have to finish tagging the prints to get more complete results, but preliminary searches gave us several dozen possibilities. One, however, caught my eye. Name's Rex Andrews, and he was in the NFL for a year."

"Wide receiver out of Michigan, left early to enter the draft, as I recall." Toni hopped into the room, tossing out tidbits of information. "Do you mind if I join you two?"

Rynn smiled and nodded at the open spot on the couch. Pearson looked up at Toni with a surprised expression. He switched his attention to Rynn. "She's good. It took me twenty minutes poking around the Internet to find that much. You know anything else, Toni?"

She took a seat on the end of the couch, sharing it with Pearson. "About Rex? He was a bust. He was a finalist for the Biletnikoff Award his junior season and then went pro. Green Bay tabbed him in the late first round, but he rarely saw the field that year. For whatever reason, he fell apart in the pros. Then he got into some trouble spending his newfound millions. Club brawls, DUIs, I think there may have been an assault charge. Anyway, between that idiocy and his lack of productivity on the field, Green Bay had enough. He was cut and as far as I know, no one else picked him up."

Rynn smiled at her walking football encyclopedia. Even if football was her career, Toni continued to display an impressive memory for player statistics.

Pearson shook his head. "That's amazing. How do you keep all those players straight? I wasted so much time looking that stuff up when I should have just come to you."

Toni smiled, obviously flattered. "It's what I do. It's my job to know everything about every player, owner, coach and manager in the league. And to know about the up-and-coming talent from the colleges. I do my homework to build my business." She paused. "And beyond that, football is a passion for me."

Pearson turned to Rynn. In a conspiratorial whisper that was clearly audible, he said, "That much football expertise? This one's a keeper." He made a show of winking at her, chuckling when she and Toni laughed.

"So why are you talking about Rex? I only just heard his name as I was entering the room," Toni explained. Her question was phrased innocently, but her tone suggested she knew he was somehow tied to the case.

Rynn sighed. Time to return to the file in front of them. "Pearson thinks Andrews might be the other guy involved in these crimes. A partial fingerprint has connected him to the scene of Wednesday night's attack."

"He has a criminal record, although nothing approaching the degree of murder and attempted abduction," Pearson added.

Toni's expression darkened slightly. "I knew I didn't like him much three years ago when he flirted with being a professional," she mumbled.

Something Toni had said tugged at Rynn's attention. She leaned forward to search through Pearson's notes. When she pulled the file toward her, Pearson questioned her heightened interest. "What are you looking for?"

Rynn flipped through the papers, not finding what she sought. "Have you had any further contact with the detectives responsible for the Quinn case?" she asked.

Pearson shook his head. "No. They never gave us anything that would help with our case, so I focused on our two bad guys."

Rynn nodded. "Understandable." Facts swirled through her brain, almost taunting her with a connection that was still out of reach. "Toni, you said Andrews played for the Packers?"

Toni nodded. "Yes. Why?"

Rynn mulled the idea bouncing around in her head. "When we were observing the Quinn investigation, I remember noticing how much Packers paraphernalia he owned. Maybe he had some association with the players there when Andrews was on the team."

Pearson looked thoughtful. "Okay, maybe Andrews encountered Quinn while he was in Green Bay. We have confidence that our killers are targeting gay persons with some connection to NFL players. At least, we know Rocker's boyfriend was a victim and you heard them spew plenty of homophobic remarks when they attacked Toni. But that still doesn't tell us who's behind this, or how Tommy Rocker was even found out."

Rynn leaned back in her chair, a new memory teasing at her mind. "Say that again."

Pearson looked at her, perhaps surprised by her reaction. "Which part? Rocker's boyfriend or the homophobic slurs?"

Rynn remained silent, thinking. Pearson waited for her to chase down her memories.

"Boyfriend," she finally told him. "They said something about killing fruitcake boyfriends." She trailed off, desperately trying to remember, but the memory wouldn't come into focus. "Damn it, I'm just not sure what else he said."

"You're sure you heard one of them say 'boyfriends' specifically?"

Rynn replayed the voices in her mind again. "Yes."

"Maybe we can get the lieutenant to let us try the detectives up north again. If Quinn was dating an NFL player, that fact could significantly narrow our pool of potential victims. Not to mention open up a whole host of people who might know something."

"Even just based on what I heard, I think we can narrow the pool."

Pearson shrugged. "Sorry. Once we get a more definitive ID on Andrews, I'll get a BOLO out on him. But having been involved with the attack and then watching his accomplice get shot, I'd be surprised if he does anything but hang low for a while." He paused. "Since we now have a theory about who's being targeted, is there any way to warn other potential victims?"

Rynn thought about the idea. "I don't know. Boyfriends of NFL players? Toni," she turned to face her, "any idea what size group we could be talking about?"

Toni blew out a frustrated breath. "Just gay players? I know maybe a dozen, twenty at most."

Pearson seemed startled by her estimate. "You actually know of at least a dozen gay NFL players?" he asked incredulously.

Toni met his stare. "Yes. Are you really that surprised? There are over two thousand players in the NFL, if you count scout teams. Even though I doubt gay players make up the ten percent that's often thrown out for general populations, I'm sure there are plenty I don't know."

Pearson shook his head in disbelief. "I guess I'm guilty of stereotyping my own minority, but we're not usually the buff, tough, macho type."

Toni laughed. "Ever heard of bears? Football is a great outlet for the pent-up aggression that some of these guys feel from being forced to live in the closet. A few have come out after they retire—I'm sure Daniel will someday—but while they're suiting up? Public opinion would squash their careers." After a moment's silence, she spoke again quietly. "I can give you names. They'll all hate me if anything ever gets out, but if it saves a single life, then it's worth it."

Rynn smiled, recognizing the nobility of Toni's offer. She wasn't sure, but she suspected news of her breaking client confidentiality, even if to protect innocents, would probably be very damaging to her career. Reasonable people would understand, but not everyone was reasonable.

She shook her head, frustrated. "I don't see what good knowing possible targets does us, not when the pool is that large. Even if you gave us fifteen players' names, we would have to contact each of them, identify anyone they might be involved with, contact them, and then what? What would we say? You might be the target of a possible serial killer, but we don't actually know much yet? The pool would almost surely cross multiple jurisdictions, so we wouldn't be able to assign protection. We need to figure out a way to solve this before the killers strike again."

Pearson nodded his agreement, although she was aware of the agitated helplessness reflected in his expression. "No, you're right. As much as I'd like to know those names, my personal curiosity doesn't justify a breach of confidence. Really, we're still premature in labeling the Boden and Quinn homicides as serial murders, anyway. Two is barely enough. But taking into account what Rynn heard that night last week, we can assume more attacks are planned."

Toni sighed, seeming relieved by their decision. Rynn placed a hand on her knee. Toni frowned. "If it changes, if those names would make a difference, all you have to do is ask."

Rynn managed a slight smile. "I know. Thanks."

She, Toni and Pearson talked about the case a while longer. She and Pearson agreed to dig up everything possible on Rex Andrews since he was their only lead, and to continue piecing through the evidence in the hope of figuring out whom he and Michaels were working for. There were still so many unanswered questions, but she had learned long ago just to push through.

But by the time Pearson left, she feared they weren't moving fast enough.

CHAPTER TWENTY-SEVEN

It had been six days since the wreck. Toni was getting ready for bed, having very quickly gotten used to the comfort of sleeping in Rynn's arms. In fact, with Rynn insisting on keeping other activities to a minimum until her shoulder healed, the time they shared snuggled together in bed was one of the best parts of her day.

She had, of course, taken time to communicate with her office and some of her clients. With the exception of Daniel, they were ignorant of the case. The fact that she had been in a car "accident" was more than enough reason for her to stay away from the office. Besides, with all the wonders of modern technology, she was nearly able to run her business remotely.

Rynn was still downstairs, but she'd said she would be up shortly. Toni slipped out of the baggy sweats she'd worn all day around the house and into the tiny boxers she preferred to sleep in. Actually, she preferred to sleep naked, but she was pretty sure Rynn might have a heart attack if she came up the stairs and found her like that.

She smiled at the thought and tested her shoulder again, moving gently, pushing the limits of her strength and motion. Maybe, once her strength returned enough to live up to the promises implied by crawling naked into Rynn's bed, she would indeed surprise her that way.

It would be fun.

Toni was still thoughtfully considering her shoulder when she heard Rynn's light footfalls coming toward her. She lowered her arm, holding back the evidence of her recovery so that she could surprise Rynn in a few days. She smiled again at the idea of Rynn finding her waiting in bed, naked and wanting, and shook her head.

"What's up?" Rynn asked, catching the private movement when she entered the bedroom.

"Nothing. Just thinking about something."

Rynn paused and studied her. "And you're not going to share?"

Toni grinned. "Nope."

Rynn eyed her suspiciously, but shrugged and accepted the response. Toni hopped over to climb under the covers, while Rynn ducked into the master bathroom to slip out of her jeans and into the boxers she'd been wearing to bed. She wished Rynn wouldn't leave the room to undress, but at the same time, she was grateful. Despite her protests, she knew her body was not quite where she needed it to be for the intimacy she had planned.

"You're grinning again," Rynn pointed out as she stepped from the bathroom, now sporting soft cotton boxers and an oversized T-shirt.

"And I'm still not going to tell you why," Toni replied.

This time, Rynn rolled her eyes. "Fine." The word might have been curt but for the smile that accompanied it.

Toni scooted further into bed, making room for Rynn to slip in next to her. With the familiarity of a long and tender relationship, though they'd only been sharing a bed a few nights, she snuggled comfortably into Rynn's arms, her head resting on Rynn's shoulder. She loved the way Rynn stroked her hair as they lay together. Curled safely into Rynn's side, she sighed her contentment.

Rynn placed a small kiss on her forehead, and rested a cheek against her hair. "That sounded like a good sigh," she observed.

Toni nodded her confirmation and wrapped her arm tightly around Rynn's waist. "I'm so comfortable here with you. It's amazing."

"Mmm-hmm," Rynn agreed.

She and Rynn lay quietly together without speaking. Toni thought about the possibility of falling asleep like this every night for the rest of her life. She felt a warmth welling in her chest at the idea. *Maybe this is what it's like. What couples like my parents feel, making it last for a lifetime together.*

Maybe it was because sleep threatened and her mind wandered, but the thought of her parents also conjured an image of family holidays. Memories of past gatherings drifted through her mind, followed by visions of future celebrations. Rynn was perhaps the best part of those visions.

Family holidays. Christmas. Thanksgiving. With a return to consciousness, she realized Thanksgiving was in just two days. "Rynn?" she whispered, unsure if she was still awake.

"Hmm?" came the soft reply.

Toni suspected Rynn had drifted into half-sleep as well. "Are we doing anything for Thursday?" she asked, wondering briefly if it was presumptuous on her part to assume they would spend the holiday together. She hoped they would.

"What's Thursday?" Rynn questioned, stirring slightly and sounding a little more awake.

"Thanksgiving."

"It is? Already?"

Toni felt Rynn shift against her. She lifted herself slightly to meet Rynn's gaze. She smiled on seeing the normally sparkling green eyes now cloudy with sleep. "Yes. Already. Do you usually do anything special for it?"

Rynn's eyes drifted closed. "No. Actually, I haven't really celebrated Thanksgiving in recent years. Not since…well, I guess not since my parents died."

Toni lifted her hand from Rynn's waist and passed her fingertips along Rynn's strong jaw. She brushed a stray piece of Rynn's messy blonde hair away from her face, wondering if this might be a delicate topic. Rynn didn't seem upset, but she wasn't sure. "Would you rather not celebrate?" she asked as she rested her head back on Rynn's shoulder.

"Hmm?" Rynn was clearly fighting sleep and took a second to answer the question. "Oh, no, we can do something if you'd like. It just seemed like a family holiday to me, and well, without my parents, I guess I didn't really feel like I had a family. Until you." The last part was barely whispered.

Toni wondered for a second if she'd heard correctly and if sleep had claimed Rynn as she finished speaking. Raising her head, she found Rynn's gaze on her, no longer holding any shadow of sleep. Rynn thought she was family? Why would she honor her that way?

She raised her head enough to close the few inches separating them and pulled Rynn into a deep kiss. She let her eyes fall closed and tasted the sweetness of Rynn's mouth.

They'd shared quite a few kisses together in bed, most fueled with a heated fire of what they couldn't yet share, but this was different. This kiss lingered, soft, gentle and full of the words neither one of them had said. She had resisted the urge to even consider the possibility of what this kiss now locked into reality. This kiss was one of forever, and in this kiss, she fell deeply in love.

CHAPTER TWENTY-EIGHT

Rynn looked up as Toni hopped into the living room the next morning.

Toni leaned against the doorframe and asked, "Steve, what are you doing for Thanksgiving tomorrow?"

Rynn and Pearson were going over the case file yet again. She smiled at the way Toni had adapted to getting around the house. Sometimes, Toni still kept the crutch with her, but once the doctor had given her permission to put some weight on her foot after her checkup the day before, she mostly used some combination of limping and hopping.

It was, after all, a walking cast, Toni had argued when Rynn tried to convince her to rely more on the crutch. If the doctor wanted her to stay off it completely, he would have said so. She wasn't sure this was a good idea, but as long as it didn't hurt—and Toni insisted it didn't—then she couldn't really see the harm in it.

"What's that?" Pearson looked up, his concentration on the file broken.

"Thanksgiving. I was just wondering if you had plans. You mentioned at one point that you moved from Cleveland, and I wasn't sure if you had any family in the area."

He smiled. "You have a spectacular memory, don't you?"

Toni's shrug reminded Rynn of what that simple gesture meant in terms of how much she had healed. "I guess so."

"To answer your question, no, I don't have any family in the area. Last year, I spent Thanksgiving alone with some take-out turkey and good ol' NFL games to keep me company. Why? Are you and Rynn making plans?"

Rynn caught Toni's mischievous glance. "Well, I don't know about Rynn, but I'm making plans," Toni said. "I'm even going to drag her to the grocery store in a little bit. I'm starting to get cabin fever from being locked in this house all the time."

Rynn raised a brow in surprise. "Wait, this is the first I've heard about going to the grocery store. I ran out and picked things up on Sunday, and you didn't mention needing anything else."

Toni rolled her eyes. "That was before I decided I was going to cook us Thanksgiving dinner."

Rynn's other brow shot up to join the first. "You're cooking? Thanksgiving dinner?"

Toni laughed. "Yes, I'm cooking. And as I recall, you liked my cooking."

Rynn's mind drifted back to the other meals they'd shared. Yes, she definitely liked Toni's cooking. "How are you going to get around the kitchen? Isn't that a lot of time on your foot? I don't think you hopping around a grocery store is a great idea either," she protested. "Why don't you make a list and I can go get the stuff?"

"Stop fussing. I'll be fine." Toni hopped over to where Rynn sat in the recliner. She leaned down and placed a sweet kiss on her lips. "I adore you, but I don't trust you with dinner. I've seen how well your kitchen is stocked."

Pearson piped up. "You know, after seeing some of the crap she eats for lunch in the squad room, I can't say I blame you."

Rynn chucked a pen at his head.

He ducked with a laugh. "I would love to join you ladies tomorrow."

"Good. I'm going to finish trying to figure out Rynn's kitchen. Honestly, I'd swear she's never cooked something that didn't come with instructions on the box." Toni glanced at Rynn and left the room.

Rynn kept silent a moment, still gazing thoughtfully at the kitchen door. Toni was cooking Thanksgiving dinner for them? Her thoughts drifted to the night before, when she and Toni had lain in bed together and the subject first came up. Had it really been six years since she had celebrated Thanksgiving? Yes. It had always been her parents' thing. She hadn't made a conscious decision to not observe the holiday, but in the years she'd been alone, she hadn't felt like she had something to celebrate. But now? Was there anything that she was more thankful for than Toni? No, the beautiful woman in the next room had rapidly become the best part of her life.

She considered the previous night again, lingering on the kiss. She had never known anything so powerful before. It didn't seem possible that a simple kiss could carry so much emotion.

"I take it things are going well between you two?" Pearson's question broke her reverie.

She closed her eyes a second before turning to answer him. "Yeah." She nodded. "Yeah, you could say that." She felt Pearson studying her, looking for more of an explanation. He had become a good friend. She realized with some surprise that she'd known him only a few days longer than she'd known Toni. Things had changed so much for her lately. "I'm glad you're coming tomorrow. It'll be good to have you," she said.

"Well, judging from your expression when Toni mentioned the last time she cooked, I'm guessing the pleasure will be all mine," he said. "She's really gotten to you, hasn't she?"

Rynn met his searching gaze. "Steve, I think I'm falling for her." It was the first time she had said the words out loud, and having spoken them, she was certain beyond any shadow of a doubt. She was falling in love with Toni.

Pearson nodded, still smiling. "Yeah, I thought as much. Good."

"Good?"

"Yes, good. She's gorgeous, funny and smart. Apparently she cooks. More than that, she's good for you. You light up every time she comes into the room."

"I do?" Rynn blinked. Pearson had pointed it out before, but she still found it odd to hear that her feelings for Toni were so obvious. Even after weeks of him ragging on her, she still thought he was just poking fun.

"Yes, you do."

She sighed. "Yeah, I guess I probably do."

She and Pearson didn't speak for a few minutes until she forced her mind back to work. "Okay, enough chat. We need go over the case one more time before we head to the station."

She was not looking forward to her psychiatric evaluation, but thought it was better to get it out of the way. Maybe then she'd be able to return to work for real.

The next morning, Rynn awoke feeling strangely chilly. She twisted uncomfortably in her bed, not quite conscious, but feeling something was missing. The bed felt cold, empty. Then it hit her. *Toni?* Confused, she sat up, looking around the room with sleep still heavy in her eyes. She rubbed the heels of her hands against her face, trying to scrub away the drowsiness.

After a quick stop in the bathroom, she lumbered downstairs looking for her missing companion. While passing through the living room, she was hit with an absolutely amazing smell, a delicious scent wafting from the kitchen that hadn't been in this house in years. *Damn. Turkey.* She closed her eyes and took in a deep breath of the mouthwatering aromas.

She pushed her way through the kitchen door and found Toni bending over the oven door, poking at something inside, large and covered in foil. The angle afforded her a breathtaking view, accented by the fact that Toni still wore the tiny boxers she'd been sleeping in. The sight of Toni's long, perfect legs made her pulse quicken. Even the cast from Toni's left knee down didn't hinder her beauty.

Rynn leaned against the wall to catch her balance and her breath. The idea of sneaking up behind Toni and embracing her passed through her mind, but she thought better of it, considering the many ways that could go wrong next to a hot oven.

After a bit more poking at the turkey, Toni finally drew back and stood upright, closing the oven door behind her. She turned with a smile. Rynn melted even more at the beautiful sparkle in Toni's eyes than she had at the sight of her stunning body. Suddenly finding her mouth dry, she bit her lower lip and swallowed a wave of desire.

Toni glanced at her and must have read her mind. She grinned suggestively. "Good morning, Sleeping Beauty," she said.

Rynn's voice didn't seem to be interested in cooperating, so she continued to stand in silence.

Toni hopped over and slipped her arms around her waist. "You're talkative this morning," she teased.

Finally, Rynn found her voice. "I'm sorry. It's just…you take my breath away."

Toni smiled tenderly and leaned in for a kiss. Rynn felt the hunger flare in her, and she opened her mouth, longing to deepen their kiss.

Toni responded in kind, but before things went too far, she pulled away. "Slow down, sweetheart. I've got way too much to do before dinner this afternoon to get distracted."

Rynn protested, but Toni slipped from her grasp.

Rynn caught her and pulled her back, placing a kiss on Toni's neck, then capturing her earlobe with her teeth, tugging gently in a way that drew a soft moan from Toni's parted lips.

"My God, Rynn." Toni twisted in her arms to face her. "Do you have any idea what you do to me?"

Rynn raised an eyebrow. "If it's anything like what you do to me, then I've got a pretty good idea."

She held Toni's gaze, the need and desire strong between them. The heat coursing through her threatened to erupt. Her rational mind reasserted itself. Toni had managed to get a turkey prepared and in the oven, which meant…

She took Toni's hand, leading her toward the door. "Come with me."

Toni's eyes seemed to darken with desire, but she held back. "No."

Rynn turned to her, nearly pleading, and tugged at Toni's hand, but she broke free.

"I know you don't cook," Toni said, "so you probably don't understand what all I've got going here, but there is no way I'm going to let you distract me into ruining this meal."

Rynn scrunched up her face, not sure she could wait any longer. She tried to distract herself by looking over the bowls arranged on the counter. "Is someone coming I don't know about?"

"No," Toni replied. "I talked to Kaya—it would have been a nice opportunity to introduce you to her—but she's out of town for the holiday."

Rynn moved toward her. "Do I have competition?"

Toni scoffed and stepped smoothly into Rynn's embrace. "Kaya is a friend from college. More a wingman than a prospect."

With Toni in her arms again, any other women were instantly forgotten. Rynn wasn't sure how long she could wait to show Toni how she felt.

Her need must have shown in her expression, because Toni kissed her gently, careful not to stir any smoldering passions. Breaking away, she murmured, "Nothing naughty until after dinner and we're alone. Besides," she added, "I'm going to need plenty of time for what I have planned for you."

Rynn felt her body come alive and turn to putty, all at once. Renewed heat shot through her. She wanted to take Toni right there. Or surrender herself to Toni's designs. She might have done exactly that had Toni not been saved by the bell when a timer on the counter sounded. Toni moved from her arms and busied herself over a bowl of mystery food on the counter.

Rynn sighed. She couldn't really complain. After a moment to make sure her knees wouldn't give when she tried to walk, she turned and left the kitchen.

They had time.

* * *

Toni glanced at the clock when the doorbell rang. Pearson arrived at one o'clock sharp with not just a bottle or two of wine, but half a case.

"Wow, man, who all did you think was coming today?" Rynn greeted him with a smile as Toni hopped over to give him a warm hug once he set the box down.

"Hello, Toni." He returned her embrace before answering Rynn. "I wasn't sure, and I didn't know if you wanted red or white. Besides, I figured between dinner and football, a bottle each wasn't unreasonable."

Toni grinned. "Football, food and wine? Sounds perfect."

She limped back into the house, watching as Rynn picked up the box and carried it into the kitchen. She took a seat on the couch and patted the spot next to her.

"Something smells absolutely delicious," Pearson observed when he sat down, obeying her silent invitation. "Do you cook often?"

"When I can. It's a passion my grandmother passed to me, but with my job I don't usually get a chance to go all out like this."

Rynn returned, holding three glasses of wine. "I felt like red first—pinot noir—although we may switch depending on the pairing rules with Toni's feast." She passed around the glasses and took her seat in the recliner. "So who's playing today?"

Toni answered. "Well, I can guarantee that the Lions and the Cowboys are at home. There's a late game too."

"Lions got the Browns. Interconference game on Thanksgiving. Guess the schedule planners felt like something a little different this year," Pearson said.

Toni looked at him. "Are you a Browns fan, since you used to live in Cleveland?"

He shrugged. "I don't know. I guess. I was kind of pissed off at all things Cleveland after I left there, so even my love for the Browns faded."

Toni picked up the remote control, turned on the TV, and flipped through the channels. "I think that game has already started." Finding the right station, she added, "Sorry, Steve, looks like the Browns are losing."

He just shrugged at the 7-0 score. "Well, like I mentioned, I'm not a huge fan anymore."

Toni studied him, wondering at the mix of anger and sadness in his eyes despite the indifference in his voice. Would she be pushing too much to ask? Or maybe, having carried some secret with him since moving, he would want to talk about it. Only one way to find out.

"Steve, do you mind if I ask what happened? In Cleveland?" Toni watched his reaction carefully, unsure whether she was treading unwelcome waters. His hesitation prompted her to add, "If I'm being nosy, just forget I asked."

He still didn't respond, his gaze remaining focused on the TV screen although, she suspected he wasn't really watching the game at all.

She was about to change the subject when he let out a heavy sigh. "You know, I was with Cleveland PD for twelve years." He paused. "It wasn't that different from most police departments, I think. The guys tended to be macho, a bit over the top, but they're good guys. Guys willing to put their lives on the line every day.

"I wasn't out. Not for the longest time. I guess it was police culture. I was one of the guys and afraid that would change if they knew I was gay. But that fear took a back seat when I met Jason. He'd been loitering in the coffee shop across from the station one evening when I left work and felt like a caffeine boost. He was just finishing up his coffee, kind of people watching out the window, and for some reason our eyes met when I walked in."

He paused. Toni had a feeling he'd tried not to think about these memories in a long time. She knew what it felt like, the first time setting eyes on someone and knowing they were going to be special. Her mind flashed to a different police station, not that long ago.

"We hit it off right away. Jason had a wicked sense of humor that just brought out a joy in me I hadn't felt before. We connected. I really thought that I'd found my soul mate.

"The one thing we didn't talk about was family. I didn't think too much of that. My sisters are okay, but my parents are still somewhat uncomfortable with the fact that I'm gay. So when Jason never wanted to talk about family, I figured they were part of a painful memory and let it slide. That's probably why it took almost eight months before I realized he was my chief's son."

Toni caught the impact of that revelation. Glancing at Rynn, she saw surprise in her expression as well.

Pearson went on, "To me, things felt a little off after I found out. I don't know, maybe it shouldn't have mattered, but I felt like he'd been lying to me. Knowing that I knew his father, that I worked for his father, he'd gone out of his way to keep that information a secret. That didn't sit well with me, but we worked through it.

"It was almost a year after that before the shit hit the fan. Overnight, the whole attitude in the station changed toward me, like I was carrying some horrible, contagious disease. The guys stopped talking when I entered the room. They hurried through their business if I happened to be in the locker room. It wasn't hard to figure out that I'd been outed, but I didn't know how."

His jaw set. Pain flickered in his eyes, still trained across the room. "That night, I called Jason. He didn't answer, but I wasn't worried. He often worked late, and I was feeling in a tough guy cop mood. I didn't need to cry out my sorrows on my boyfriend's shoulder." He shook his head, the pain shifting to anger. "For a week, I got nothing but cold shoulders and suspicious stares at work. At first, I was angry about it, but that rapidly gave way to worry the longer I was unable to reach Jason. When I got called into the chief's office, I was practically panicking, terrified something had happened. He and I had never talked about my relationship with his son. I didn't even know if he knew. When I walked through the door, I felt the wind knocked out of me. Jason was sitting there with his father, an expression cold as ice on his face.

"'Take a seat, Pearson,' the chief said to me. I could hardly take my eyes off Jason. Too many questions raced through my mind to understand any of it. I managed to settle into a chair, managed to tear my eyes from my lover and look at the chief. 'It's come to my attention that we have a little situation here,' he said. I still couldn't speak, I was just so confused. I don't know, maybe I should have seen it coming."

Toni reached over and took his hand. The contact made him jump slightly. His gaze finally left the wall in front of him. He looked at her. "I thought he loved me. I know he loved me. But when it came time to defend our love to his father, he crumbled. He made his choice, and I was left with nothing. The chief looked at me and said, 'My boy here tells me you two have been involved. Well, I can't for the life of me see what spell you got on him, but it ain't about to continue. My boy ain't like that, and I won't have no faggots in my station. So you best pack up your effects and get on out of here, before we have to go through the scandal of arresting one of our own for sexual assault on an innocent man.'"

Toni didn't want to believe it was possible, but she knew the reality all too well. "Oh, Steve. I'm so sorry," she whispered in sympathy, trying to comfort him.

"Jason never said a word. Before I left, his eyes dropped to his lap. Two years together, and he wouldn't even look at me. Thirty-two years old, and he let his father walk all over everything we had." Pearson shook his head. "I packed my things and I was gone within the hour. After a week wondering what I should do next, I told my sisters that I had to leave. I gave Roxie the keys to my house, told her to sell it if she could, and I got in my car and drove west. I stayed with a buddy in downtown Chicago for a few weeks before I came across the job opening for a detective here in Kane County." He shrugged. "So that's why I left Cleveland. That's why I'm bitter toward the city. And that's why I stayed completely closeted, not dating even once since I got here." He dropped his gaze. "I'm not sure I could date just yet, anyway. It takes a while to recover from something like that," he added, his voice barely above a whisper.

Toni pulled him into a strong hug, offering him the comfort he'd lived without for so long.

He allowed himself to be held for a moment before pulling back. "Enough of this sad, sappy shit. I still have some masculine pride. Let's watch some overly aggressive Adonises jump each other's bones."

Toni chuckled, "Yeah, I suppose football is a good distraction." Leaning close, she whispered, "Are you okay?"

"No," he answered. "But I'm getting there. I'll be okay in time." He squeezed her hand. "Thanks."

Toni nodded and settled back on the couch. She felt Rynn's hand on her knee and smiled at the tenderness she saw in Rynn's gaze, and the silent promise: *I will never do that to you.*

"Besides," Pearson spoke again, his voice now taking on a cheerful, almost teasing lilt. "It's not like I'm the only one in the room who's had a run-in with a co-worker's kid."

Rynn's eyes went wide in surprise. She recovered and turned an icy glare on Pearson. "Oh, you wouldn't, " she threatened.

He grinned.

"I think it's time to eat," Rynn said, bolting up and making a hasty exit to the kitchen.

Toni and Pearson both laughed at her retreat.

* * *

"Thanks, again, Toni. Everything was delicious." Pearson hugged her one more time as he stood by the door, ready to leave.

Watching them, Rynn realized she didn't think she had ever hugged Pearson. She resisted scrunching her nose at the thought. She liked Pearson well enough, but they were partners. Hugging was…she wasn't sure why hugging Pearson seemed a strange idea.

"It was our pleasure. We're glad you were able to make it," Toni said graciously.

Rynn was warmed to hear Toni speak for them both. It felt so right to have Toni there. Even Toni's use of plural words— *our pleasure* and *we're glad*—were little recognitions of the bond they shared. Each one filled her with a deep, tender feeling.

Pearson hitched his chin toward her in farewell and they said their goodbyes.

Rynn watched him walk through the dark to his car before gently closing the door behind him. She stepped over to Toni, pulling her into a strong embrace. With a kiss, she whispered. "He was right, you know. Everything was delicious." Another kiss. "You are amazing. I haven't had a Thanksgiving like this in…well, I guess I'm just trying to say thank you."

Toni smiled. "I'm glad you liked it. I wanted this to be special for you."

Rynn felt a wave of joy wash through her. What had she ever done to deserve such a wonderful woman? She couldn't say anything, just smiled her thanks and hoped Toni could read the tenderness in her eyes.

Toni took her hand and led her back into the room. They sat together on the couch, and Toni reached for her glass, which still held a bit of wine.

Two football games had been enough for Rynn, so she grabbed the remote and flicked off the TV. Right now, she just wanted to hold Toni in her arms.

"I take you're not interested in the late game?" Toni asked, snuggling into her embrace.

She mumbled that she was not, nuzzling her face into Toni's neck. "Thank you again. For today," she whispered.

For a little while, she sat with Toni, quietly enjoying her presence while Toni sipped the rest of her wine. She took comfort in the feel of Toni in her arms. Small talk eventually crept in. Although she believed she would have been happy to sit silently with Toni for hours, she never felt like talking to Toni was trivial. It didn't matter what they talked about, the conversation was easy and enjoyable.

Sometime later, Toni stirred. Rynn realized she'd drifted to sleep. She turned her head to meet Toni's smoldering gaze. The heat ignited a fire in her that instantly stole her breath away.

"Tired?" Toni asked softly, a slow smile forming on her perfect lips.

Rynn was certain Toni knew exactly the effect she had on her. She shook her head, unable to speak. Together, she and Toni rose from the couch and climbed the stairs to the bedroom.

Rynn felt her insides burning. The feeling was so much more powerful than mere desire. She had never imagined she could feel so strongly.

Reaching the bedroom, she pulled Toni into her arms and kissed her deeply, passionately, both elated by and terrified of her emotions. She needed to let Toni know. "Toni, I..." She broke off, wanting to confess her love, but the words caught in her throat. She was suddenly afraid Toni might not feel the same.

"You don't need to say anything." Toni's arms snaked around Rynn's shoulders and she kissed her again. "I want you," Toni whispered against her lips. "Take me."

Rynn didn't need to be asked twice. She hungrily found Toni's mouth, claiming her kiss as she pushed Toni backward onto the bed. She slid to her knees between Toni's legs and her hands found their way under Toni's thin cotton blouse. Remembering the reason their passion had been halted before, she wondered briefly if Toni had worn a button-down shirt on purpose. She caressed Toni's warm, soft skin while continuing to kiss her. Raising her hands along Toni's sides, her thumbs slipped under the fabric of Toni's bra and gently stroked the swell of her breasts.

Toni pulled her mouth away. "Take my shirt off."

Rynn obeyed. She withdrew her hands. Her fingers quickly worked the buttons of the blouse. Then the delicate lace of Toni's bra was the only thing left between her hands and the nipples that strained at the fabric. She carefully removed the loose shirt, still wary of Toni's injured shoulder, but Toni reassured her with a look that said this time there would be no stopping.

Rynn slid her hands around Toni's waist, inching her fingers upward to unclasp the bra. When the undergarment fell away, her breath caught when her gaze fell for the first time on Toni's bare skin, luminous in the dim bedroom light. "So beautiful."

She claimed a perfect breast with her hand, lowering her head to capture the other nipple with her mouth. Toni's moan of pleasure stirred the heat coursing through her body and drew out a matching sound from deep within her.

"I want to feel your skin against mine," Toni breathed, tugging at the bottom of Rynn's pullover. "Please."

With one smooth motion, Rynn drew her shirt and sports bra together over her head and tossed them haphazardly on the floor. Toni let out a faint purr and touched her skin, her delicate fingertips leaving a trail of fire across her chest.

Toni shifted farther onto the bed, pulling Rynn with her so she straddled her body.

Consumed by hunger and passion, Rynn's mouth found Toni's in a kiss. Toni's hands wove their way into her hair. She gently settled her weight on top of Toni and slid her thigh between Toni's legs. Through the loose cotton pants Toni wore, she felt a surge of heat and knew her own wetness was mirrored there, waiting.

Rynn let her mouth slip away from Toni's. She kissed her neck and traced her collarbone with her tongue. She wanted to touch Toni so badly, she thought she might burst from the need. "Are you sure you're ready?" she whispered, her lips at Toni's ear, her teeth nibbling on her lobe.

"God, yes." Toni's reply was barely more than a gasp.

Rynn smiled. She fingered the waistband of Toni's pants, then slipped her hands inside and forced the pants down from Toni's hips. They caught on Toni's cast. She chuckled when Toni impatiently kicked them away.

Rynn's hand rested on Toni's hip, her fingers playing with the lace of Toni's panties. She caught Toni's glance. Staring into Toni's eyes, darkened with desire, she found she couldn't breathe. Her heart pounded wildly, seemingly deafening in the quiet of the bedroom.

Toni had just kissed her when they were interrupted by the intruding ring of a phone.

"Shit." Rynn pulled away, but Toni caught her arm.

"Let it go. Rynn, please." Toni's eyes pleaded as much as her words, but Rynn couldn't ignore the call.

"I can't. I have to check it. My job. If someone's calling me this late…" She let the sentence die, pulled herself away from Toni, and dug the phone out of her jeans pocket. "Callahan."

"I hope you're ready to get back to work," Pearson said.

Rynn listened to Pearson and ran a frustrated hand through her short blonde hair. When she spoke, it was to end the call. "I'll meet you there." She flipped the phone closed, resisting the impulse to shatter it against the wall. Why tonight? Why did this have to happen tonight? She pinched the bridge of her nose, trying to hide the frustration and growing anger before turning back to Toni. "I'm sorry, but I have to go." She hated the look that flickered across Toni's stunning face, a fight for control between disappointed frustration and rising concern.

"What is it?" Toni sat up.

Do not tell civilians anything. Rynn's mind screamed protocol at her, but Toni was involved. "There's been another murder."

CHAPTER TWENTY-NINE

When Rynn finally pulled up to the address Pearson had given her, he was already there talking with another man, a stranger in his mid-to-late thirties. She walked over to them.

Pearson turned and made the introductions. "Detective Callahan, this is Darius Hart, the victim's brother. He was the person who notified us tonight."

She listened as he and Hart spoke for a few more minutes before he motioned Rynn to join him in the house.

"No sign of forced entry," Pearson noted when they passed into the hallway.

He led her toward the back of the house. Rynn noted her surroundings as they walked. It was a relatively small house, clean and tidy, with a dining room and sitting room off either side of the hallway where they first entered. It appeared to have been decorated rather stylishly.

All of the house lights were on. Rynn nodded to a CSI who looked up as she and Pearson entered. They passed a small bathroom and a stairwell leading to the floor above and moved into a single large room at the rear of the house. She noted the kitchen to her left, behind the dining room, but her attention was quickly drawn to the casual sitting area to the right, where a team of people hovered over the mangled body of Zachary Hart.

"Jesus..." Rynn couldn't help the quiet exclamation that escaped her lips.

She'd seen some brutal crime scenes, but this was horrific. There was a shocking amount of blood, some splattered across the room, a level of violence she'd seldom seen. The victim's body lay crumpled in the middle of the room, unnaturally slumped on his side. His torso was bare and his lifeless brown eyes stared at the ceiling. The slashes across his face and chest were similar to those she'd seen first with Boden and later, Quinn.

A CSI approached. "Detectives, I think you should see this." He gestured for them to follow him back in to the kitchen and nodded at an open cabinet drawer. "We've taken photos, but we wanted you to see it before we bag it and take it in."

"What do you make of this?" Pearson asked, waving at the item in front of them.

Rynn looked down at the note. *Third Down. And so far, your defense is weak.* The words were written in a jarring pink shade in a smudged but feminine script. "Is that lipstick?" she asked, leaning in to take a better look.

"Sure looks that way."

Returned to her full height, she looked at her partner. "This is an interesting twist, considering the profiles of Andrews and Michaels. It might be our first significant clue on the identity of 'the boss.'"

"Lipstick might point to a woman," he suggested.

"A woman, a drag queen, someone trying to frame either of those two. Anything is possible."

The lipstick was odd, but she'd also learned not to have many expectations when in came to criminal minds. She continued, "I'm sure CSI will run a full battery of tests on it."

"You don't think we'll get anything from it, do you?" Pearson asked.

"No, but leaving a note and taking responsibility for the first two homicides is certainly more cocky than our perpetrators have been so far. Maybe they're getting arrogant and we'll catch a break."

"But lipstick?"

Rynn shrugged. "We could get lucky. All lipsticks are different. Cosmetics companies pride themselves on their individual formulas. If we can identify an exact brand, maybe we can narrow down where it's sold."

Pearson stared at her skeptically. "Seems like a long shot. And since when do you know anything about cosmetics companies? I've never seen you wear an ounce of makeup."

Rynn laughed. "Just because I don't touch the stuff doesn't mean I don't know anything about it." She turned to leave but added, "I once dated a makeup sales manager. She used to rave about the differences between brands. I think she may have had dreams about the perfect eyeliner. Somehow I made it through three whole dates before ending things with her."

She heard Pearson laugh behind her. "Yeah, I can definitely see that working out well."

Rynn passed back through the hallway and stepped into the dark night. It was well past three a.m. before she returned home. She quietly slipped up to the bedroom and found Toni asleep. Toni looked so peaceful, deep in dreams. She leaned in the door and watched her, still in awe of the feelings stirring inside her every time she set eyes on this amazing woman.

With a smile and a slight nod to herself, she pushed off the doorframe to change out of her clothes and into her boxers and oversized T-shirt. She climbed gently into bed next to Toni, careful not to disturb her slumber. As soon as she hit the bed, Toni turned and snuggled into her side, never waking.

Rynn smiled. Had anything else ever felt so right in her life?

* * *

Toni woke up, warm in Rynn's arms. She relished the feel of Rynn absentmindedly stroking her hair. For a moment, she wanted nothing more than to snuggle deeper into Rynn's embrace and just stay there, safe and comfortable. With a contented sigh, she opened her eyes.

Rynn reclined against the headboard, gazing at a tattered photograph, lost in thought. The sight nudged Toni awake a bit more. She'd learned quickly Rynn was not a morning person.

"Is everything okay, sweetheart?" she questioned, trying to keep the concern from her voice.

Rynn stirred, smiling down at her. "Good morning." She dipped her head to give Toni a gentle kiss.

Toni noted the deep concentration fading from Rynn's expression. After returning the kiss, she waited, still seeking an answer to her question.

Rynn glanced back at the photo before setting it on the bedside table. "Yeah, everything's fine. Just thinking about this new development."

Toni nodded, her gaze drifting to the photo Rynn had set aside. "Who is that?" She wasn't entirely sure she should ask.

Rynn hesitated, seeming to consider the matter. She picked up the photo and held it so Toni could see. "The guy on the left is our victim. Zachary Hart." Rynn paused, her voice heavy with sadness. "The guy on the right is his brother, who found him last night. Darius. This was taken when Zachary got them a pair of Bears tickets last fall."

Toni studied the photo, some lost familiarity tugging at her memory. Had she met Zachary Hart before? No, she couldn't place him. "You'll be looking into Bears players, then, won't you?"

Rynn smiled. "Exactly what I was thinking. You know, you probably would have made a pretty good detective yourself." She kissed the top of Toni's head and rested her cheek there. "That will be one of the first things we follow up on. Any suggestions?"

Toni knew Rynn was asking for insider information, which she would readily have given had anything come to mind. "I'm

sorry, I don't know. He looks familiar, somehow. But I can't..."
She sighed, frustrated. "I know of two other closeted players
with the Bears, but one just broke up with his boyfriend, Luke,
and the other, as far as I know, is still happily involved with
Travis."

Rynn set the photo aside.

Toni tried to place the man in the photo. Where had she
seen that face before? "I wish I could be of more help," she
whispered, raising her face to nuzzle into the side of Rynn's
neck.

Rynn sighed. "Don't worry about it. We'll figure it out."

"I'm guessing this new case is going to force you to go into
work today?"

Rynn nodded. "Yes. I'm waiting to get a call that I've been
fully cleared to return to duty. Last night I had a temporary
clearance, but with another victim, I expect they'll accelerate
the process. Chances are, I'll have to work all weekend."

Toni didn't much want to spend the time alone, but she
understood the demands of Rynn's job. "I've been thinking
about that. I think I'm going to return to work myself on
Monday. No one had any complaints that I took the week off,
considering I was in a serious car 'accident' last week." She
shrugged, trying to keep the bitterness and especially the fear
hidden. "But I think it's time I go back."

Rynn reached up to gently brush a stray lock of hair off her
face. "Are you sure? I don't want you to rush into things."

"Yes, I'm ready." A thought occurred to her. She no longer
had a car and couldn't have driven yet anyway. "Do you think
you could drive me?" she asked.

"Of course. I was planning on it anyway, once you did decide
to go back. At least until we get this case wrapped up. I want to
check out security in your office building. Can I convince you
to accept a security detail?"

That she might not be safe at work wasn't something she
had permitted herself to consider. Bad enough the police
suspected the men who attacked her had staked out her
apartment—the excuse for her staying with Rynn, although she

suspected ulterior motives on both their parts—but that the killers might have tracked her to work was a frightening idea. "Should I be worried?" she whispered.

Rynn took a deep breath. "I don't know. But I don't want to risk it."

Toni couldn't help tensing slightly as reality crashed in on her. It was way too early in the morning for such sobering thoughts.

Rynn must have felt her tension, because she immediately placed another kiss on her head and rubbed a soothing hand along her back. "You don't have to worry about that now, sweetheart. You're completely safe here. Those men have no way of tracing you to me. We'll figure things out for Monday, okay?"

Toni nodded against Rynn's chest. She wished they could just spend the day together. "What time is it?"

"About seven thirty."

Toni sighed. Surely Rynn would have to leave soon. "What time do you need to go?"

Rynn didn't respond immediately. "I'm not sure. I can't go in until they say I'm allowed. Hopefully by lunch, I'll get a call. In the meantime…" She didn't finish her thought.

Toni grinned at Rynn's quirked eyebrow. "What are you scheming?" she asked, although she knew full well where Rynn's thoughts had gone.

Rynn responded with a kiss, hungry and passionate. Toni opened her mouth under Rynn's demanding pressure, welcoming in her tongue.

They broke apart. Toni stared into Rynn's blazing emerald eyes.

"I want to finish what we started last night," Rynn murmured, brushing soft lips gently against her mouth.

Toni merely nodded, heat and hunger instantly boiling inside her. She moaned softly when Rynn's mouth found her neck, working kisses along her collarbone and causing waves of desire to crash through her body. She welcomed the feel of Rynn's warm hands slipping beneath her loose T-shirt. When those hands closed on her breasts, she closed her eyes to the pleasure.

"God, Rynn," she gasped. "I want to feel you."

Rynn nodded, lips lingering on Toni's throat. Without warning, Rynn pulled away, shed her T-shirt, and carefully lifted Toni's shirt off in a smooth, gentle motion.

Toni smiled, her hands automatically drawn to touch Rynn's perfect, soft breasts. She watched in fascination as Rynn's nipples hardened immediately under her fingertips. She cupped her palms around them, loving the way Rynn reacted to her touch.

Rynn's eyes closed. Her body pressed closer to Toni's. Rynn rolled on top of her, slipping a thigh between her legs. She opened under Rynn's insistent movements. Their hips rocked together, matching in rhythm, urgent and hungry.

Rynn lowered her head, claiming Toni's nipple with her mouth.

Toni moaned with pleasure. Her hands slid down to Rynn's hips, pulling her closer. She pushed her fingers under the waistband of Rynn's boxers, craving the hot flesh she knew was waiting for her. "Take these off," she whispered, her lips at Rynn's ear.

Rynn obliged, discarding the last of her clothing. She sat back, allowing Toni a view of her strong, toned body.

Toni's breath caught. She stared, overwhelmed by the feelings sweeping through her. Desire fought with tenderness. Both emotions told her Rynn was the woman of her dreams.

Rynn tugged on Toni's panties, a pleading look in her eyes.

She's asking permission? Even with everything that's already passed between us? My God, she's incredible! Toni nodded, giving Rynn a little help by shoving the garment down herself.

When Rynn settled back on top of her, their naked bodies connecting fully for the first time, Toni thought the simplest touch might take her over the edge. When Rynn's mouth found hers again and their tongues met, fast and strong, she knew she'd never felt so alive before.

Rynn's fingers slid delicately along her hip, slipping between them and caressing her center.

She arched against the power of Rynn's gentle touch. "Please."

Rynn took Toni completely, her fingers slipping inside.

Toni lost all semblance of control. She and Rynn moved together, Rynn setting a pace and motion she eagerly matched. Rynn's lips devoured hers, catching her scream as her orgasm shook her. Rynn didn't stop, her hand working strongly. She bucked against Rynn when another wave ripped through her body. Her strength gone, she shuddered, weak in Rynn's embrace.

Rynn slowly, gently withdrew her fingers and held her close.

"My God," Toni breathed, barely finding the air to form words. "You weren't joking when you said this would be worth the wait."

Rynn smiled, deep emotions revealed in her expression.

That passionate look infused Toni with strength. She rolled them over, settling her weight in between Rynn's legs. With a promising grin, she leaned close, whispering, "Your turn," before sucking Rynn's earlobe into her mouth.

Rynn moaned softly, responding readily to her touch. She teased Rynn, tugging gently with her teeth before releasing Rynn's ear and tracing her mouth down Rynn's neck and across her throat.

Her lips closed over Rynn's nipple. Rynn rose against her touch, urging her on. She held Rynn tightly, her hands wrapped around strong shoulders, moving over the taut muscles of her back before making their way lower, cupping Rynn's ass and pulling her close.

Rynn surged against her, matching the rocking rhythm she set.

Toni flicked her tongue against Rynn's breast and traced her fingers across her body, grazing Rynn's inner thigh and slipping between them. She found the wetness she'd known would be there. Her fingers moved as through silk, slipping into Rynn as her body arched. She pumped in and out, feeling Rynn's muscles tighten.

She and Rynn moved together as one. She stretched Rynn's pleasure as long as she could, until with one more movement, Rynn's cries of ecstasy rang out as she peaked.

Toni found Rynn's mouth, feasting on her sweet lips. She moved inside Rynn again.

Rynn responded once more. "Toni, God, yes."

Rynn's words fueled her movements. She found herself teetering on the edge of another orgasm as she strove to give Rynn release.

As if Rynn were reading her thoughts, she shifted below her, forcing a leg between hers so she straddled Rynn's thigh. Her fingers were still buried deep within Rynn. The pressure of Rynn's thigh against her center triggered an eruption. Aware of Rynn's orgasm, she climaxed with her, an explosion of color and heat and pleasure erupting behind her tightly closed eyes.

Spent, Toni collapsed with Rynn, holding her tenderly, breathing hard, her heart pounding.

After a moment, Rynn raised her head enough to kiss Toni gently. "My God," she breathed against her cheek.

Toni lay tangled in Rynn's arms and the sheets, enjoying the afterglow of their incredible lovemaking.

Soon the exhaustion settled in, and Toni curled into Rynn's arms, drifting off into a well-earned sleep. Just before she sank into the darkness of dreamless rest, she felt Rynn kiss her forehead and tighten her hold around her.

CHAPTER THIRTY

Rynn drifted in and out of a peaceful sleep. As much as she wanted to stay in bed with Toni all day, she knew she had to go in to work, sooner rather than later. Toni dozed in her arms, and she reflected with immeasurable tenderness on the powerful lovemaking they had shared. Never before in her life had anything felt so perfect. Never before had anyone touched her the way Toni had.

She reluctantly turned to check the clock, suppressing a disappointed groan that it really was time for her to get up. She would surely get a call soon, and there was no way she could go to work without a shower. Even so, she hated to separate from Toni.

After a moment longer, she carefully extracted herself from Toni's tangled embrace. Once up, she gently tucked Toni in, wrapping her securely in the soft cotton sheets. She kissed the top of Toni's head, breathing in the sweet scent of her hair.

Quietly, almost instinctively and before she fully realized what she was saying, she whispered, "I love you." She hadn't intended to say the words out loud, but they were as right as holding Toni in her arms. She wasn't sure she'd ever before said them with such truth and conviction.

She stepped away from the bed and rushed through a shower, keeping it cold to help her regain her focus. After she finished, she checked on Toni one more time and went downstairs. Her timing seemed perfect since her phone rang just as she entered the kitchen. Her instructions were as expected—time to get back to work—and she quickly left the house.

She rang Pearson as she drove, and they started to discuss the case.

"I keep thinking about the note left behind this time," Pearson said. "Why do that? Why suddenly start giving clues?"

Rynn shrugged. She slowly stopped the Tahoe at a red light. "I don't know. I've thought about that too. That note may not have had many words, but it was loaded. Not only does it confirm this is the third kill, is also hands us the football link on a silver platter. That's something we've obviously kept out of the media, so the killers would have no way of knowing we'd already pieced that fact together."

"I thought that too, at first, but actually, I think it might make sense because they think we don't know. I mean, think about it: if we didn't already know, that note wouldn't have made any sense. It may not obviously have been a football reference. We just jumped to that immediately because of what we already know. As far as the public is concerned, we've not even acknowledged linking the first two. But say the killers assume we link all three, but without knowing the victims were connected to NFL players. We end up sitting there, scratching our heads, trying to read something into that note. Even with the football connection, maybe we waste time investigating high school and college football. Maybe we go through the hoops of questioning hundreds of people involved in local football on various levels."

Rynn considered his hypothesis. A twist on a red herring? "It's possible. So you think we're just starting to see typical serial killer arrogance? They believe they've got us beat, that we're not even close. Now they're just rubbing it in? Catch-me-if-you-can?"

"I think that's exactly what we're seeing," Pearson confirmed.

"No mention of the attack on Toni, though. Going after her still doesn't fit the rest of the scenario. But if you're right about this note, that might also explain the accelerated timing and violence. It's so uncommon for serial killers to trust someone. We know Andrews is working for someone else. I'm not sure 'the boss' will fit the typical profile."

"Or perhaps because 'the boss' has someone else doing their dirty work, they think that gives them an extra layer of protection."

Rynn arrived at the station and whipped the Tahoe into a parking space. Sighing, she told Pearson she was there and would see him in a moment. Flipping the phone closed, she mulled over his theory. She saw the note in her mind. Deliberate? Arrogant? Sloppy? Possibly yes to all three. Was it enough of a break to finally get these guys? She needed more concrete facts.

She walked briskly into their office, tossing a greeting nod toward Pearson. "Okay, I want to know everything about Zachary Hart. What have we got?"

She and Pearson reviewed what they knew and the connections to the other murders. After a moment, Pearson paused. "Is there any chance you asked Toni about our new dead guy?"

Rynn nodded, the glow from her morning with Toni lingering. "Actually, I did. No luck. Even showed her the picture that Darius gave us last night. She seemed to think he was familiar, but couldn't place him. She did rule out his involvement with the other gay Bears she knows."

Pearson seemed both surprised and disappointed. "How many gay Bears are there?" His tone was incredulous.

Rynn made a face at him. "Apparently, Toni knows three, counting Rocker."

Pearson still seemed shocked. "I know, I should be about the last person to talk, but really? Three closeted players on one NFL team? That would average to nearly a hundred gay players across the league."

Rynn shrugged. "Is it really so hard to believe? Toni already told us she knew of maybe twenty, and even a hundred across the league is what, less than five percent of players?"

He shook his head. "I know, but…" He let his sentence die unfinished.

They returned to work. She and Pearson pored over the files, tossing details and ideas back and forth, and arranging interviews. Nothing further came to light.

After a few hours, Pearson looked up with a tired sigh. "Let's take another look at the idea that 'the boss' could be a woman. How much weight can we put behind something like a lipstick note in feminine script?"

"It might say a lot about a suspect, but it isn't really enough in and of itself to indicate gender. I think it's more indicative of a flair for the dramatic."

Pearson shrugged. "Or maybe watching too many Lifetime movies."

She smiled. "Could be. Female serial killers are so rare compared to their male counterparts. Sometimes they are inadvertently omitted from initial suspect lists. Another aspect that trends away from a female is the sexuality connection. Typically, males are more driven by sexual motives, while females serial kill for power or financial gain."

Pearson considered that. "There are always exceptions to statistics, but even if this were such an anomaly, why would a woman have it out so bad for gay men who date NFL players? What could possibly be the motive?"

She shrugged. "I don't know. Then again, we don't know that Hart was dating a football player. There must be more to it." She glanced at the clock and saw it was already nine thirty. "Let's keep at it one more hour."

CHAPTER THIRTY-ONE

By the time she got home to Toni on Sunday night, Rynn was exhausted. Any relaxation and recovery she'd had the week before, even from the wonderful day they'd had on Thanksgiving, had rapidly faded. Since Friday, she and Pearson had worked double shifts trying to figure out anything they could on Hart's murder.

She smiled warmly when Toni stepped out the front door to greet her. She quickly hopped up the few steps and slipped easily into Toni's arms. They kissed tenderly for a moment before Toni shivered lightly in the cold. She realized Toni wore only a long-sleeved T-shirt and sweatpants. With a flourish, she ushered her into the warmth of her home.

Once inside, Toni helped her remove the bulky jacket. "All I need is your touch and I'm on fire." Toni kissed her deeply.

Rynn felt heat ripple through her body. When they broke apart, she found herself breathless. "You know, between my job during the day and coming home to you at night, I don't think I've slept since Thursday," she murmured against Toni's mouth.

"Well, we can't have you collapsing from exhaustion, now can we," Toni teased. "That's why I'm going to feed you and pamper you and get you to bed, straightaway."

Rynn smiled. "Food and bed, I can do. Straight, however, is strictly out."

Toni rolled her eyes and pulled her into the living room. "You're cute, you know that?"

Rynn feigned insult. "Cute? Really? I don't know about that. What about witty or clever?"

Toni pushed her onto the couch. "Well, maybe. But for now, I'm just sticking with cute."

Rynn made a face and stuck out her tongue.

Toni just laughed and stepped toward the kitchen. "I thought you might be getting sick of leftover turkey, so I scrounged in your freezer and found some ground beef. How does a burger sound?"

Rynn showed her appreciation with an admiring look. "That sounds great."

Toni grinned. "In that case, give me a few minutes to cook them and I'll be right back."

Rynn settled on the couch and reflected on the changes in her life over the past few weeks. She drifted in and out of awareness, lost in pleasant thoughts.

"Oh, no, no, no." Toni came in, chuckling.

Rynn shook herself awake, yawned, and stretched. "Hmm. Seems the couch is a bit too comfortable for me right now."

Toni held out a hand and helped her to her feet. "Then why don't you come out to the kitchen and sit with me. Dinner will be ready soon."

She and Toni chatted idly while Toni finished cooking and they ate together. Afterward, she washed the few dishes and let Toni lead her upstairs. Sitting on the edge of the bed, she felt conflicted between her arousal and her exhaustion.

"Toni, maybe tonight, we just..." She let her voice trail off. Just what? Just sleep? Just snuggle? She sighed. Snuggling always sounded good.

Toni placed a gentle kiss on her head. "Sweetheart, I know you're tired. Why don't you change clothes, and we can see how fast you fall asleep in my arms."

Rynn followed Toni's instruction, pulling on her boxers and baggy shirt, and sliding under the sheets.

Toni ducked into the bathroom. When she returned, Rynn couldn't help the catch in her breath when her gaze fell on Toni's gorgeous body. She had forsaken the shorts the past two nights, opting instead to sleep only in her panties and a long T-shirt when she wore anything at all. Tonight, when Toni returned to the bedroom, Rynn took in her perfect legs, disappearing under the edge of the cotton hem.

Toni chuckled. "That look doesn't say tired to me."

Rynn flushed, painfully aware of her body's signals. "I know. You just...You're stunning."

"Thank you. But I think we need to turn out the light so you can get some sleep." After flicking the light switch, Toni climbed into bed and into her arms.

Their bodies fit together perfectly. Rynn breathed in the sweet scent of Toni's hair. Despite her claim that she was too tired, she felt a surge of desire. She kissed Toni gently on the forehead, her brain trying to remind her body of her exhaustion.

"Rynn?"

"Hmm?"

"Your heart is racing. Are you okay?"

Rynn smiled. "Yes, sweetheart. I'm fine." Amazing, really. *Just having you in my arms always makes my heart pound.* She drew her finger up to Toni's face, gently stroking her jaw before raising her head to kiss her fully on the lips.

Toni returned her kiss, initially soft, but pulled back when Rynn turned the kiss hungrier, catching Toni's lip with her teeth. "I thought you were tired?"

"I am." Rynn found Toni's mouth again.

Toni parted her lips to her insistent tongue. After a moment, Rynn moved her mouth against Toni's jaw, searching for her throat. "I just can't seem to resist you."

Toni murmured, "Do I need to sleep in the guest room?"

"Don't you dare leave me," Rynn breathed. "I need your hands on me."

Toni pulled Rynn closer. "No, not tonight."

When Rynn tried to protest, Toni captured her mouth, her tongue commanding her attention for a moment before breaking away. "Since you've decided I'm irresistible, tonight I want something different."

Toni shifted in her arms and rolled on top of her, supporting her weight on her right shoulder and snaking a hand down her body. With a swift movement, Toni pushed up her T-shirt and found her breast with her mouth.

When Toni grazed Rynn's nipple lightly with her teeth, she felt her whole body ignite. "Oh, God, Toni."

Toni smiled against her breast and flicked her tongue against her nipple. Rynn responded with a sharp intake of breath. The heat and wetness concentrating at her center demanded attention. She grasped Toni's hand, guiding it lower.

"No." Toni pulled her hand back, instead claiming Rynn's other breast. "I told you, tonight I want something different." At her confused moan, Toni whispered in her ear, "Tonight, I want to taste you."

Rynn felt like she might come just from those words.

Immediately, Toni shifted, her mouth finding Rynn's breast briefly before kissing a trail down her flat stomach. Toni used her teeth to tug her boxers down an inch, but she couldn't bear the slow, torturous sensuality. She wriggled out of her shorts, then pulled off her T-shirt and yanked at Toni's in the same movement.

Toni obliged, removing the garment.

Rynn slid up higher on the bed. Toni wrapped her arms around her waist, pulling her hips forward, and licked tentatively, teasingly at her center. She bucked against the touch, seeking a rhythm, seeking Toni's mouth. She closed her eyes tightly to the sensations, her hands tangled in Toni's hair, urging her onward.

Toni suckled her and slipped a tongue inside her, and Rynn keened her pleasure. Toni worked Rynn, her movements skilled, strong, relentless. She teetered on the edge. When Toni slipped her fingers inside, her world exploded. She screamed Toni's name, and that scream seemed only to encourage Toni further. A hot tongue moved over her, pulling more pleasure from her. Another scream ripped from her throat as all thought, all reason left her.

Rynn collapsed, gasping for breath. Toni rested against her lower body, head laid on her stomach. She pulled at Toni weakly, wanting to take her in her arms, but not having the strength.

Toni smiled and moved so they could kiss, and Rynn tasted herself on Toni's lips. She fought against the sleep that threatened to overtake her.

Toni kissed her gently. "Rest, my love. Rest with peaceful dreams."

* * *

Toni loved waking up in Rynn's arms. They lay tangled with each other, and she couldn't think of anything more intimate than the embrace they shared. Making love was powerful—no, with Rynn it was more than powerful, it was earth-shattering—but this? This was intimate in a whole different way.

She felt Rynn stir, tightening her hold. She smiled at Rynn's protective instinct and managed to wiggle around enough to find the bedside clock. They'd agreed the night before to set the alarm for seven o'clock, even though on workdays she typically got up much earlier.

She saw the alarm would sound in three minutes. She had learned about Rynn's habit of waking as late as possible, giving herself just enough time to grab a quick shower and get to work. This morning, Rynn would alter the pattern, instead taking her to work and checking some things with building security.

Toni took a deep, contented breath, nuzzling her face into the base of Rynn's neck. Waking up this way gave her a better understanding of people who talked about lingering in bed and being reluctant to get up. She'd even started to drift back to sleep when the alarm screamed.

She laughed when Rynn automatically slapped at it, blindly trying to shut it off. Even in a half-asleep state, Rynn found the clock quickly and slammed the snooze button.

Toni chuckled. "Good morning, beautiful," she whispered, raising her face to place a gentle kiss on Rynn's cheek.

Rynn smiled and mumbled something inaudible. She rolled on her back, pulling Toni on top of her, and squeezed her like a human teddy bear.

"Time to get up, sweetheart," Toni said.

Rynn grunted, obviously reluctant to move.

Toni persisted, finding Rynn's semi-conscious stupor amusing and adorable. "Did you sleep well?"

Another grunt, although this one had a distinctly affirmative tone.

Finally, Toni had an idea she thought might wake Rynn up pretty quickly. "Tell you what, I'm going to go shower. If you can drag yourself out of this bed, you should join me." She smiled when Rynn's eyes cracked open and continued, "I just need a minute to wrap my cast, and then I'll be naked…and hot…and wet…" She punctuated each word with a kiss, before deftly slipping out of Rynn's arms and onto her feet. "Don't keep me waiting too long, okay?"

Rynn grabbed futilely as she retreated.

She smiled when Rynn appeared at the bathroom door before she'd even completed preparing her cast. "I thought you weren't a morning person," she said.

Rynn rolled her eyes and muttered something, still not willing to speak.

Toni finished wrapping her cast, swished some mouthwash, got in the shower, and turned on the hot spray.

Rynn stepped in behind Toni, her hands immediately finding her body.

Toni soaped Rynn intimately, playfully, running the bar gently over her soft skin. She heard Rynn's sharp intake of breath when she passed the soap over her breasts.

Rynn clamped her hands over Toni's. Taking the bar of soap from her, she returned the sensual wash.

Somehow, they both managed to get fully clean. Rynn leaned in for a deep, hungry kiss as they embraced under the hot water.

Toni welcomed the kiss, but at the same time knew they had to get moving. "Rynn, baby, come on. We have to go," she murmured her resistance against Rynn's cheek, trying to step back.

Reluctantly, Rynn released her hold. They managed to get ready without further delay. At least not much, Toni thought.

A little while later—Toni was mildly surprised she and Rynn managed to make it out of the house without returning to bed—Rynn pulled the Tahoe into the parking lot of her office park building.

As they entered her office together, she caught Rynn taking an appreciative look around. Maybe she was spoiled after years of being in the same location, but glancing around the stylish suite, she realized her surroundings had a high-class attitude. A plush area rug spread over the hardwood floors under their feet. Dark mahogany paneling ran up the walls.

Toni hated the normal overhead fluorescent lighting that so often glared in office buildings. She'd made sure there was none of it in her suite, opting instead for high quality light fixtures lining the rooms and an occasional floor lamp. Smiling at Rynn, she asked, "You like it?"

Rynn raised a brow and nodded. "It's certainly better than the hole I work in."

Toni walked up to the front desk, Rynn following right behind.

Her startled assistant jumped to her feet. "Ms. Davis, you're back!"

Toni introduced Rynn to Kari. The three women spoke a few minutes before Toni led Rynn into her private office.

Rynn soon left to check around the building, mentioning she wanted to talk to the lobby doorman. After a while, apparently satisfied with the security, she returned to kiss Toni goodbye. "Are you sure you'll be okay here all day?"

Toni nodded. "Yes, of course. I'll be buried in paperwork all day, trying to catch up from being away."

"Okay, then. I'll be back to pick you up, say six o'clock?"

"Sounds good."

"All right. I'll see you tonight. You'll call me if you need anything?"

Toni rewarded Rynn's concern with a grin. "Yes, sweetheart, I'll call. But I'm sure I'll be fine."

Rynn stole one more quick kiss before walking out the door.

* * *

"Damn it!" Rynn muttered in frustration.

They had nothing. The autopsy report for Hart had come back that morning. The ME's conclusions were in line with what they'd expected. The brutality of Hart's injuries matched more closely with Quinn's than with Boden's: more bruising, more aggressive cutting, but otherwise consistent. The biggest discrepancy was no injury to Hart's knee. The lack did nothing to advance their investigation, only confirmed what they already knew.

"Pearson? Have we heard back from the lab about the crime scene evidence?" she asked.

He glanced up. Exhaustion had worn him thin, too. He rubbed his eyes briefly. Rynn was sympathetic to the burning from staring at a computer screen too long. "Yeah, I talked to the head tech a little while ago. He's processed all the fibers they pulled. Still working on the prints, but so far it looks like mostly matches for Hart or his family. The lipstick on the note is another story, though. I guess he's run it through his machines and found some unusual, extremely high quality and expensive component chemicals that usually only appear in top-of-the-line makeups. He has one of the junior techs working with him to contact major pharmaceutical and beauty product companies, trying to find an exact match for us so we can trace it back to specific retailers."

Rynn nodded. She knew they were getting close. Just one break was all they needed.

When five thirty p.m. rolled around, she was both relieved and aggravated that it was time for her to call it a day. She could stay and spin her wheels all night, but Toni would be waiting for her and she needed to clear her mind anyway. "Pearson, go home. Take it easy. We'll hit it again in the morning."

Her partner nodded. "Yeah, you're probably right."

She shut down her computer, pulled on her jacket, and headed out to the parking lot with him.

"You have any good plans for the evening?" he asked conversationally as they walked out.

"I'm thinking pizza, beer and football sounds about right."

He laughed. "You know, you'd fit in just fine with some of the good ol' boys club members I've worked with over my career."

She shrugged. "Yeah, except those guys tend not to be too fond of women joining the club."

He shook his head. "It's because you intimidate them. Strong men welcome strong women. You can hang out in my clubhouse anytime."

She smiled at him. "Thanks, man."

Later, at Toni's building, when Rynn stepped out of the elevator, Kari waved her in to Toni's private office.

Toni was on the phone, leaning against her giant mahogany desk and gazing out the window. She turned, smiled at seeing Rynn, and gestured that she'd only be a minute.

Rynn sat in a chair in front of the desk and watched Toni, smiling at the confidence her lover expressed. Toni seemed very much at home, very much the ruler of her elegant domain. Although Toni leaned casually against the desk, she could envision her full of energy, pacing in front of the large plate glass windows showing incredible views of the city in the distance.

Finished with her call, Toni limped across the room to give her a kiss.

"Mmm. I could get used to hellos like that," she said.

Two hours later at home, Rynn tossed half a slice of pizza back in the box on the coffee table. "Seems my eyes are bigger than my stomach tonight," she mumbled.

Toni laughed. "I'm not sure how. That was, what? Your fourth slice?"

She grinned and shrugged. "Meh, I was hungry." Turning her attention back to the game, she was pleased to see Pittsburgh up on the Patriots by seven. "So by cheering for the Steelers, I'm not making you go against any of your guys, am I?" she asked.

Toni smiled at her. "Doesn't bother me. I have players on both sides tonight. One Steeler and two Patriots. In fact…" She left her thought unfinished.

The room fell quiet. Rynn glanced at Toni, concerned by the sudden concentration in her expression. "Is everything okay, sweetheart?" She reached across the couch and grasped Toni's hand.

Toni gazed thoughtfully at the TV screen, her face showing confusion and concern.

"Toni?"

Toni started, bringing herself back to the present. "Rynn, do you still have that photo from the other day? The one of the man who was killed last week?"

"Zachary Hart?" Rynn asked in surprise.

Toni nodded.

Rynn rose from the couch and walked over to the closet. Pulling the photograph from her coat pocket, she crossed back through the room and handed it to Toni. She watched, worried and fascinated, as Toni studied the photo for a moment.

Toni squinted her eyes, her uncertainty evident. "I…I'm not sure. But when you showed this to me the other day, I thought he looked familiar. And now, I wonder…"

Rynn tried to wait patiently for Toni to gather her thoughts, but she suddenly found herself anxious and excited. What were the odds that Toni might give them a break in this case? "You recognize him?"

Toni shook her head slowly. "I—I don't know. If he is who I think he is, I only met him once, and briefly at that. There was a publicity event last year for the Bears, and he might be the man Levi introduced me to. I'd tried to think of Bears, or even Packers—anyone who might live in this area—who might have been dating this man. But I didn't think of Levi." She paused, obviously struggling to pull a forgotten memory into focus.

"Toni, who is Levi?"

Toni glanced up from the photo and gestured at the TV screen. "Levi Gregory. The Bears traded him to the Patriots last offseason. Tight end. He's one of my guys."

"Can you give me contact information, anything to get in touch with Levi as soon as possible?"

"Of course. Hand me my phone and I'll give you his private number right now. Obviously, he's at the game, but I'll give you any information I have."

Rynn nodded. "I'll get in touch with him first thing tomorrow, then."

Toni settled back on the couch. "I'm not sure, Rynn. I could be wrong. But it's possible." She looked pensively at the photo. "Then again, I don't know." Her voice was quiet, barely audible.

Rynn felt grateful for Toni's help. She reached for Toni, pulling her into an embrace.

They shifted into a comfortable snuggling position, Toni's back to her chest so they could both see the television. She wrapped her arms around Toni, holding her close. "Thank you." She kissed Toni again and settled in to watch the rest of the game.

CHAPTER THIRTY-TWO

The first thing Rynn did Tuesday morning was call Levi Gregory.

After a moment, a deep strong voice answered the phone. She took a breath and mentally crossed her fingers. "Mr. Gregory, I'm Detective Rynn Callahan, Kane County P.D., outside of Chicago."

Levi hesitated. "Hello, what can I do for you?"

"Did you know a man named Zachary Hart?"

"I…no, that name doesn't ring a bell." His voice cracked at his denial.

Rynn knew he was hiding something. Making a split-second judgment, she decided to try to get him talking using sympathy. She softened her voice. "Mr. Gregory, he's gone. I need you to tell me the truth so I can bring him justice."

He remained silent.

Come on Levi, talk to me. What Rynn heard next caused her throat to tighten.

Levi sobbed into the phone. "It's my fault. I should have insisted he move here with me, damn the consequences. He didn't want to move, and I didn't push it, because I was afraid people might piece it together if we were seen with each other in two different cities. The rumors were already starting, and I got scared. I let him step back, let him stay behind. If he'd come with me, he would still be alive right now."

"No. This is not your fault. He was murdered, and there's nothing you could have done." Rynn paused, giving him time to compose himself. "I'm sorry to intrude on your grief, Mr. Gregory, but I need to ask you some questions about your relationship with Mr. Hart."

Levi took a few sharp, staccato intakes of breath and regained control. "Yes. Yes, of course, I'll tell you anything. It's the least that I can do now for Zach."

"Just tell me about your relationship. When and how did you meet? How long have you been together? Anything like that."

Levi talked while Rynn quietly listened and took notes. He provided an alibi without being prompted. She doubted it would be difficult to corroborate. By the time he got to his trade last season to the Patriots, his sobs had calmed, but the regret never left his voice.

"If he'd just come with me. Or maybe if I'd taken retirement and stayed with him." He fell silent again.

"Mr. Gregory, how many people knew of your relationship with Mr. Hart?"

He considered her question. "I don't know. Not many, I think. I am deep in the closet because of my career, and Zach, he was only out to close friends and some family. Being closeted, it's rough. A painful topic, so we didn't discuss it very often."

Rynn turned his statement over in her mind. The "boss" had ties to the NFL, based on the targets being hunted. That meant it was more likely to be someone entering the picture from Levi's side of the relationship rather than from Zachary's. "Did anyone on your team here know? Or anyone in the front offices?"

Levi sighed. "Yeah, a couple of the guys knew, but they seemed cool. When I was in Chicago, there was one instance I still remember vividly. There was this chick in the front office, she cornered me once and told me she'd seen me out with Zach. I was terrified, thought she was going to try to blackmail me. Instead, she just leaned in and whispered 'Stay strong. We'll all be equal someday.' I think it took me a full ten minutes to understand what she'd said and start breathing again. Funny how you remember details like that," he went on. "I was just standing in one of the complex corridors, trying to catch my breath. I think that's the first time it actually struck me how god-awful the paint scheme is in the Bears complex. Everything is that wretched blue and orange. Almost blew it myself when V. strutted down the hall and glared suspiciously at me as Janie walked away."

Rynn paused in writing her notes. "Who's V.?"

"V.? Vanessa Carter. She must have glared at me a good minute, as if she was trying to figure out why I would waste breath on a front office clerk. She thought she was someone special, but I never had any time for her. She seemed to read people well, though, so she knew Janie had at least surprised me. Guess she figured I wasn't worth her time, because she eventually sauntered away."

Rynn's mind raced. He was certainly not the first person she'd heard talk disparagingly about the owner's wife, but Vanessa Carter's presence didn't seem like a coincidence. Her Barbie doll figure, full pouting lips, arrogant self-centeredness, and the sneer they'd received when she was introduced as Toni's date that night at the ball—all of it came flooding back into her mind. "Did Mrs. Carter ever say anything to you about it?"

"No, she preferred to chase the stars, not a tight end on his way out. Worked just as well for me. I wouldn't have wanted to fend off an STD from that whore."

Rynn chased ghosts of conversations in her mind. Was this the crack in the case she'd been waiting for? But she had to finish talking to Levi. "Mr. Gregory, is there anything else that you think might be important for me to know?"

"No. I can't think of anything. I just can't believe he's gone. I wish…I wish I'd done so much differently."

"Mr. Gregory—Levi—I'm sure you did the best you could. Zach loved you. Don't regret the time you shared."

The man's voice cracked again. "No. I don't. I…Thank you."

Rynn said goodbye, ended the call, and pushed back in her seat. She took a deep breath and started to rise to find Pearson just as he walked in the door.

"Rynn, we've got a break," he said. "The lab identified the exact lipstick. It's an exclusive product, only sold in one boutique in North Chicago. Apparently, they're an elite dealer—who knew cosmetics lines had elite dealers?—and they sell this product for two hundred dollars a tube. At that price, we might get lucky and a sales associate will remember a purchase."

Her excitement matched his energy. "We've got more than that. I think I have a suspect." At his astonished stare, she grinned. "I've got enough to bring her in for questioning, but let's follow this up first. If we can tie her to the lipstick, I think we might be able to get a warrant."

* * *

Toni left a short message at the tone as instructed.

She had mentioned to Rynn this morning that one of her other Bears players had a boyfriend in the area, and they had agreed it was time to talk to him. Rynn suggested it might be better if she got in touch with Malakai Johnson to caution him about the danger his boyfriend might be in, that way there'd be less likelihood of panic. Coming from someone he knew and trusted meant he wouldn't be suspicious of a police investigation or have to face fears of being outed.

Toni had agreed, but so far, she'd been unable to actually reach Malakai, which was frustrating. Her message had been noncommittal, but she'd told him it was important and he should please call her as soon as possible. Chances were he was at practice or in the weight room.

By midafternoon, she toyed with the idea of calling Malakai again. She knew Rynn had said there was unlikely to be a problem right away, but she remained anxious to speak with him.

Maybe she'd try later that evening, she decided.

* * *

As Rynn and Pearson drove to the North Chicago boutique, they filled each other in on the discoveries they'd made that morning. The more they talked, the more her gut told her that Vanessa Carter was "the boss." Now they just had to put together enough evidence to lock her up.

Vanessa was a society figurehead—or at least she perceived herself as one—so that might reduce her chance of being a flight risk. With her money, she'd have access to the best lawyers, but celebrities didn't often abandon their adoring fans. Her arrogance in leaving a note at the latest crime scene suggested that being caught was probably the furthest thing from her mind.

"Damn, it really looks like this adds up. Oh, man, do I want to nail 'em!" Pearson bounced in his seat, clearly excited.

Rynn wondered if he showed this level of joy every time he closed a case, or if this one had become personal for him. She couldn't deny it was certainly personal for her.

She parked her Tahoe and entered the small store, Pearson right behind her. The woman at the counter was tall and elegant, wrapped in a silky, flowing dress that looked like it cost a small fortune. She wondered if the snooty woman's neck was stuck at that angle from years of looking down her nose at people. She also wondered how much of the attitude was an act. Surely someone with enough money to be that stuck-up wouldn't be working as a sales agent in a boutique, no matter how high end the apparel.

She and Pearson flashed their badges. Pearson took the lead, asking about the specific lipstick the lab had identified.

"Oh, yes," the woman replied. "We pride ourselves on being an elite dealer for that line of beauty products."

Rynn was amused. The woman had used the exact terminology Pearson had mocked back at the station. She hid her smile.

The woman launched into a pitch about antiaging qualities, moisture locking compounds, and a scientifically tested glossy finish that would bring extra sparkle to a woman's smile.

Pearson cut her off. "How much of this particular product would you say you sell?"

"Well," the woman replied, clearly offended at having been interrupted, but unwilling to make a scene. "Not everyone can afford the best in beauty products. That particular lip finish sells five to eight units per month."

"Five to eight units? As in cases?"

"No, no, my dear man." The woman had apparently lost her patience. "Five to eight individual sales."

Rynn's brow rose slightly. This was good news for the investigation. "Would you be able to turn over sales records for this product from the last, say, three months?" she asked.

The woman appeared highly affronted at the suggestion. "Our sales records are entirely confidential. Credit information is very sensitive, and we value our customers' privacy to the utmost degree. I simply can't release those records without a court order."

Rynn and Pearson released matching sighs of frustration. "We'll arrange for that shortly, then," she said. "In the meantime, can you at least describe for me any sales of that item you remember? Did anyone seem unusual in purchasing that product recently?"

The woman considered the questions. Evidently deciding that was acceptable, she said, "Well, there was one that seemed odd to me. A woman, one of our regulars, purchased a tube, maybe two weeks ago. It struck me as odd for two reasons. One, because this woman typically uses a darker shade—the color really doesn't quite complement her complexion ideally—and two, because she paid with cash. Mrs. Carter always pays with her Black MasterCard, but I wondered if perhaps she might be giving it as a gift and wanted her friend to have the option of returning for cash back. That would be most considerate of her."

"I'm sorry, did you say Mrs. Carter?" Rynn asked. She had to be sure.

"Yes, Mrs. Vanessa Carter. Stunning woman, and so gracious. Surely you've heard of her work with the Bears Foundation charities. I understand she and her husband give substantial sums to the program."

Rynn met Pearson's eyes. *Bingo.* "Thank you, ma'am, you've been a great help."

The woman seemed confused. "Will I be seeing you back to collect the sales records?"

"Someone will be in touch," Pearson replied.

She and Pearson offered polite goodbyes before retreating from the store.

"We've got her." Pearson grinned from ear to ear.

Rynn couldn't help matching his expression. "Call it in to the DA, get our arrest warrant, and we'll go pick her up right now."

Pearson nodded. "Any idea where she lives? We can start driving."

Rynn smiled. "Actually, I know the exact place."

* * *

Toni looked up from the papers she'd been shuffling when Kari buzzed on the intercom. "Ms. Davis? Malakai Johnson is here to see you."

She was surprised. She had been anxiously anticipating his phone call, but she hadn't expected him to come in person. "Send him in."

A moment later, the giant man popped cheerfully through her door. She stood and gave him a polite kiss on the cheek in greeting.

"Toni! You're looking sexy as always!" Malakai seemed genuinely pleased to have the opportunity to visit. "Got your message, and since I had some things to do around this part of town, I thought I'd just stop in and see you."

She smiled warmly. Malakai was one of her favorite clients. Though they maintained a strictly professional relationship, nothing like the friendship she shared with Daniel, she was happy to see him. He always exuded strong emotions. When he was laughing and cheerful, he was a pleasure to be around. Today seemed to be one of those days.

He flopped into one of her visitors' chairs, causing the large mahogany furniture to groan under his sudden bulk.

And that's why I need the solid, sturdy furniture. She stepped back around to her side of the desk.

"Now, hang on there," Malakai suddenly said, hopping up with more agility and energy than a man his size should possibly possess. "Are you limping? And, wait just a second, missy! Is that a cast on your foot?" He leaned eagerly toward her, clearly wanting to hear the story behind the battle scars.

Toni settled in her seat. "Indeed I am, and indeed it is. I was in a bit of a car wreck two weeks ago. I'm afraid I broke my foot."

"Aw, damn, Toni! I hadn't heard! You're doing all right, now, aren't ya?"

"I'm doing much better, thank you." She studied his warm smile. Malakai was a big man, although for an offensive tackle, he was fairly average. The shock of dark hair atop his head went perfectly with his toothy grin to give him an almost boyish appearance.

She and Malakai exchanged pleasant small talk for a little while, until she decided it was time to get to the point. "Kai, there's something I need to talk to you about." She paused, suddenly unsure how to start. "Are you still seeing Travis?" she asked.

He was obviously surprised by the question but answered quickly. "Sure am. Can you believe it's been two years this winter?"

Toni smiled at the shift in his tone. At the very mention of Travis, he seemed to soften.

"Why do you ask?" he added.

She relayed the information she and Rynn had agreed to share with him, the central message being that Travis should be extremely careful and take all precautions to be safe. She even suggested he consider hiring personal security.

While she spoke, a dark cloud settled over Malakai's face. By the time she finished, she wasn't sure if it was rage or fear. "Someone has been killing men who…I knew I wasn't alone, I couldn't be the only one. But you're telling me there are three men dead, and Travis might be…?"

"Yes. Which is why you need to talk to him. Make sure he's careful in the coming weeks until the police sort this out."

Malakai shook with disbelief. "No way am I gonna let anyone hurt Travis." He ripped a cell phone out of his pocket and punched a speed dial button.

"Malakai, I'm sure he's fine for now. You can talk to him tonight. I just want you to make sure he's careful." Toni wasn't sure what reaction she'd expected, but she didn't think this was it. Malakai's mounting aggression was indicative of the killer instinct that made men warriors on the gridiron.

"He's not answering." Malakai punched another number. Toni tried again to tell him that the threat was not immediate. "Travis always takes my calls." He jumped to his feet. "Come on, we're going to check on him."

We? She was taken aback. "Malakai, I've got work to do here and my ride will be coming to get me soon." Was he panicking?

"No, Toni, you've got to come with me and make sure he's all right. Then you need to tell him what you just told me. Make sure he understands how serious this is."

"Kai, come on. I'm sure he's fine. It's the middle of the day! Maybe he's just wrapping up things at work and tossed his phone in his briefcase or something."

"Toni, please, you gotta come with me."

"But Rynn's coming to get me in an hour," she protested.

Malakai turned to her. "The banker from the ball? Good. Tell her to meet us at Vincenzo's. I'll treat you to dinner once we pick up Travis and I know he's okay."

She was mildly surprised that he remembered Rynn, who must have made a positive impact. Dinner out did sound nice. What was the harm if it calmed his nerves a bit?

He apparently sensed her hesitation. With a little more arm twisting, he talked her into it. After all, she reasoned to herself, it might be good for Rynn to meet Kai and Travis, and for her to fill them in on whatever details she felt were appropriate.

"All right, fine. You've convinced me," she said. "Let me just call Rynn and tell her where to meet us."

Toni was disappointed when Rynn's phone went to voice mail. She left a quick message explaining what had happened and where she and Malakai were going, with the instruction to meet them at Vincenzo's at six o'clock.

She shut down her office for the day, grabbed her coat, and followed Malakai out.

CHAPTER THIRTY-THREE

City traffic was ridiculous. It took Rynn nearly two hours to drive from the boutique to the mansion residences in the North Shore. The only good thing about the delay was that the DA's office succeeded in processing their warrant in that time.

"Okay, so how are we going in? Immediate arrest or try to chat her up first?" Pearson asked.

"Let's try to get her talking, see if we can establish any animosity toward gays or anything like that. She might be too proud to talk once we've got the cuffs on her," she replied.

"Could be. My guess is she might still think she's three steps ahead of us until we make the arrest. We might get lucky with some gloating hints."

She nodded and killed her Tahoe's idling engine right in front of the Carter mansion's massive front door. She stepped out of the car, hardly surprised to find a man dressed like a classic, stereotypical butler had come out and now waited silently for them to approach.

"May I help you?" he drawled when she and Pearson came to a halt.

Rynn resisted the urge to show her skepticism at the show of formality. She flashed her badge. "We're here to discuss some things with Mr. and Mrs. Carter. Are they available?"

The butler scrutinized their badges rather intently. After a long moment, he stepped back and actually bowed. "Please follow me." He turned curtly and strode purposefully into the house.

Rynn and Pearson were shown to a parlor and asked to take a seat while "the master" was notified of their visit.

Some fifteen minutes later, a stately older gentleman came into the room, leaning on the butler's arm. "Officers." Lawrence Carter nodded and took a seat in a chair opposite them. "Charles tells me you'd like a word."

Rynn considered the butler, standing stoically behind Lawrence's chair. *I wonder if his name is really Charles, or if that's just a good butler-like name?* Turning to Lawrence, she asked. "Is your wife available this afternoon?"

The old man shook his head slowly. Rynn was struck by how weak he appeared compared to the outgoing youth and power she remembered from Vanessa. He seemed in poor health, to say the least. Despite his age, he had a full head of white hair, neatly combed straight back and oiled.

"I'm afraid Vanessa is out for her usual afternoon shopping," he said. "She frequently goes to the boutiques in town or takes tea with one of her friends." Rynn thought she detected a slight British accent, particularly when he mentioned taking tea. "I rarely see her until later in the evening, if at all." He sighed wearily. "My wife doesn't seem to have the patience nor the devotion to spend her days with her weakened husband, although this is hardly a new development since my heart surgery."

Rynn glanced at Pearson. Vanessa wasn't here. What would be the best way to handle the situation? Wait for her to return? Pearson made the slightest gesture toward Lawrence. Okay, so they'd talk to the husband in the meantime.

"Forgive me, Mr. Carter, but it doesn't sound like you're all that close to your wife." Her statement was intended to lead him and see what sort of beans he might spill.

He contemplated her a moment before responding. "Generally, I consider myself an excellent judge of character. It has been perhaps my best tool in a lifetime of business management. Ness, however, has the distinct honor of being one of few who have fooled me. Our relationship deteriorated rapidly after our vows, and I don't often see her anymore. When I do, we have little in common and even less interest in sharing our lives with each other."

"Mr. Carter, you paint such a bleak picture, I can't help wondering why you're still married." She was beginning to think delicacy wouldn't actually be required. He seemed simply indifferent to his wife, willing to answer honestly whatever questions might be asked.

"I imagine I'll divorce her eventually, once my health improves further. For now, I simply have more important things to concern me."

"Do you have any reason to suspect your wife has ever been unfaithful?"

Lawrence looked at her demurely. "Surely you've not come the whole way to the North Shore to discuss my wife's indiscretions?" When neither she nor Pearson spoke again, he went on. "I do not *suspect* that she's been unfaithful. I *know*. But as I said, it means little to me. Upon realizing I'd been duped, I admit to some initial consternation. However, most of my emotional connection to Vanessa, either good or bad, has faded. She lives here, she spends my money, and in time I will have her removed. Until then, I don't pay her much mind."

His indifference astonished her. "Would I be accurate in assuming that Vanessa frequently leaves the house, day and night, without accounting for her whereabouts?"

Lawrence nodded. "Yes, indeed. I suspect she goes off to meet clandestine lovers and the like on a regular basis. She's grown bolder in recent weeks, even going so far as to meet with young men in the pool house. I really don't care to trouble myself with her shenanigans." Despite his initial protest about discussing Vanessa's "indiscretions," his comment betrayed his aloofness.

Rynn glanced at Pearson. Once they had Vanessa Carter in custody, fingerprinting the pool house might give them connections to the men working for her. For now, the focus was on Lawrence Carter. "Mr. Carter, do you know much about your wife's background?"

He scoffed. "My dear, I may have allowed some romantic naiveté to color my view of Vanessa before we wed, but my vision was not so clouded as to forgo an investigation into her past. In some way, I think her past was one of the things that drew me to her. I know now that it was an act, but Ness portrayed the most delightful sweetness mixed with just a hint of tenacity. I believed it to be a result of her troubled childhood.

"You see, her father left her mother and Ness when she was quite young. It seems he had struck up an erotic affair with another gentleman and decided to pursue his own happiness away from his wife and young child. Nowadays, such an event may not be viewed with quite the same level of scandal, but I always suspected it left quite an impression on Ness. I asked her about it once. In our entire courtship that was one of the few subjects I learned was taboo. She seemed aggravated I had even learned of the incident. Who knows? Perhaps it was just part of the game to trap me, the idea she loved me as the protector and provider she'd not had in her childhood. That's how I convinced myself she could really be interested in a man so much her senior."

Rynn looked at Pearson in a meaningful but wordless exchange. Vanessa had reason for a grudge against gay men? Lawrence Carter had just handed them a motive on a silver platter.

"Mr. Carter, do you believe your wife to be capable of violence?" she asked.

The old man studied her carefully before responding with an inquiry of his own. "Am I to take that to mean you are not simply looking to speak with Vanessa today?"

"That's not what I said," she answered with firm calm.

He considered her further. "I see. Well, should that have been the case, I would hardly have been surprised. Ness, I have come to learn, has a bit of a proud temper. She does not take kindly to the suggestion that she is in reality anything less than what she is in her mind."

Rynn turned to Pearson and tossed him the slightest shrug. He nodded and spoke. "We plan to arrest Vanessa for her role in several recent crimes. With this knowledge in mind, would you care to make any additional statement?"

Lawrence shook his head mildly with a look of deep sadness. "I truly do not know how I could have judged her so poorly. The police will, of course, have my full cooperation, though I don't know what help an old codger like me might offer." The elderly man paused and drew a shaky breath. "Officers, I find this conversation has weakened me terribly. If you'll excuse me, I would like to return to my chambers. Charles will provide you with whatever assistance you may need, or perhaps food or beverage. I assume you'll be waiting for Vanessa to return?"

Rynn glanced at Pearson. He nodded. She rose from her seat to shake Lawrence's hand as he stood to take his leave. "Thank you for your assistance, Mr. Carter. I'm sorry for any pain our news has brought."

He took Rynn's hand between his own. His palms were warm and soft, belying his age and a life of comfort. "My dear, I have known for quite some time that Vanessa was not as I had hoped. It does pain me to hear how badly she has faltered, but I cannot align myself with her any longer." He squeezed her hand before releasing her and accepting Charles's help to move to the door.

Rynn sank back into her chair and glanced at her watch. It was nearly four thirty. It would take at least an hour to make it back to Toni's office.

Pearson turned to her. "I know you have to pick up Toni, so why don't you head on out? I'll call a patrol unit, and we'll wait for Mrs. Carter to return. Tomorrow morning, we'll have our suspect in custody and just the loose ends to tie up."

Rynn was momentarily torn. She wanted to be there when they slapped the cuffs on Vanessa Carter's delicate wrists. But love proved a stronger pull than vengeance. She accepted Pearson's suggestion. "You sure you don't mind lagging behind?"

He laughed. "Are you kidding? I want to cuff her myself. I wouldn't miss it."

She nodded, knowing the feeling, but Toni would be waiting. "All right. I'll see you bright and early, then."

CHAPTER THIRTY-FOUR

Pulling into the parking lot of Toni's office complex with two minutes to spare, Rynn noted she still hadn't heard anything from Pearson. Stepping out of the car, she pulled out her cell phone and was surprised to discover the battery had died. *Damn*. She never let that happen.

She entered the elevator and rode to Toni's floor. Stepping from the cold steel lift, she noticed the lights were turned down dimmer than the night before.

Kari stood behind her reception desk, pulling her jacket around her thin body. She jumped when she turned around and saw Rynn approaching. "Oh! Ms. Callahan! You startled me." She flushed slightly.

Rynn frowned. "I'm just here to pick up Toni. That's all."

Kari seemed uncertain and confused. "But Ms. Davis left over an hour ago. I assumed she'd notified you."

Toni left? Damn it, of all the days for my cell phone to die! Rynn was nonplussed. "Battery died. How did she leave? She can't have driven."

Kari made a half-shrug. "She left with Mr. Johnson, said something about the measures she would take to keep a client happy. She didn't say where they were going."

Rynn sighed. "Can I use the phone before you lock up? I want to give her a quick call."

Kari nodded and moved the receptionist's phone within her reach.

She quickly punched Toni's number into the phone. After five rings, it went to voice mail, so she hit reset and dialed her own voice mail. The mechanical voice made her especially irritable as it droned, "*You have two…new…messages.*"

She tapped her fingers impatiently, punching through the menus to get to what she needed. Finally, she heard a beep and the message she expected from Toni.

"*Hey sweetheart. Malakai stopped in to see me just now and he's worried that he can't reach Travis. I'm going with him just to prove that Travis is fine, and then Kai has invited us to join them for dinner. Can you meet us at Vincenzo's at six o'clock? I thought you might appreciate the opportunity to talk with them yourself. Kai said it's just twenty minutes to Travis's house. We'll swing by, pick him up and meet you. See you soon, baby.*"

Another beep. The electronic voice returned to rattle off Toni's cell number. "*Message left at four…thirty-eight…p…m.*"

Rynn sighed. Well, she was late for dinner.

"*Message…Two: 'Hi sweetheart, me again. Just wanted to give you the dinner information in case you beat us there. Kai made the reservation in Travis's name. Travis Winters. Party of four for six o'clock. I missed you today. I'll see you soon.'*" Beep.

Rynn hung up the phone. "Kari, thanks for your patience. Can I keep you here just a minute longer?" At the woman's resigned nod, she asked for a phone book and quickly flipped to the number for Vincenzo's Italian Trattoria. After a young woman made a formal greeting, she hurried to speak.

"Hi, my name is Rynn, I'm supposed to be meeting a party there and I'm running late. Can you just let them know I'll still be twenty minutes and not to wait for me?"

"What's the name of the party, ma'am?"

"Travis Winters."

The line fell silent. At last, the woman said, "I'm sorry, the Winters party has not yet arrived. I'll make a note to let them know you called. Is there anything else I can do for you this evening?"

"Wait, they haven't arrived?" Rynn checked her watch. Quarter after six.

"No, ma'am."

"I see. Well, please let them know when they do."

"Yes, ma'am."

Rynn set down the receiver in its cradle. If Toni and the rest of her party were running late themselves, why hadn't Toni left her another message? She turned back to Kari. "Thank you."

In silence, she followed Kari out of the building.

Her mind spinning, Rynn tried to quell the fear rising in her throat. She'd gotten no message from Pearson, either, so as far as she knew, Vanessa Carter and her stooges were still loose. Now Toni was missing—*No, she's not missing, I just don't know where she is. There's a difference*. Nevertheless, she was unable to get in touch with Toni, whose last communication indicated she was going to another potential victim's home. All three prior victims had been killed in their homes. Toni had just gone to the possible next one on the killer's list.

Arriving at the restaurant a short while later, Rynn ripped her Tahoe into the valet lane and parked. "I'll be back in just a minute, guys," she called to the bewildered drivers approaching her car as she dashed inside. She cut the line and moved to the hostess station. Ignoring haughty indignation from the patrons behind her, she spoke quietly to the startled woman holding menus. "The Winters party. Have they arrived?"

The woman looked at her dumbly. When Rynn gestured her impatience, she glanced down. "No, I'm sorry, they never showed. It's our policy to hold a table for half an hour and then …"

Rynn didn't wait to hear the rest. She dashed out the door as quickly as she had entered, waved at the valet, got in her Tahoe, and tore out of the drive. She arrived at the police station in less than two minutes.

When she unplugged her phone from the dash, it beeped meekly at her. One new message. "Please be Toni. God, please be Toni."

"Rynn, it's Steve. I've been here two hours and there's no sign of Vanessa. Just thought I'd let you know."

Rynn swallowed the rush of fear that hit her. She punched in Toni's number. Five long rings, and then voice mail. *Damn it!* She ran into the station, finding the officer on duty for the evening shift. "I need an address, right now. Possible victims in danger. Travis Winters. Find him."

The officer spun into action, no questions asked. It felt like forever, but a few minutes later, Rynn had an address and sprinted out the door. She considered backup, but what would she tell them? She didn't know. She wasn't willing to be delayed.

Tearing the Tahoe through town, she dialed Pearson's number. "Steve, it's me. I can't get hold of Toni. My last message from her said she was going to another NFL boyfriend's house."

"What?" Pearson's tone told her he immediately understood the significance of her statement.

"Please, tell me you've got Vanessa."

"Rynn, no. She never came back."

"Damn it! Travis Winters." She rattled off the address. "Leave the second officer at Carter's and let's pray I'm wrong. How fast can you get there?"

"In a patrol car? I'll throw on the lights and be there in twenty-five minutes. Thirty max."

"All right. I'm on my way. ETA fifteen minutes."

"Rynn, don't do anything stupid. I'm sure she's fine."

Rynn hung up without answering. *Please God, let her be okay. Let me be wrong.* She shot through town, fighting down the sick feeling growing in her gut.

She had to get there. Fast.

CHAPTER THIRTY-FIVE

Toni stirred, an ache blistering behind her eyes. She sat in an uncomfortable chair, her body stiff. She groaned and tried to lift her arm to rub her head, but found she couldn't. Her wrists were tied behind her. Before she even opened her eyes, memories crashed in.

Malakai had been aggravated and worried when he couldn't reach Travis. She'd had to remind him at least three times on the drive to Travis's house to slow down or they might not make it at all. She hadn't been the least bit worried until they arrived and found the front door swinging open. There were lights on in the back.

Malakai had stood stunned on the front sidewalk a moment before rushing inside. Toni had had no choice but to follow him into the house. Hopping on her casted foot, she'd only just caught up to him when she'd caught movement in the darkness to their right. Malakai had suddenly crumpled at her feet. Another movement and the rest went black.

She knew she was in trouble. At the same time, she also knew she was still alive. Surely, her head would have stopped pounding if she were dead. She kept her eyes closed a moment longer, testing the ties binding her wrists. She couldn't move her arms, she'd already realized that. She discovered her legs were bound too.

Finally, she opened her eyes. The room was dimly lit. She looked around quickly, but the sharp movement sent a throb through her head. She couldn't stifle the whimper that escaped her throat.

Malakai lay on the floor in front of her, in the corner of the room. Looking at him in the gloom, she saw a small pool of blood near his head. She feared the worst until she realized she could make out the slight movements of his chest rising and falling weakly. She glanced away, her eyes falling instead on Travis, tied in a chair not three feet from her. He was bloodied, bruised and obviously unconscious.

"Toni Davis. Fancy meeting you here." She didn't quite recognize the sugary sweet, feminine voice purring from behind her. "Had I known you would walk willingly to me not two weeks after our first attempt to get you, perhaps Cutter needn't have died. Such a shame."

The voice was familiar now, but darker than she remembered, filled with cold malice. Just as the name attached to the voice floated into her mind, Vanessa Carter stepped in front of her.

"What's a nice dyke like you doing in a place like this?" Vanessa sneered.

Toni was shocked and confused. Her head throbbed.

Vanessa drifted across the room to turn on another light. "Oh, I'm sorry, do you have a headache? Isn't it frustrating how bright lights can aggravate a bad headache?" She chuckled cruelly, redirecting the light to shine right into Toni's eyes.

"What is this, some kind of Hollywood interrogation?" Toni murmured, squinting.

Vanessa threw her head back and laughed. "You hear that, Rex? She has a sense of humor. Perhaps she won't find things so funny once she sees what we have planned for her friends."

Rex Andrews stepped out of the shadows and approached Travis. He pulled a knife from his pocket and pressed it to the unconscious man's chest.

"What are you doing to him? Stop!" Toni's plea was hardly above a whisper, but it echoed loudly in her ears.

"Stop?" Vanessa scoffed, feigning incredulity. "Why ever would I want to stop? That's the whole reason I'm here. To execute the faggots who have corrupted the men of my league."

Toni couldn't believe her ears. Instinct told her to keep Vanessa talking. She didn't know the time, but it had to be after six o'clock. Surely Rynn was looking for her. "*Your* league?" she challenged.

"Yes!" Vanessa spat, turning on her. "I will fix it, eliminate the fools who have tainted its gladiatorial glory."

"By killing innocent men?"

"Innocent? They have committed countless perverse crimes. I will punish them and return purity to my league!"

My God, she's lost it. Toni faltered.

Vanessa sneered again and turned to Rex, who stood over Travis. "Begin."

"Wait!" Toni pleaded desperately.

To her surprise, Rex listened.

Vanessa glared at her, a shocking, dark hatred blazing in her eyes.

Toni asked the first question that popped into her mind. "Why their boyfriends? Why not go after the players themselves?"

Vanessa stepped back, her rage cooling, replaced by arrogance. "Well, if I were to harm the players themselves, particularly the Bears, it would damage my husband's business. That old coot is not long for this world. When he dies, his assets will pass to me. So you see, it really is in my own self-interest to leave the players unharmed. Besides, their deaths would be noticed and the publicity would stunt my mission. I couldn't let them die heroes, but no one notices when an anonymous faggot is eliminated."

Her words made Toni ill. Between her nausea and her splitting headache, she was afraid she might vomit. "What will you do with me? With Malakai?" she asked.

"You will be accompanying my men back to their accommodations. Perhaps they might even be so kind as to give you lessons in the pleasures a man can provide." Vanessa's face twisted in a sick, deranged grin. "Certainly better than that banker bitch you had the audacity to bring into *my* house!"

Toni heard a low, dark chuckle behind her that added to her fear. Someone seemed appreciative of Vanessa's horrible suggestion. She fought to keep from vomiting.

Vanessa turned and gazed thoughtfully at Malakai. She studied him, even stepping toward him. She addressed the unconscious man. "You…you do present me with a dilemma. What to do with you? I hadn't intended to harm players, but I suspect you've been told what's going on. If you know my plan, I can't very well let you walk away and blab about it." She nudged him with the toe of her stiletto, an expression of disgust painting her face as if she were kicking away garbage someone had left in her path.

Toni strained to hear Vanessa. She could barely make out her words.

"No, because you rushed in, you force me to act. You are a threat to my mission, and threats must be neutralized." She confronted Toni. "Who knows? Perhaps the publicity of the hit-and-run death of an NFL athlete will garner sympathy. Perhaps the team will unite around the tragedy and actually play with some heart." She scoffed. "Lord knows they could use a kick start. They're pathetic. We'll be changing that once I am an owner."

Toni shook her head, her disbelief growing with each word Vanessa spoke. "Why me? Why keep me alive? What's your interest in me?"

Vanessa laughed. "Why, Toni, don't you know how important you've been to my mission? Closeted gay athletes aren't easy to locate. Tommy Rocker revealed himself when he was so blinded by his pathetic Patrick that he actually declined my advances. Me! He said he wasn't interested in me! Have you seen the wretched fool mope around the locker room since I removed his so-called lover?" She laughed as she defiled Patrick's memory. "Rex here was good enough to tell me about a former teammate in Green Bay who appreciated a variety of unusual sexual fare. Sending him and Cutter to dispatch Derek Quinn was easy. After that, I'll admit, I ran out of despoilers. How fortunate that you did me the wonderful favor of showing up at my party and throwing your perversion in my face with your *date*. You, a well-respected agent in the league. And that Tommy Rocker was your client made me wonder. I realized you might be useful to me. Perhaps, with some persuasion, you might lead me to the others. Surely you would have access to the network of miscreants. When Rex failed to bring you back to me, losing Cutter in the effort, I was enraged! And then you disappeared altogether. Where have you been hiding out? No doubt with that other bitch." Her eyes were wild while she rambled about her actions.

"Well, despite their failure—" Vanessa paused to glare coldly at Rex, who shifted uncomfortably, a shrewd look in his eyes, "—I used your name and your connections to trace others. Your secretary has been very helpful, by the way. I've been working my way through the list of players you represent, either finding them acceptable or, when they prove guilty, tracking them until I could eliminate their partners.

"Which really leads us to here and now, doesn't it?" Vanessa laughed and switched her attention to Travis's limp figure. "Why have you stopped, Rex? Finish your task."

Toni watched as Rex hesitated. Finally, he nodded and raised his knife to Travis's chest.

"Very good, Rex," Vanessa gloated, circling the room and moving behind Toni's chair.

Toni shuddered when Vanessa clapped a hand on her shoulder. She closed her eyes. Whatever happened next, she couldn't watch.

* * *

Rynn peeled the Tahoe around the corner and onto the right street. Nearing the address, she braked, slowing the vehicle nearly to a halt. If her fears were right, she needed the element of surprise on her side. She parked two houses down, and drew and checked her weapon. Six in the clip, one in the chamber. Safety off.

She approached the house. The front door hung open. Her breath caught. No one left their door open in the dark on an early winter night.

She quickly circled the perimeter, hoping to see something, anything to tell her what, or who, she was up against. The only lights in the house were in the back rooms on the first floor. She saw a shadowy figure move across a curtained window and loped back to the front, climbing the front steps soundlessly and entering the house.

The hallways were dark. No surprise there. She crept silently but quickly toward the occupied room's door where she heard a woman's low voice. "Finish your task."

Rynn froze. A few more words were spoken, but she couldn't make them out. She couldn't wait any longer. A silent prayer raced through her mind when she kicked open the door.

CHAPTER THIRTY-SIX

Rynn charged through the door into the room. A dark shadow. The flash of a long knife. She fired at the hulking figure of Rex Andrews. He fell against the wall, clutching at the curtain and sliding down heavily in front of the window. Another sudden movement in the back of the room. A raised gun. She aimed and loosed two more shots. The unidentified male slumped, his gun clattering from his hand.

Her gaze darted around the room, cataloging and assessing. Toni sat tied to a chair a few feet in front of her, wide-eyed, but very much alive. She wanted to run to her, but was frozen to the spot by the threat of a gleaming blade at Toni's delicate throat.

Vanessa Carter laughed. "Why do I now get the impression you're not a banker after all?" She crouched directly behind Toni, the knife in her hand. She kept herself well shielded by Toni's body.

Rynn had no shot. She checked the rest of the room, her eyes never leaving Vanessa for more than a split second. Malakai lay crumpled on the floor, just inches from the door. Another man—she assumed it was Travis—was unconscious, tied to a folding chair. Apart from Andrews and the second man she'd shot, there was no one else. She strained to hear if anyone might come running.

She let her gaze flick briefly to Toni and suppressed a surge of adrenaline. Toni was alive, albeit with a cut on her brow and terror gleaming in her dark eyes. Rynn could breathe again.

"Not feeling conversational? Ms. Smith, wasn't it? Although I suppose you wouldn't have used your real name at my party," Vanessa said.

Rynn didn't speak. Furious at the threat to Toni, she kept her gun trained on Vanessa.

Vanessa laughed—a cold, cruel sound.

"Let her go." Rynn said, interrupting Vanessa's mockery. "Let Toni go, and I won't kill you."

"Oh, please! Whoever you are—some sort of cop, I presume—you've got to have more sense than that. I can see you don't have a shot that doesn't go through Ms. Davis first, so it seems to me that I have all the leverage." Vanessa inclined her head toward the blade at Toni's throat, its deadly point pressed into Toni's soft flesh. "You disagree?" she challenged. She tensed her hand.

Rynn felt herself blanch as a tiny bead of blood appeared on the knife's tip.

Toni's eyes closed briefly. When she opened them, Rynn saw her searing pain and fear.

"No. Stop. I agree," Rynn said. "What do you want?"

Vanessa snarled. "That's more like it. Do what I say and *I* won't kill *her*. At least, not yet. You won't be so lucky."

Rynn's heart pounded. She knew Pearson was on his way, but time seemed to crawl as slowly as the blood trickling down Toni's throat. "Fine. Tell me what to do. Just don't harm her."

"Well, for starters, I don't like having that gun in my face, so why don't you put it down?"

Rynn hesitated. Without her gun, she had nothing.

"*Put it down!*" Vanessa screamed, her rage no longer contained.

Rynn squatted slowly and placed the gun on the floor.

"Now slide it toward me."

Rynn obeyed, noting Toni's ankles were bound to the legs of her chair.

"Are you a cop?" Vanessa snarled the question.

Rynn nodded.

"Then you should carry handcuffs. Do you?"

Rynn nodded a second time and rose to her full height.

"Good. See those pipes behind you? On your knees, hands behind your back. Cuff yourself to them, and do be careful not to burn yourself," Vanessa mocked.

Rynn's gaze returned to Toni. Their eyes met for a brief moment.

Vanessa shouted, "Do it!"

Rynn moved slowly, buying time and not wanting to startle Vanessa into cutting Toni any worse. She pulled her handcuffs from the small pouch on her belt, showing them to Vanessa. She stepped backward toward the pipes, never turning her back on the evil woman dictating her movements. She considered faking it, but Vanessa appeared unstable. If the woman checked the cuffs, both she and Toni could be dead in a heartbeat. She sank to her knees. The sound of the cuffs clicking closed echoed in the otherwise silent room.

The low, slow laugh bubbling from Vanessa's throat chilled Rynn's blood. Vanessa rose from behind Toni, finally moving the blade from her neck. Rynn felt some relief, but she knew she'd only deflected Vanessa's violence.

Sure enough, Vanessa stepped around Toni and picked up Rynn's gun. She raised the weapon, taking careful aim at Rynn's chest.

"God, no, don't hurt her!" Toni begged pointlessly. She bucked against her chair, tears streaming down her face, unable to do anything to stop Vanessa.

"Say goodbye to your cop, Ms. Davis."

Rynn locked gazes with Toni's, not knowing if she would ever see anything else.

Toni screamed when the shot rang out.

CHAPTER THIRTY-SEVEN

The sound of shattering glass told Rynn her gun hadn't fired the shot, since there was no glass between her and Vanessa Carter. A second and third shot sounded. Vanessa collapsed, shock and confusion the last expressions on her face.

"Toni! Toni!" Rynn called.

Toni screamed hysterically when Vanessa fell in front of her. Clearly, she had no idea what was happening.

"Rynn! Rynn, you okay?" Pearson called from outside the shattered window.

"Yeah, Steve! Thank God you made it. Room's clear, get your ass in here!" She struggled against her cuffs, wanting to rush to Toni, take her in her arms and comfort her. "Toni! Toni, look at me. I'm okay. You're okay. Steve's here."

Toni quieted. Tears poured down her face. Her breaths were uneven. She appeared on the verge of a panic attack.

"Toni, look at me," Rynn repeated. "Are you hurt? Did they hurt you?"

Toni swallowed hard. "No. I'm okay," she gasped. "You're okay?"

"Yes, Toni. I'm okay." Rynn kept her voice tender, calming, until she saw Toni's breath even out. "We're okay, Toni." The realization sank in for her as well. She smiled. "We're okay," she repeated.

Pearson came inside. "Good God," he said, looking around the room. He seemed almost unsure what to do first, then he snapped into action, dropping to his knees to unlock Rynn's cuffs.

As soon as she was free, Rynn darted over to Toni, wrapping her in a strong hug. "I'm here, baby, I'm here. You're okay." She kissed Toni, desperate to reaffirm she was alive.

"Oh, God, Rynn. I thought she'd shot you. I thought..." Toni's breath caught. She broke down in sobs. "I thought she'd killed you. I don't know how I could have survived. I love you so much, Rynn, and I thought I'd lost you."

Rynn held Toni tightly. Her heart pounded. "I love you, too, Toni. I was afraid that I wouldn't make it in time. I was so afraid..." Tears streaked down her face. She held Toni close, lost in their embrace.

EPILOGUE

Five months later.

Rynn strolled into the dimly lit living room. "You know, I never really understood why the draft is such a big deal."

Toni smiled and held open her arms, welcoming Rynn into her embrace. Together, they curled up on the couch in front of the television, a perfect fit. They kissed.

Toni pulled back slightly, her lips still brushing Rynn's. "Today sets the tone for the futures of these teams. Get the right player, get a little lucky, and it can make all the difference for the next dozen years."

Rynn nodded and nuzzled her mouth against Toni's neck. "Speaking of futures…"

Toni shifted to look into her eyes. Rynn's breath caught at the beauty and passion reflected back at her. Her heart raced. Toni's eyes seemed to darken further with desire. She felt the familiar fire rip through her body as the sweet scent of Toni's breath invaded her senses.

"Love me, Rynn." Toni's whispered command set Rynn's blood boiling.

"For the rest of my life." Rynn captured Toni's mouth and let the undeniable, unquenchable heat take control.